PENGUIN BOOKS

TAMAS

Bhisham Sahni was born in 1915 into a d   najist family
in Rawalpindi (now in Pakistan). H   , then went
to Government College. I   n Master's
degree in English Li   join his
father's import bus   cided to
teach at a local colleg   e involved in
the activities of the In

After partition in 19   ..ed to settle in India and
Bhisham Sahni took the   .o India—he settled down in Delhi
and began to teach at a Delhi University college. His first collection
of short stories, *Bhagya Rekha* (Line of Fate) was published in 1953.
In 1957, Bhisham Sahni moved to Moscow to work as a translator at
the Foreign Language Publishing House. He worked in the USSR for
nearly seven years, during which time he translated twenty Russian
books into Hindi. He returned to India in 1963 and resumed teach-
ing in Delhi. He edited a literary journal, *Nai kahaniyan,* from
1965-1967 and began working on *Tamas,* a novel based on his
experiences as a young man, in 1971.

Bhisham Sahni won the Sahitya Akademi Award for *Tamas* in
1975. He has also won the Distinguished Writer Award of the Punjab
Government, the Lotus Award of the Afro Asian Writers' Association
and the Sovietland Nehru Award. So far he has published five novels,
eight collections of short stories, three plays and a biography of his
late brother, the actor and writer Balraj Sahni. Many of his books
have been translated into various languages.

Bhisham Sahni is married and has two children; He lives with his
wife and daughter in New Delhi.

*

Jai Ratan was born in Ludhiana in 1971. He was educated at the
Forman Christian College in Lahore, from where he took a Master's
degree in English. He is a founder member of the Writer's Work-
shop, Calcutta.
He has translated extensively from the Hindi, Urdu and Punjabi and
has also edited and been published in several anthologies.
Jai Ratan lives in New Delhi.

BHISHAM SAHNI

TAMAS
(DARKNESS)

Translated from the Hindi by Jai Ratan

PENGUIN BOOKS

Penguin Books India (P) Ltd, 72-B Himalaya House 23 Kasturba Gandhi Marg.
New Delhi 110 001. India
Penguin Books Ltd, Harmondsworth, Middlesex, England
Penguin Books USA Inc., 375 Hudson Street New York 10014 USA.
Penguin Books Australia Ltd, Ringwood, Victoria, Australia
Penguin Books Canada Ltd, 2801 John Street, Markham, Ontario, Canada L3R 1B4
Penguin Books (N.Z.) Ltd, 182-190 Wairau Road, Auckland 10, New Zealand
First published in Hindi by *RajKamal Prakashan* 1974
First published in English as *Kites Will Fly* by Vikas Publishing House 1981.
Revised English translation published as *Tamas* in Penguin Books 1988
Reprinted 1990 (twice), 1991, 1992
Made and printed in India by Ananda Offset Private Ltd.
Typeset in Garamond by Wordtronic, New Delhi.

Introduction

A traumatic historical event usually finds the artistic/literary response twice. Once, during the event or immediately following it and again after a lapse of time, when the event has found its corner in the collective memory of the generation that witnessed it. The initial response tends to be emotionally intense and personal in character, even melodramatic. On the other hand, when the event is reflected upon with emotional detachment and objectivity, a clearer pattern of the various forces that shaped it is likely to emerge. *Tamas* is the reflective response to the partition of India —one of the most tragic events in the recent history of the Indian sub-continent.

Bhishamji witnessed the turbulence of the period as an adult. That was a period of intense turmoil — people sacrificing their lives for the freedom of the country, people dying fighting. The unprecedented communal violence provoked by the callous manipulation of religious sentiments of different communities by the elements who chose to use religion as a weapon to achieve political objectives heightened his sensitivity towards human suffering and also strengthened his commitment to secularism. *Tamas* had to wait twenty-three years after partition to be born. Perhaps, because the initial response was shock and numbness. As a writer, Bhishamji is rarely given to a sentimental and dramatic response to immediate events. His creativity is characterized by deep reflection upon and understanding of the complexities and nuances of reality.

As a novel *Tamas* is episodic in structure, which, from the point of view of literary craftsmanship may not exactly be considered flawless. Yet, as a piece of literature it reveals the vision of one detached yet passionate, quietly reflective yet emotionally intense.

A work of fiction with an immediate historical event as a backdrop invariably invites questions like how far does the work reflect true history? In the case of *Tamas*, the question becomes all the more delicate because it involves three different religious communities who were either the victims, or the aggressors, in different parts of the country, during partition. In 1974 when the novel was first published, surprisingly, no such questions were raised. However, when the television mini-series based on *Tamas* and two other short stories by Bhishamji ('Sardarni' and 'Zahud Baksh') was shown from 9 January 1988 it evoked an unprecedented response all over the country, both emotional and political. Several questions were raised — Why *Tamas* now? Why dig up old graves of tragic memories when the country was constantly tense with apprehensions of communal violence? Amidst the allegations of being biased against the Hindu community and unjustifiably glorifying the Communists and thus distorting history, fears were expressed that the uneducated, poor and insecure 'common man' might find it highly inflammatory and that a fresh wave of communal strife might sweep the nation. A petition was moved in the Bombay High Court praying for the discontinuance of the telecast on the plea, among others, that ... the film would have a deleterious effect on the minds of people at large who in the majority were illiterate and particularly on the youth of the country . . . No one was going to learn anything from *Tamas* and religious slogans would poison the minds of the young.'

In their by now famous judgement Justice Bakhtawar Lentin and Justice Sujata Manohar of the Bombay High Court said . . . *Tamas* is an anatomy of that tragical period. It depicts how communal violence was generated by fundamentalists and extremists in both communities, and how innocent persons were duped into serving the ulterior purposes of fundamentalists and communalists of both sides; how an innocent boy is seduced to violence resulting in his attacking both communities; how extremist elements in both communities infuse tension and hatred for their own ends at the cost of intercommunal harmony, how realisation ultimately dawns as to the futility of it all, and finally how inherent goodness in human nature triumphs and both communities learn to live in amity. They have learnt it the hard way. *Tamas* is in equal measure against fundamentalists and extremists of both communities, and not in favour of hatred towards any one particular community. Both communities are treated equally for blame as they are for praise. The message is loud and clear, directed as it is against the sickness of communalism.'

The Supreme Court of India, upheld the Bakhtawar Lentin-Sujata Manohar judgement and observed. . . 'It is out of the tragic experience of the past that we can fashion our present in a rational and reasonable manner and view our future with wisdom and care. Awareness in proper light is a first step towards that realisation. It is true that in certain circumstances truth has to be avoided. *Tamas* takes us to a historical past — unpleasant at times, but revealing and instructive. In those years which *Tamas* depicts, a human tragedy of great dimensions took place in this sub-continent — though 40 years ago it has left lasting damage to the Indian psyche. It has been said by Lord Morley in *On Compromise* that it makes all the difference in the world whether you put truth in the first place or in the second place. It is true that a writer or a preacher should cling to truth and right, if the very heavens fall. This is a universally accepted basis. Yet, in practice, all schools alike are forced to admit the necessity of a measure of accommodation in the very interests of truth itself. Fanatic is a name of such ill repute, exactly because one who deserves to be so called injures good causes by refusing timely and harmless concession; by irritating prejudices that a wiser way of urging his own opinion might have turned aside; by making no allowances, respecting no motives, and recognising none of those qualifying principles that are nothing less than necessary to make his own principle true and fitting in a given society. Judged by all standards of a common man's point of view of presenting history with a lesson in this film, these . . . could have been kept in mind. This is also the lesson of history that naked truth in all times will not be beneficial but truth in its proper light indicating the evils and the consequences of those evils is instructive and that message is there in *Tamas* ... There cannot be any apprehension that it is likely to affect public order or it is likely to incite the commission of any offence. On the other hand, it is more likely that it will prevent incitement to such offences in future by extremists and fundamentalists.'

Apart from the judiciary, a large number of democratic, progressive and secular individuals and groups, trade unions, students organizations, womens' groups, scientists, film societies and political parties like the Communist Party of India (CPI) and Communist Party of India (Marxist) expressed their solidarity and support for *Tamas* in strong and unequivocal terms.

In the midst of the raging controversy Doordarshan, India's State-controlled television network, stood by its decision to complete the telecasting of all the six episodes.

As cinema *Tamas* has been hailed variously as a 'milestone', 'a major achievement', 'an extremely relevant historic document', 'a work with epic dimensions' and 'a masterpiece'. It has also been condemned as 'simplistic', 'overdrawn', 'inflammatory', 'irrelevant', 'a distortion of history' and 'exploitative commercial cinema'. This was to be expected.

A subject as potentially explosive as partition will always raise strong emotions. All I can personally say about the TV version of *Tamas* is that it refocussed the attention of the public on the grim consequences of communal politics and the significance of secularism to preserve our democratic system and national unity.

Bhishamji is a committed secular humanist. In *Tamas*, as in all his major works, he provides an insight into the contradictions of human nature, the complexities of a fanatic mind, the subversive nature of communal politics, the terror of religious fundamentalism, the undercurrents of faith and hope in the midst of the most violent of tragedies. When I read the novel for the first time, I was deeply moved by its simplicity of expression, its honesty of observation, and the deep compassion of his secular vision. As a film-maker, I only made a humble effort to retain these qualities in my film version of *Tamas*.

For me, who has deep impressions of the holocaust of partition, (my first memories of fright, panic and blood are from that period), *Tamas* is more than just a mini series or a film, it is an act of faith. As a novel *Tamas* is more than a work of literature. It is a grim reminder of the immense tragedy, that results whenever the religious sentiments of communities are manipulated to achieve political objectives. It is a prophetic warning against the use of religion as a weapon to gain and perpetuate political power.

Bombay   *Govind Nihalani*
March 1988

A clay lamp stood flickering in the alcove. Its tiny flame drooped and again winked back into life. Two bricks had fallen from the wall where it joined the roof, making a hole in it. As the wind blew in through the hole the lamp would waver, casting lurid shadows on the wall. Then the little flame would straighten up on its own, sending up a thin column of soot which, after licking the arch of the alcove, dissipated itself in the air. Nathu was breathing hard, his chest heaving like a bellows. He suspected it was his breathing that made the lamp flicker.

As Nathu sat there, his back resting against the wall, his eyes again turned towards the pig. The pig squealed and, rushing up to the slimy garbage heaped in the middle of the room, feverishly started rummaging through it with its purplish snout, its small, beady, red-rimmed eyes fixed intently on the heap. For the last two hours, Nathu had been trying hard to overpower the beast. Three times its snout had fastened on his leg and a searing pain had shot through his flesh.

Its eyes fixed on the floor, the pig would trot along the wall as if searching for something. Then it would suddenly squeal and move away. Its small tail curled over its back like a whiplash. Rheum, oozing from its left eye, had trickled down to its snout. As it walked, its belly swayed heavily from side to side. By constantly trampling over it, the pig had scattered the garbage and now the stink of rotting food, the foul breath of the pig and the acrid smoke of the lamp hung in the damp room. There were clots of blood on the floor but no signs of injury on the pig's body. It was as if Nathu had been plunging his knife into water or sand. He had succeeded several times in sticking his knife into the animal's belly or under its shoulder; as the knife came out a few drops of blood would trickle out and fall on the floor. But that was all: the flesh, it seemed, had the knack of remaining miraculously whole. Every now and again with an angry grunt, the pig would lower its head and aim its snout at Nathu's leg. Then it would resume walking along the wall or attack the garbage again.

Nathu cursed his fate. What a sinister brute had fallen to his lot to tackle; ugly, big-bellied, with a jungle of bristles on its belly and white hair around its snout, thick and stiff like a porcupine's.

Nathu had heard somewhere that the easiest way to kill a pig was by pouring scalding water over its body. But where could he get boiling water at this time? Once, when tanning a hide, Nathu's companion, Bheku, the tanner, had told him in passing·that one should go for a pig's hind legs and twist them, making the animal roll over. While it was struggling to get back to its feet, one should cut open its jugular vein. The pig would die.

Nathu had attacked the pig, time and again, using all the devices that he could think of. All to no avail. Instead, he had hurt his own knees and ankles. It was one thing to tan a hide and quite another to kill a pig. He cursed the evil moment when he had agreed to take the job in hand. Even now, had he not taken the money in advance , he would have pushed the animal out of the door.

Nathu had been washing his hands under the tap, after finishing the day's work, when Murad Ali had appeared.

'Our Veterinary Doctor requires a dead pig,' he had said to Nathu.

'A dead pig? What for, Master?' Nathu had looked at Murad Ali, surprised.

'A lot of pigs escape from the piggery and run all over the place. Entice one of them into your room and kill it.'

Nathu had looked hard at Murad Ali. 'I've never tried my hand at killing pig, Master,' he had said. 'I'm told it's a difficult job. I'm afraid I won't be up to it, *hazoor*. If it's a question of skinning it, I'm at your service. But killing a pig, only the piggery people can kill pigs.'

'If I wanted to get the job done by them I wouldn't have come to you.' Murad Ali had said, taking out a crisp five-rupee note from his pocket and thrusting it into Nathu's side pocket. 'It's not much of a job for you,' Murad Ali had tried to sound very casual.

'The veterinary doctor wants a pig. I couldn't say no to him, could I? You come across many pigs running about in the vicinity of the piggery, on the other side of the cemetery. Catch hold of one of them. If those people create trouble, the veterinary doctor knows how to deal with them.'

Giving Nathu no opportunity to refuse, Murad Ali had turned to go. 'You must finish the job tonight,' he had said swinging his cane against his leg. 'The *jamadar* (sweeper) will come at dawn and carry away the carcass in his cart. Don't forget. The pig is to be delivered at the veterinary doctor's house. I'll tell the *jamadar*. Understand?'

Nathu had gaped at Murad Ali's face, astonished by the request. But the note in his pocket had stopped him from protesting. 'It's a Muslim locality,' Murad Ali had warned Nathu. 'If any one sees you, there's bound to be trouble. Be careful how you go about your job. I don't like it myself, but orders are orders. I can't defy the veterinary doctor, can I?' Tapping his leg with his walking stick, Murad Ali had walked away with a swagger.

Since Nathu had to deal with Murad Ali every day he was in no position to refuse him. When a horse, a cow or a buffalo died in the city, Murad Ali would let him strip off the animal's hide for which Nathu paid him eight annas or a rupee. It was worth paying Murad Ali for no one ever tried to take the hides away from him. Murad Ali was a man of some influence. Being an employee of the Municipal Committee he had easy access to the high-ups and rubbed shoulders with all kinds of people.

It was a common sight to see Murad Ali swaggering along the city roads. Dark, thickset and short-statured, he would appear at any place, in any lane, on any road of the city without any apparent reason. Small, penetrating eyes, pointed moustache, long khaki coat, going down to his knees over his *salwar*, turban over his head, a walking stick in hand. The totality of impressions added up to what was known as Murad Ali. Take away his stick or his turban and the picture would become woefully incomplete.

Murad Ali had blithely walked away, leaving Nathu in a quandary. To lay his hands on a pig and to slaughter it—it wasn't going to be easy for Nathu. He thought of going to the piggery and telling them that the veterinary doctor wanted a pig and it was their business to arrange it. But he immediately dismissed the idea as impracticable. He knew he would not be able to face the people at the piggery. For a start, how was he to bring the pig into his room? It certainly wasn't going to be easy. He had seen stray pigs hovering over garbage heaps. Maybe he could lure one into his room with garbage! So he carried garbage in big heaps and scattered it outside the courtyard, in front of the door, and inside his dilapidated room. The evening shadows had started descending when he saw three large pigs emerging from behind a dung heap. Making a detour of the stagnant pond and the cluster of bushes they wandered towards Nathu's room. One of them raised its snout, sniffed the air, and entered the courtyard. Nathu immediately closed the door of the courtyard and, running forward, opened the door of his room and then, lifting his *lathi*, manoeuvred the pig into his room. To prevent the pig from squealing and attracting its owner's attention, Nathu brought more garbage into the room for it to gorge on.

Having secured the animal, Nathu entrenched himself outside the door and smoked one *bidi* after another, waiting for nightfall. After a long patient wait, when it was finally dark, he ventured back into the room. In the dim, wavering light of the clay lamp he saw that the garbage lay scattered all over the floor, filling the room with its stench. Then his eyes fell on the big, powerful brute. It looked huge and forbidding. His heart sank. He felt like flinging the door open and letting the pig out.

More than half the night was gone and the pig was still very much alive, still gobbling up garbage. There were a few clots of blood on the floor and a few scratches on the pig's belly. Almost playfully the pig had succeeded in clamping its snout on Nathu's legs every now and again. Otherwise, the scene had undergone no significant change. The pig was in fine fettle whereas Nathu was bathed in perspiration and breathing heavily. He sat there looking balefully at the pig and wondered how he could extricate himself from his predicament.

Far away, the clock in the Sheikh's Tower struck two. Nathu got up in alarm; glared at the pig. Planting its feet on a heap of garbage, the pig urinated and then resumed its walk, round and round the room. The clay lamp again winked and the shadows danced ghoulishly on the wall. The situation remained unchanged for a while. Lowering its head, the pig would abruptly stop to sniff at the garbage and resume its circumambulations. Then it would squeal and dash off across the room, its tiny, little tail twisting into a knot and then uncurling itself like an insect.

'I wish I knew what to do!' Nathu thought in angry frustration.

'This brute is going to be the death of me.'

He decided to make one more attempt to catch hold of the pig's hind legs and roll it over on the floor. Holding the knife aloft in his left hand, he cautiously moved to the middle of the room. Having reached the end of the room, the pig was now walking along the left wall. Seeing Nathu approaching, instead of fleeing, the animal suddenly turned and made for him. Then it stopped in mid-gallop with a grunt, as a prelude to charging its tormentor. Nathu cautiously retreated, step by step, his eyes fixed on the pig's snout. Still facing Nathu, the pig stalked forward. No, Nathu knew he had no chance of grabbing the animal's hind legs. The pig's small eyes glittered with hate; it seemed to be getting desperate. It was already past two. What Nathu had not been able to achieve in the course of the long night, there was little chance of his accomplishing in the remaining two hours before dawn. The *jamadar* could come any moment with his cart. If that happened how would he face Murad Ali? From a friend he could turn into an enemy. He could stop giving him hides, have him ejected from his hovel and even get him beaten. He knew so many ways of harassing a person. Nathu felt helpless. To go for the pig's legs was a risky affair. It might get frantic and bite him. Or, in its frenzy to get its legs released from his hold, it could kick out at him and injure him.

It made Nathu angry. 'It's going to be either me or the pig!' he muttered. Retreating towards the alcove, he pulled out one of the slabs which was loose, and went back to the middle of the room. Holding the stone slab over his head, he stood stiffly erect, watching the animal. The pig had lost interest in him and was sniffing at the rind of a water melon, its red eyes blinking, its small tail waving at its back. If the animal stood still like that, the slab could cause it considerable injury and it would be slowed down effectively.

Taking aim, Nathu hurled the slab at the animal. The lamp wavered, the shadows on the wall shook. The slab hit the pig squarely, but on which part of its body Nathu could not tell, for he had turned his face away as he let go of the slab. The pig grunted loudly as the slab hit it. But, to Nathu's surprise, the pig still seemed unhurt in any significant way.

Suddenly, the pig grunted again, and walked to the middle of the room, its belly swaying from side to side. Nathu stationed himself at the door opening into the courtyard. Under the wavering light of the lamp he could see the pig, a solid black mass, walking ponderously towards him. It looked as though the slab had hit it on its head and, feeling dazed, it was having difficulty seeing. Nathu felt scared. Was the pig going to charge him? It could bite him, maul him badly. Quickly opening the door he slipped out of the room.

'I'm done for!' he muttered to himself, as he stood leaning against the courtyard wall. The streaming wind came as a relief. The stench in the room and its stuffiness had been getting intolerable. As the wind blew against his perspiring body he felt alive again.

'This job will be my undoing!' he said to himself in despair. 'What is it to me if the veterinary doctor does not get a pig! I've done my best. Tomorrow I'll return the five-rupee note to Murad Ali and fold my hands before him. "*Hazoor*, this job is beyond me." I'll tell him. He can't do me any harm. For two days he will go about grim-faced. On the third day I'll place my head at his feet and he'll relent.'

Nathu lingered in the courtyard. The moon had come out, softening and rearranging the perspective of the familiar scene around him. Some distance from where he stood ran the dirt road. Throughout the day, one could hear the creaking of the bullock carts and the jingle of bells around the bullocks' necks as the carts passed along the dirt road. But now the road lay deserted and quiet. Across the road, wild berry trees, thorny bushes and cactus plants grew along the steep slopes that descended to the *maidan*, beyond which lay the graveyard. Behind the graveyard stood the huts inhabited by low caste grave diggers. The grave-diggers would get roaring drunk at night and start raving, frightening Nathu who lived in a nearby hovel with his wife.

Nathu suddenly thought of his wife sleeping in the tanners' *basti* (settlement). If he had not got himself involved in this racket he would have been sleeping by her side; with her firm and lush body in his arms? He knew she must have been waiting for him till late at night, for he had come away without leaving word with her. Even a separation of one night was too much.

Nathu felt that his body had gone so limp that even while standing he could take a short nap, resting his head on the courtyard wall. It was so peaceful outside that the knife in his hand looked old, almost an anachronism. If only he could run away without having to go back to the room! Tomorrow when the Purbia swineherd passed that way and saw the garbage scattered all over the place, he would at once guess that his pig must be loitering somewhere in the vicinity and it would take him no time to locate the truant and chase it back to the piggery.

Nathu again thought of his wife. Oh, how he missed her! A few sweet words from her lips would have eased his tormented mind. He wished he could extricate himself from his present ordeal and join her at the tanners' *basti*.

The Sheikh's clock struck three, sending a shiver through Nathu's body. His gaze travelled to the knife in his hand. What was he doing standing here while the pig was still alive? Soon the *jamadar* would arrive with his push cart. What would he tell him? A pale yellow had streaked the eastern sky. It would soon be dawn. And here he was, his task far from accomplished.

His head in a whirl, he went to the room and pushing open the door, cautiously peeped in through the narrow opening. A whiff of stench assailed his nostrils. In the dim light of the lamp, he saw the pig standing in the middle of the room, looking listless and exhausted as if constant walking had sapped it's strength. Here was the opportunity Nathu had been waiting for to fell the brute and end the whole thing.

Closing the door behind him, Nathu stood under the alcove and steadily looked at the pig. The pig lifted its snout and looked in Nathu's direction. It looked furious. The slab of stone lay some distance behind the pig. The lamp flickered, casting unsteady shadows in the room. Then the pig stirred and tried to walk. Nathu looked at the pig in surprise. Yes, it was moving, steadily advancing towards him, its belly swaying from side to side. Then it stopped and made a strange throaty sound. Holding his knife on the ready, Nathu sat down on his feet, watching the pig all the time. The pig took a few more steps forwards, its snout limply hanging between its legs. But before it could reach Nathu, it lurched to one side and collapsed on the floor. Its legs shook, violently and then stiffened. The pig was dead.

Nathu put his knife down. His eyes were still fixed on the pig. Somewhere in the neighbourhood a cock flapped its wings and crowed. Then Nathu heard the rattling sound of a push cart on the dirt road. He heaved a sigh of relief.

Chapter 2

At the start, only a handful of people had assembled for the morning singing party. But as the party wound its way through the bazars and lanes more people joined up, yawning and scratching their bellies.

There was still a nip in the air. The members of the party, who had joined early, had arrived swathed in thin blankets and the more aged among them had protected their heads and faces with knitted woollen caps.

The clock in the Sheikh's garden struck four. There were only three people standing in front of the office of the Congress Committee, the starting point of the singing party. They were waiting for the others to arrive. Two men, apparently members of the CID (the secret police) in plain clothes, stood a little apart from the group, watching it.

In the distance, a light twinkled in the dark. Taking a turning at the end of the Burra Bazar, a man came walking towards the group, a hurricane lantern in his hand. In the arc of light thrown by the lantern only the man's pajamas were visible, creating the illusion that two legs were walking along with the torso missing.

'Here comes Bakshiji,' Aziz said, recognizing the owner of the pajamas from a distance.

Bakshiji was a stickler for punctuality. To him, four o'clock meant four on the dot; neither a minute less nor a minute more. But this morning he was himself late.

Yes, it was Bakshiji, the Secretary of the District Congress Committee. Phlegmatic, growing in years, his body had already started showing signs of age, but even so nothing happened unless he was around.

As Bakshiji drew nearer, Aziz recited a couplet which held that there was one thing in common between a preacher, a priest of the mosque and a torch bearer: They showed light to others but themselves moved in the dark.

'I slept late last night,' Bakshiji said defensively as he came up to the others. 'I couldn't wake up in time. I don't see Master Ram Das here. Hasn't he come?'

'He must first milk his cow,' Aziz replied promptly. 'How can he come without milking his cow?'

'When he was seeking a rise in his salary he came bouncing along even at eleven in the night. Now he has got what he wanted. So why should he care?'

In the distance they saw a tall man, clad in white, coming from the direction of the Naya *mohalla*. Seeing them, he quickened his pace.

'Here comes the Man of Truth!' One of the party greeted the newcomer. 'Mehtaji, you look every inch a leader.'

Mehtaji looked around. He wanted to know where Ajit Singh, Desraj, Shanker, Master Ram Das and various others were. Then he turned to Bakshiji. 'I knew four o'clock would be too early for the party. I told you so.'

'If you tell them four, it's only then that they assemble at five,' Bakshiji said. 'If you had asked them to come at five they would have assembled long after sunrise. Mehtaji, you're in the habit of pulling up others but you're yourself the worst defaulter.' Bakshiji put his hand into his waistcoat pocket under the blanket and produced a packet of cigarettes.

'Mehtaji, even from a distance you look a leader.' Aziz said, taking another dig at Mehtaji.

A hint of a smile broke through Mehtaji's grave expression. 'The other day when I was standing at the bus-stand someone mistook me for Pandit JawaharLal,' Mehtaji said, placing his hand on Aziz's shoulder. "Is that Pandit Nehru standing over there?" I overheard the man asking his companion. Well, people often make this mistake.'

'You've a majestic bearing, a grand personality!'

'The only thing is that I'm slightly taller than Pandit Nehru.'

'Mehtaji, did you take your bath before coming?' Kashmirilal asked.

'What a question to ask! I never stir out of the house without a bath. Summer or winter, I must observe this rule. Kashmirilal, if you ask me, no one should be allowed to join a singing party unless he has taken a bath. And I know you haven't even washed your face.'

'I washed my face last week,' Kashmirilal said, a mischievous gleam in his eyes.

Their attention was drawn by a sound coming from the direction of the slope leading up to the Congress office: 'Left! Left! Right! Left!'

'Lo and behold! our General has also marched up!' Bakshiji said. They all started laughing.

The light of the hurricane lantern first fell on the General's worn-out shoes. It was difficult to make out whether they were shoes or bedroom slippers. They seemed to be a cross between the two. His khaki trousers started six inches above his ankles. He wore a khaki tunic, also abbreviated like his trousers. He had pinned all the Gandhi and Nehru medallions that he could lay his hands on, onto his breast pocket, embellished with assorted coloured ribbons and strings. His tunic was crumpled and hung loose on his shriveled body. What made his face so conspicuous was his unkempt, moth-eaten, beard. He wore a loosely bound khaki turban on his head.

The General was the one person among the party who had regularly courted imprisonment during the Freedom Movement. He went about making speeches, whether there was a meeting or not, and often came in for rough handling. But that never deterred him from performing his self-imposed duties. A swagger stick under his arm, he would take one *mohalla* (locality) after another in his stride. If a *tonga* (horse-carriage) was hired to go round the city to make public announcements on behalf of the party, the General was invariably one of the three who constituted the announcement team. He was the first to speak at all meetings, though his hollow, hoarse voice did not carry beyond the first two rows.

'General, yesterday you showed your back at that meeting,' Kashmirilal said.

Recongnizing Kashmirilal's voice, the General focused his small, beady eyes on him and pressed his swagger stick under his arm.

'I've no truck with men like you, specially in the morning,' he said glaring at Kashmirilal. 'Keep yourself at a distance from me.'

'This is no time for jokes,' Bakshiji said to Kashmirilal in a severe voice. 'Leave the General alone.'

But the General was already in full cry. 'I'll expose you to one and all,' he said in a threatening voice. 'I know you hobnob with the Communists. The other day I saw you feasting on *chaina murgi* with the Communist, Devdutt at the hunchback sweetmeat seller's shop.'

'That's enough, General,' Bakshiji said in a placatory tone. 'Don't expose him any further.'

Just then Shankerlal appeared on the scene, the ends of his broad pajamas flapping. The darkness gradually grew thinner and thinner. On the right, one more layer of darkness had fallen from over the high wall of the bank building. Across the road, adjacent to the Arya School building, jets of smoke rose from sweetmeat shops. From the side lanes emerged the early morning walkers on their morning constitutionals. They cleared their throats and brandished their walking sticks as they briskly walked along the road. They were all men, though an occasional woman, her face covered, could be seen going towards the gurudwara or the temple.

Bakshiji lifted the hurricane lantern and blew it out.

'This is how you greet me, Bakshiji? A fine welcome, indeed!' Shankerlal, the public announcer, said. 'You blew out the lamp the moment I arrived.'

'What do you want the light for?' Bakshiji said. 'For people to admire your looks or Mehtaji's?' Then he added as an after-thought, 'It would have been a waste of oil. The lantern does not belong to the Congress Committee. It belongs to me, it's my property. If you can get me the necessary sanction for oil from the Committee I'll burn it day and night.'

Shankerlal, who had taken his position behind Kashmirilal, said under his breath, 'If you can burn cigarettes without permission why do you require permission for burning kerosene?'

Bakshiji had heard Shankerlal's remark but he swallowed his anger and ignored him. He considered it beneath him to bandy words with persons like Shankerlal.

'You're the boss,' Shankerlal tried to drive the point home. 'Why should you, of all persons, require any permission?' Without waiting to find out if his jibe had registered, he turned to Mehtaji. 'Jai Hind, Mehtaji!'

'Jai Hind!'

'I hadn't seen you.'

'These days you don't care to take notice of me. You've become too big. Your bag? Haven't you brought your bag?'

'What have I to do with my bag at the morning singing party?'

'Wah! A bag comes handy anywhere. One never knows when one may run into a candidate for life insurance.'

Mehtaji made no reply. Besides his involvement in the Congress activities he also did life insurance business.

'Shanker watch what you say,' Bakshiji said, 'Mehtaji is three times your age. You must have some regard for elders.'

'Did I say anything wrong? I only asked him why he hadn't brought his bag. I didn't ask him if he had succeeded in getting fifty thousand rupees off Sethi.'

Shanker a blunt man, did not believe in mincing words. In fact, he was famous for his cutting remarks. By alluding to the fifty thousand rupees, he had touched Mehtaji on a raw spot.

Mehtaji had been President of the District Congress Committee and had spent sixteen years in jail. He wore spotless white khadi. Only a bold man like Shanker could dare to insinuate anything against him. As rumour went, Sethi had agreed to take a life policy for fifty thousand rupees through Mehtaji who, in turn, had promised to get Sethi a Congress nomination at the forthcoming Assembly elections.

'Mehtaji, don't take any notice of this loud-mouthed fellow,' Bakshiji said 'He only knows how to trot out canards.'

'I never said that Mehtaji has promised to get Sethi a nomination ticket. Only the Provincial Committee has the right to do so at the recommendation of the District Committee. If the local President and the Secretary come to some secret understanding between the two of them—well, that's too bad. We won't let that happen. I know the President and the Secretary are hearing what I am saying. If big contractors and money-bags manage to wangle tickets in this manner that will be the end of the Congress.'

Mehtaji walked away and began talking to Kashmirilal. Bakshiji lighted another cigarette.

Mehtaji and Shanker never agreed with each other. The feud had started from the day the District Committee nominated its delegates to the Lahore Conference at which Pandit Nehru was to preside. Mehtaji had not included Shanker's name in the Conference. To add insult to injury, the Conference had organized a big community lunch from which Mehtaji had excluded Shanker, though he had bought tickets for the other delegates from the Party fund. Though it had irritated Shanker he hadn't been able to do anything about it. Somehow he had managed to find his way to the lunch session. At lunch Mehtaji and Shanker had happened to be sitting facing each other. Shanker had been gobbling up his food like a hungry wolf, making a spectacle of himself.

'Shanker, eat like a human being!' Mehtaji had admonished him. 'You are bringing a bad name to our District Committee.'

'Mehtaji, you've no right to talk like that to me,' Shanker had retorted. 'I've spent my hard-earned money on this food. I've not bought it with Congress funds. We shall thrash the matter out when we are back home. I know how to deal with people of your type.'

True to his word, on returning from Lahore, Shanker had had a big tiff with Mehtaji. The election to the Provincial elections of the Congress Committee had been about to take place. Each District Committee had the right to nominate four candidates for election. Mehtaji proposed Kohli's name as the fourth candidate. But for Shanker Kohli would have certainly been nominated. At the meeting of the Scrutiny Committee Shanker had suddenly stood up.

'Pardon me, I want to ask a question,' he had said.

Mehtaji had realized Shanker was spoiling for trouble. 'It's a meeting of the Scrutiny Committee,' he had said. 'You can ask me any number of questions afterwards.'

'I am not asking you. I'm asking the Scrutiny Committee.' Shanker had stood there, dramatically poised, waiting for the Chairman's permission to speak.

'What do you want to know?' the Chairman had asked.

'May I know what rules govern the nomination of candidates?'

'Talk some sense. This is no time for fooling around.'

'Mehtaji, I'm not asking you. You had better keep quiet.'

'Let him have his say,' the Chairman had said. 'Yes, Shanker *bhai*, so you want to know the rules?'

'As far as I know, a Congress member is required to pay an annual subscription of four annas, he must wear pure handspun khadi and he must daily ply the spinning wheel. Am I right?'

'Yes, Shanker *bhai*, you're correct.'

'I'll request Kohli Saheb to stand up for a moment.'

A hush had fallen on the room. .

'Excuse my impertinence, every member has a right to put a question to the Scrutiny Committee.'

Mehtaji had growled.

'Mehta Saheb, you're not the Chairman of this committee. Your writ can't run here. Well, Kohli Saheb, will you please stand up for a moment?'

Kohli had stood up. 'You wear khadi, don't you?'

'What's going on here? Come to the point. What are you driving at?'

'May I see your pajama cord?'

'Why? Why should you?'

'It's an insult to a member.'

'Mehta Saheb, I'm not doing this for fun. You've no business to interrupt when the Chairman is here. Kohli Saheb, please show your pajama cord.'

'And if I don't.?'

'You have to. Your pajama cord has an important bearing on the point I'm going to make.'

'Show him, *yar*. That's the only way to shut his big mouth. It seems a lot of loafers have infiltrated the Congress.'

'What did you say, Mehtaji? If I'm a loafer, by the same token you're a scoundrel. I know everything inside out. Well, Kohli Saheb...?'

'You want me to untie my pajama cord before everybody?'

'Who's asking you to untie it? I'm just asking you to show it.'

'Show it to him *yar*, and be done with it.'

Kohli lifted the flap of his achkan and then the front of his kurta. Under it a yellow pajama cord dangled. Shanker had jumped forward and caught hold of the cord.

'Have a good look, friends!' he had cried. 'It's not made of handspun cotton yarn. It's machinemade and of artificial silk. You may see it for yourself, if you like.'

'So what? How does it really matter?'

'You want to nominate for election a person who violates the basic rules with impunity? Has the Congress really no rules?'

The members of the Scrutiny Committee had looked at one another. They had had no alternative but to strike Kohli's name from the list of candidates. Since that day Mehtaji had developed a great dislike for Shanker.

Bakshiji was getting restive. Master Ram Das had not shown up, nor had Desraj. Who would lead the singing? In the singing party they must have someone who sang well. Of course, Bakshiji himself could sing. But what about those who were paid for the job by the District Committee?

'I tell you, Mehtaji, Ram Das will not show up until we have covered three lanes.' Bakshiji said. 'He will say that the calf drank all the milk. See? That's the kind of interest they have in their jobs!' Then he turned to the others standing around him. 'Kashmirilal, we can't wait any longer. Better start.'

Kashmirilal, who enjoyed having fun at others expense, at once turned to the General.

'General, let's have your speech!' he said. 'We must have a speech before we launch forth on our singing.'

Immensely pleased, the General marched up, swinging his stick, and got up on a rock by the roadside.

Bakshiji was furious. 'Kashmirilal, is this the time for a speech?' he asked testily. 'If you're not serious about it,let us call off the whole thing.' He stepped forward towards the General. But the General had already started his speech.

'Come down, you!' Bakshi said, gesticulating wildly. 'We don't want to have your lecture so early in the day. Ask the fellow to come down, yar!'

'Nobody can stop me from speaking!' the General said, as he stood firmly perched on the stone. He began his speech:

'Gentlemen!' he said in his grating voice.

The General was only a little above fifty but many years in the British jails had sapped his vitality. Whereas other Congress men were given the 'B' class in jail, he was consigned to the 'C' category as a result of which he often fell ill for he had to eat abominable food and *chapatis* made from flour mixed with sand. But the General was not the type to submit. He never gave up wearing his uniform. There was an interesting story behind the uniform. He had attended the historic Lahore session of the Congress as a volunteer. When they proclaimed complete independence as their goal, he had danced with joy along with Pandit Nehru, on the banks of the Ravi. From that day on he had always worn the volunteer's uniform. When he came into some money he would add a whistle to the uniform or an additional tricolour cord to his shoulder pad. When hard up, which was most of the time, he could not even afford to wash the uniform. He never had any employment, nor did he ever try to find a job. He was paid fifteen rupees a month by the Congress office for public announcements. If Bakshiji tried to find fault with him he would immediately launch into a nonstop harangue. He had no home, no wife, no children. So he had no responsibilities. Every week he would be beaten up by adversaries of the Congress. When there was a *lathi* charge by the police, while others scampered away, he would stand there baring his scraggy chest and would return with a few broken ribs.

'Kashmirilal, ask him to stop!' Bakshiji fumed. 'Do you want people to laugh at us?

'Gentlemen, I'm sorry to tell you that the Presidentji of the District Congress Committee has betrayed us. Till the very end we shall stand by the pledge that we took on the bank of the Ravi in 1929. Without taking much of your time I would like to reiterate that no man can defy the mandate of the Congress. Mehtaji is an insignificant creature before us. We are capable enough of dealing with him as well as with his stooges—Kashmirilal, Shankerlal, Jeet Singh and their like.'

There was a peal of laughter.

'You can't get the better of him like this,' Kashmirilal, who had prompted the General, whispered in Bakshiji's ear. 'The more you try to stop him, the more obdurate he'll get.'

Bakshiji glared at Kashmirilal.

'If you clap he'll end his speech. Don't worry. Just clap two or three times and that will do the trick.' Kashmirilal started clapping and the others, taking their cue from him, joined in.

'Gentlemen! Without taking more of your valuable time I must take this opportunity to express my gratitude to you for hearing me with such patience. I assure you that day is not far off when our country will become independent. The Congress is bound to gain its objective. The pledge that I took on the bank of the Ravi...'

Kashmirilal clapped again.

'Gentlemen, I thank you once again. I will present myself before you some other day. Now join me in shouting, "Inquilab!"'

The audience responded with, 'Zindabad!'

'Are you starved? Don't you eat? Louder!'

The response this time was louder: 'Zindabad!'

His swagger stick under his arm, the General got down from the rock.

'Zindabad!' The shout had come from the direction of the slope. Panting heavily, Master Ram Das came into view through the morning haze.

'So, this is your idea of punctuality!' Bakshiji said to him angrily.

The reply came from Kashmirilal: 'The calf is to blame. He sucked up all the milk—and that, as you know, was responsible for the delay.'

They all laughed. But Master Ram Das remained unperturbed. 'We are not having morning singing today, are we?'

'Why not?'

'This morning has been allotted for community reconstruction work. That's what was decided, if I'm not mistaken.'

'Who decided it?'

'Last night Gosainji told me that in the morning we would undertake the cleaning of the lanes behind Imamdin's *mohalla.*'

'Don't give me that. You're just making up lame excuses because you are late.'

'I've already sent the brooms, baskets and spades over there. Some I sent last night and the others this morning. Five spades, twelve broomsticks, five iron pans, three pick-axes. They are lying in Sher Khan's house.'

'Nobody told me about it.'

'That's why I've come running. I was here earlier but there was no one about.'

'You mean you want us to clean the drains?' Kashmirilal asked. 'Are you mad? They don't have any drains there.'

'Of course, the drains are there. But they are *kuchcha* ones. None of them is paved.'

'If they are unpaved, they must have been gathering filth for years. Who's going to clean them?'

'We shall do it,'the General said in a sharp voice. 'You're a traitor, Kashmirilal!'

'One time it's one decision, another time it's something else. If Gosainji had decided it that way he should have sent word to us in time.'

It was getting brighter. More people had gathered in the expectation of joining the singing party but now it looked as though they would have to do something different.

'Let's get away from here,' Bakshiji said, picking up his lantern. 'We'll go singing from here. Ram Das, start!'

They fell into position, the General taking the lead. Kashmirilal took charge of the tri-color (the party flag).

Master Ram Das started singing in his heavy tuneless voice—the same song with which they always started the march, a song that had gone stale with repetition:

Those who are fired with a passion for freedom!

The party repeated after Master Ram Das, to the accompaniment of the staccato sound of shod feet falling on the cobbled street.

They roam about like love-lorn Majnus
High and low. In every jungle, in every desert.

Singing, they went towards Imamdin's *mohalla*.

Chapter 3

Nathu heaved a sigh of relief as he neared his lane. The lane was still steeped in darkness, though it was growing light in the distance. After his nightmarish experience it was a great relief to walk along the dark, sleepy lanes.

Some distance away, to the right of the lane he was walking on, he heard people talking in whispers. As he came closer, he saw three women sitting by the tap talking, their empty pitchers lying by their sides. They were waiting for the water to be turned on by the municipality. Nathu was reassured by this familiar morning sight. He had gone only a few steps when his foot struck against something lying in the lane.

He bent down to look and saw that the thing was a broken clay pot. Parts of it lay scattered around his feet. A shiver ran through his body. Alongside some pieces of stone, tied in a rag, lay a human image made of kneaded flour, a few thin sticks of wood jutting out of its head. Some unfortunate woman must have resorted to 'black magic' in front of a house in order to pass on her woes to a neighbour's family. Nathu was extremely upset. To step on the ingredients of 'black magic' after such a ghastly night did not bode well for him. It dismayed him, but he quickly took hold of himself. Generally, this sort of 'black magic' was resorted to ward off evil from one's child. And Nathu had no child. Comforted by the thought, he resumed his walk.

He knew these lanes well. The lane he was walking along was flanked by Muslim houses, with a few Hindu dhobis' houses in between, followed by a small block of butchers' house. The butchers had their meatshops outside the lane along a nondescript patch of road which seemed to lead nowhere. Here also lived Mahmud, who ran a *hamam* (public bathing place). Further up, there was a block of Hindu and Sikh houses; after that came

27

the houses of Muslims of the Sheikh families which stretched up to the end of the lane.

He heard words of prayer coming from within a house: 'May Allah bless every man,every family!' It was an old man praying. Then he heard the sound of the old man's coughing followed by a long drawn-out yawn. People were waking up.

He had advanced only a few steps when his right foot sank into something wet and sticky and he just saved himself from falling. As he tried to pull his leg out of the mess, a half-broken pitcher rolled away in the lane and the sharp acrid smell of dung leapt to his nose. His expression mellowed. A smile played across his face. The pitcher had nullified the effect of the 'black magic'. For some days past the summer heat had been increasing and there were no signs of rain. When the rains were delayed young boys in the *mohalla* would collect horse and cow dung in a pitcher and fling it outside the house of someone in the lane who was unusually disliked. As the superstition went this was sure to bring rain.

In front of a house, a man standing by the side of a cow, was mixing fodder, cotton seed and oil cake in a trough for the animal's morning feed. From another house,Nathu heard the clinking of crockery and the jingle of bangles. A housewife getting the morning tea ready. A woman passed by, mumbling holy words, her face hidden behind her *dopatta*, a small metal pot poised on her upturned palm, on her way to a gurdwara or a temple for the morning worship. The day had started.

Nathu saw a fakir approaching from the other end of the lane, plucking his one-stringed instrument with his fingers and singing: 'O ignorant one, the birds are awake but you are still sleeping.' Nathu had not seen the fakir before,though he had often heard him singing as he went from lane to lane. A tall old man with a close-cut gray beard, he was wearing a long cloak, a bag hanging from his shoulder, his head covered with a skull cap. Singing in a low voice, he would pass through the city lanes, never missing the days of Ramzan when devout Muslims kept fasts. Nathu placed a paisa on the fakir's palm. The fakir blessed him: 'May Allah shower His blessings on you!' Nathu resumed his walk.

Traversing the lane he came onto the open road where there was more light. From here started the *mohalla* of the hackney carriage drivers. Although he was now on the road, the scene had hardly changed except that the road was not as gloomy as the lanes he had passed through. There were three *tongas* standing by the roadside, their shafts lifted towards the sky, as if deep in prayer. Standing by a long wall a driver was scrubbing his horse down. Close by, two women were making dung cakes and sticking them against the wall. In the middle of the road a horse was slowly being walked up and down, as if it was going through the ritual of a morning walk. In the stillness of the morning, the world was gradually coming back to life.

Nathu felt as if he was out on a stroll. But despite overcoming his nervousness, he did not wish to be seen by anyone. Where would the cart be now? An unpleasant question. He stepped up his pace without knowing it. For all he knew, the cart must have reached the cantonment and would be standing outside the veterinary hospital. Nathu swore under his breath. Couldn't the pig be killed in the daytime? And why was the veterinary doctor in such urgent need of a pig's carcass? Maybe he wanted to sell the pork on the sly. What a hectic night he had been through! Sweat, the stuffy room, the pig and its malevolent grunts. Three times it had rasped the skin off his leg with its snout. By the time he had succeeded in dispatching it he had himself been half-dead. What did he care for Murad Ali? He was a free man and could go anywhere he liked. He put his hand in his pocket. The five-rupee note crackled under the touch of his hand. It was money he was after and it was safe in his pocket.

From the grazing ground he took a turn to the right. Far away, the clock in the Sheikh's garden struck the hour of four. What clear chimes and how resonant! During the day the city noise muffled their sound. But now the chimes seemed to descend from heaven. They fell on his ears like divine music. Soon after, the sound of a bell from a temple built on a high mound in the middle of the city, came ringing through the air. As the sound grew louder more people emerged from their houses and went out on their morning walks, tapping their sticks on the road as they walked. Driving his goats in front of him, a goatherd came out on his morning milk round. Nathu slowed down. He was enjoying the walk and the cool breeze.

Past the carriage drivers' *mohalla* and walking along the railing of the Committee Park, flanking Imamdin's *mohalla*, Nathu came to a slope which ended in a big *maidan*. The *maidan* was the most popular venue of the city where crowds gathered everyday to witness some *tamasha* or the other. In winter there were dog fights at which people betted heavily. If a wounded dog tried to run away, the spectators ringing the arena would not let it escape. Pig-sticking was also organized in the same *maidan*, and big circus companies—Tarabai's and Rammurti's—pitched their tents there as well. Of late, political parties, specially the Muslim League and Belcha Party had started holding their meetings there. The Congress held its public meetings near the grain market under the roofed *maidan*.

Hoisting himself up, Nathu sat down on the iron railing and taking a *bidi* out of his pocket, he leisurely lighted it and took long pulls at it.

Just then the muezzin's call rang out from the mosque behind Imamdin's *mohalla*. Through the rapidly clearly morning haze he could see houses ranged along the road in the near distance.

Nathu threw away his *bidi* and, getting down from the railing, walked towards Imamdin's *mohalla*. He suddenly remembered that Murad Ali lived somewhere near the Committee Maidan. He was not quite sure of it though; he had only seen him moving about in that locality, his thin stick under his arm.

It was strange he thought, that though he had often (reluctantly) gone near Murad Ali to pay his *salaams*, he had never succeeded in seeing Murad Ali's teeth through his black, bushy moustache—even when he laughed. Only his cheeks would puff out and his sharp penetrating eyes would recede into his dark, rotund face and glitter like a serpent's. He must slip away from there. Murad Ali had specifically asked him to wait for him, outside his room. If he happened to find him roaming about in this place, he would be very angry.

He hastily scurried into a narrow lane. Walking briskly, he turned into the next lane; he heard the sound of singing and saw a group of people at the end of the lane. He guessed it must be a party of Congressmen for there was a tri-colour flag fluttering at the head of gathering. There were about ten people in the group, some young, others old, two of them wearing Gandhi caps and another a fez cap. There were also two turbaned *sardars*(Sikhs) among them.

A man shouted in a loud voice: 'National slogan!'

Back came the response: 'Bande Mataram!'

'Say Bharat Mata ki jai!'

'Mahatma Gandhi ki jai!'

Only a moment later counter-slogans echoed at the point where the two lanes interesected:

'Pakistan Zindabad!'

'Pakistan Zindabad!'

'Qaid-e-Azam Zindabad!'

'Qaid-e-Azam Zindabad!'

Nathu turned to look. Three persons had suddenly appeared at the point where the lane turned, shouting slogans. It looked as though they would prevent the singing party from going any further. One of them wore goldrimmed glasses and had a Rumi cap on his head.

Planting himself in the middle of the lane, he said in a challenging voice: 'The Congress party belongs to the Hindus. Muslims have nothing to do with it.'

'The Congress belongs to everyone!' an old man from among the singing party replied. 'It belongs alike to the Hindus, the Muslims and the Sikhs. Mahmood Saheb, you're forgetting. Once you were also one of us.'

Walking up, the old man threw his arms around Mahmood Saheb and hugged him warmly.

Disengaging himself from the old man's clasp, Mahmood said, 'Bakshiji, I know your tricks. Whatever you may say, the Congress as a political party, belongs exclusively to the Hindus. The Muslim League represents the Muslims. The Congress cannot lead the Muslims.'

Both the parties stood there facing each other. People were talking and shouting at the same time.

'You can see for yourself,' Bakshiji said. 'We've Hindus, Sikhs and Muslims among us. There's Aziz standing over there and there's Hakimiji on his right—both Muslims.'

'They are the dogs of the Hindus. We don't hate the Hindus but we certainly hate their dogs.'

There was so much venom in Mahmood's voice that both Aziz and Hakimji felt deeply upset.

'Is Maulana Azad a Hindu or a Muslim?' Bakshiji asked. 'He's the President of the Congress party.'

'Maulana Azad is the biggest dog of the Hindus. He follows Mahatma Gandhi everywhere, wagging his tail.'

31

Bakshiji said with a show of great patience, 'Freedom will be for everybody. It will be for the whole of Hindustan.'

'The liberation of Hindustan will benefit the Hindus only. The Muslims can feel free only in Pakistan.'

Nathu saw a tall, scraggy man, in a rumpled dress, a cane tucked under his arm, step forward. 'You can only establish Pakistan over my dead body!' he cried.

Someone from among his group tried to quieten him but he was too excited to stop.

'Gandhiji said that Pakistan could come only over his dead body.' the man continued in his raucous, grating voice. 'Under no circumstances will I allow Pakistan to be established as long as I live!'

'General, don't get so worked up!'

'General, stop it! Why don't you stop?' Bakshiji cried.

Bakshiji's admonition provoked the General all the more. 'Nobody can stop me!' he cried. 'I'm a soldier in Netaji Subhas Chandra Bose's Army. I know everybody. I know you too, for what you are'.

People standing around him started laughing.

The singing party tried to advance; the man in the Rumi cap blocked its way. 'Don't come this way!' he warned them. 'This *mohalla* belongs to Muslims.'

'Why do you want to stop us?' Bakshiji tried to argue with the man. 'You go about the whole city, shouting slogans. Does anyone stop you from doing so? We're only singing partiotic songs.'

'All right, we won't debar you from entering this *mohalla*,' the man in the Rumi cap said. 'But we won't allow these dogs to go with you!' He stretched his arms out and gave Aziz and Hakimji a menacing look.

Suddenly Nathu's eyes fell on Murad Ali who was standing a little way behind the man in the Rumi cap. Nathu was shocked. Walking alongside the wall, Nathu quickly fell behind the singing party, hiding himself from Murad Ali's view. It would be terrible if Murad Ali happened to stop him. He stood stock-still for some time and then, craning his neck, looked in the direction of Murad Ali. Murad Ali was still there, intently following the arguments between the two contending parties.

Slowly Nathu began to retreat, under cover of the singing party, hoping that so long as these people kept squabbling among themselves Murad Ali would not shift his gaze from them. This was his only chance of escape. If Murad Ali happened to see him there, he would reprimand him severely and demand an explanation for disobeying his orders. Nathu withdrew until he had turned the corner of the lane and then started running.

Chapter 4

They reined in their horses as they gained the top of the hill and looked out over the broad valley stretching away from the foot of the hill. Far away, a rainbow-coloured haze hung over the horizon. The hill was approached by a broad stretch of undulating land, vaulted over by a deep-blue sky under which the pine trees seemed to be floating in the air. To their left stood a high mountain range, a mass of scintillating blue, sweeping down to the west, till it merged into the plains. On their right, they could see, through the distant haze, the dim outlines of purple peaks.

Richard had ridden up the hill with his wife, Liza, to show her the glorious sunrise. He turned and looked at Liza's face to see whether she was impressed. He had wanted to present it to her as a gift for a long time.

Liza's golden hair flew in the breeze. There was a sparkle in her blue eyes but faint circles had formed under them which might have been a result of her boredom. They might have been also because of excessive beer drinking and long hours of sleep.

Richard was doing all he could to divert Liza's mind, for he wanted to see her happy. She had returned from England after a prolonged absence of six months and Richard was anxious that the old story should not repeat itself. If she did not like the new city and took it into her head to go back to England again, life would become awful for both of them. In the evening, when he returned home after a full day's work he would find her fidgety and withdrawn and he had decided to devote the mornings exclusively to her. During the course of the week, since she had joined him, he had taken her for walks on the Mall, or to the Topi Park, or for an early morning ride. On her part, Liza was making an earnest effort to take an interest in Richard's affairs. In her capacity as the Deputy Commissioner's wife, even if she went out alone to the Cantonment or the *sadar*(cantonment), the natives ran forward to *salaam* her and attend to her needs. But she could not go on her own all the time. The Deputy Commissioner's time, in a way, was not her own and both of them had the unspoken fear that it would be difficult for them to adapt to one another.

'Beautiful!' Liza exclaimed. 'Richard, what's that peak in front of us called? Do the Himalayas start from here?'

'In a way, yes,' Richard said enthusiastically. 'Further up, the valley traverses hundreds of miles between the mountain ranges.'

'How eerily quiet!' Liza said softly.

'Liza, this valley has become a part of history. All the invaders from the North came through this valley. Those who came from Central Asia and those who came from Mongolia.' Richard was getting into his stride. 'Alexander too followed the same route into India. Further on the valley bifurcates, one route going to Tibet and the other to Afghanistan. The traders came to India along this route and the Buddhist missionaries went far afield into Asia by following this trail. This region is full of history. Over the last month, I've visited all the historic places in this region. It is of special interest to a student of history — old buildings, ancient ruins, *viharas*, forts, inns.'

Liza laughed. 'Richard, you talk as if it's your own country.'

'True, the country is not mine, but the subject is.' Richard smiled. Then he pointed his riding crop towards a mountain. 'Behind that peak, about seventeen miles away as the crow flies, we have the ruins of Taxila. You've heard of Taxila, of course.'

'Yes, I'm familiar with that name.'

'Once upon a time the place was renowned for its university.'

Liza smiled. She knew that her husband would now launch forth into a detailed description of the place, bringing out its historical importance. She liked Richard's enthusiasm. He could talk about dead stones with the same zeal, marked by a childlike curiosity, as he did about living things. Although he held the position of a Deputy Commissioner, he was a bit naive in his dealings and she liked him all the more for it. She wished she could display the same interest in a subject that was so dear to his heart.

'We have also a museum at that place. You'll find it interesting. The other day I bought a small image of Gautama Buddha from there.'

'But why another? You've already so many.'

'There was an excavation going on near the place where they had unearthed many statues and other things. The curator gave me one as a gift.'

Richard had a large personal collection of various Buddhas housed in the main hall of his bungalow, with representative samples of a cross section of India folk art thrown in for good measure. The *almirahs* were crammed with books on the subject. He had developed a similar mania while he was serving in Kenya and had flooded his rooms with samples of African art, bows and arrows, beads, birds' feathers, totems. And here he had started collecting Buddhist figurines.

Liza looked at the view again. Behind her was a dense jungle of small trees through which their horses had climbed up to the hill top.

'I find the soil here rather unusual—it's so red,' Liza said as she surveyed one of the hills in front of her. 'Don't they have roads over here? Don't tell me we are going back through this jungle!' There was a twinkle in her eye. 'Richard, show me the road by which Alexander came to India.'

'They had no *pucca* roads in those days. But there is an old road—it's not less than four thousand years old. It passes along the hill.'

Liza looked at Richard. Under the thick frame of his glasses the lower portion of his face looked so delicate. She wished that instead of talking of dead stones and ancient ruins he would talk to her about love. But Richard was engrossed in his subject. 'The people you find around this place have been living here for hundreds of years,' Richard continued. 'Have you ever taken a good look at these people? They belong to the same stock, the same features, same noses, mouths, broad foreheads, brown eyes. Yes, they have brown eyes. Haven't you marked their eyes, Liza?'

'How can they belong to the same stock, Richard? You say that all kind of invaders passed along this route'.

'No, Liza, that's what people forget.' Richard said in an excited voice as if he was going to make a vital point. 'The first lot came from Central Asia,' he said. 'And those that followed after a lapse of many centuries were also from the same stock. Their origin, so to speak, was the same. The first bunch were known as the Aryans. They came into this country thousands of years ago. The others who were known as Mussalmans made inroads into this country a thousand years ago. But their roots were the same.'

'These people must be aware of this fact.'

'No, they are not. They know nothing. That's the whole point. They only know what we tell them.' After a moment's pause he added: 'They don't know their history. They only live it'

Liza was getting bored. But when Richard was talking about something he loved he became almost obsessive about it. He loved Liza but he had no time exclusively for her. Liza would suffer in silence until she had either a nervous breakdown or another six-monthly trip to England.

'Is there a picnic spot around here?' she asked, trying to stop her husband's flow of words.

Richard was hurt. Her question seemed so out of place.

'Yes, there are many,' he said resignedly, pointing with his riding crop towards the hilltop on his left. 'There are springs and dense groves in the valley. Beautiful! The Hindus have built brick structures around the springs, making them into tanks. The springs have been named after the gods of the Hindu pantheon. There are shrines of ancient *pirs* (saints) where people light lamps at night. There are also plenty of temples and fortresses...There is a beautiful picnic spot over there.' He indicated the place with his stick. 'It has the tomb of a Muslim saint where they hold a fair at the advent of spring. Dancing women come to the fair from far-off places. The fair lasts for fifteen days. People gamble during the day and there's singing and dancing at night. I'll take you there some time.'

'Is the fair on?'

'But it is not proper to go now.'

'Why?'

'There's tension between the Hindus and the Muslims. Trouble can flare up any time.'

Liza had vaguely heard about the Hindu-Muslim problem but she hadn't pursued the subject further.

'I can't even distinguish between a Hindu and a Muslim,' she said. 'Can you, Richard?'

'Of course, I can.'

'Our *khansama* (cook)—is he a Hindu or a Muslim?'

'He's a Muslim.'

'How do you know?'

'From his name. He has a small beard. From his mode of dressing. And he says his *namaz*. A Muslim's food habits are also different.'

'Oh, you know everything, Richard!'

'Oh, no. Not everything.'

'Of course, you know a great deal. And I'm so ignorant. Tell me all about it sometime. I am so keen to learn, Richard. Your secretary—the man who came to meet you at the railway station that day. The man with those pearly white teeth. What's he? A Hindu or a Muslim?'

'He's a Hindu.'

'How do you know?'

'From his name.'

'It's quite easy, Liza. The Muslim names end with Ali, Din, Ahmed, whereas the Hindu names have a Chand, Lal or Ram at the end. Roshan Lal is a Hindu name but Roshan Din is a Muslim name. Roshan Lal is a Hindu name but Iqbal Ahmed, a Muslim.'

'I'll never be able to learn all this stuff, 'Liza said, looking disheartened.

'And the turbaned man who drives your car? The man with the long beard?' she suddenly asked.

'He's a Sikh.'

'It's not difficult to distinguish him from the others,' Liza laughed.

'Yes, all Sikh names end with Singh,' Richard said.

They started their horses down the hill. It was getting warmer. The sun had come out and the thin covering of mystery had started peeling from the atmosphere.

'One enjoys roaming about in this area, 'Richard said. 'I'm sure you'll love it, Liza. We shall go to a different place every weekend.'

Richard's horse was in front. They were crossing a dry *nullah*, strewn with boulders.

'Where will you go this weekend? To Taxila?'

Richard caught the faint note of sarcasm in Liza's voice. For Richard, Taxila was a very significant and beautiful place. He could spend hours and hours there. But Liza...? Would she like to spend her time among ruins?

'We won't be able to go there for sometime, Liza. There's tension in the city. We shall go when the situation improves. This weekend...' He did not know what to say. He himself didn't know how the situation would develop, whether he would be able to find the time to take Liza out.

'We'll go some place,' he said, as they came down from the hill and spurred their horses into a trot and were soon home.

They hadn't yet had their breakfast. Walking through many rooms they came into the hall. As the month of April approached, the servants would draw the curtains over the windows and the doors early in the morning. It made the rooms pleasantly dark and kept the heat out. The walls of the hall were lined with books, wooden pedestals being located in between on which rested the Buddha figurines. A lamp shed its light on each exhibit and brought the figures into bold relief. Old Indian paintings hung on the walls and palm-leaf manuscripts rested on the mantelpiece. A large carved stone edict rested against a wooden stand in front of the fireplace, three *moorhas*(cane stools) and a low table lying alongside it. On the table lay half-open books and piles of magazines and a lamp with a large shade, shedding light over the table, leaving the rest of the hall in darkness. By the side of the table stood a pipe stand, holding seven or eight pipes. The *khansama* had instructions to place a stove and tea things near the table, for Richard was fond of preparing his own tea. This was Richard's favourite spot where he would light his pipe and then browse through his books.

Wearing an old coat with leather patches on its elbows, baggy corduroy trousers, thick blackframed glasses, a pipe held between his lips, Richard looked like the curator of a museum, as he went from room to room, his arm around Liza's waist, describing the figurines which he had acquired in her absence.

He stopped in front of a Buddha.

'The most fascinating thing about a Buddha is what they call the Buddha smile,' he said. 'It lurks round its lips. To show the smile to the best advantage the Buddha's face should be kept at a particular angle under the light. Wait, I'll show you.' Richard moved the statue slightly to the right and then turned on the light. 'See, Liza!' he said excitedly. Liza saw that the Buddha's face had lit up with a smile—serene, subtle, with a touch of irony.

'The smile always lurks around the corners of the lips,' Richard said. 'If you shed light at an angle of forty-five degrees, it breaks through to the surface. If I shift the angle the smile will fade away.'

Liza turned to look at Richard's face. How strange men could be! With what enthusiasm they talked about stones and ruins. A woman would not display her learning with such ebullience, she thought, not herself at any rate. She squeezed Richard's arm and rested her cheek against his shoulder.

'It's the most beautiful thing about all the Buddhas. A smile keeps playing around the corners of their lips.' Richard bent down and kissed Liza's hair.

Looking at Richard, as he moved leisurely from one room to the other, it was hard to believe he was the highest official of the district. In his house he was nothing more than a student of history and a connoisseur of the country's art. But when he occupied the official chair he became a mouthpiece of British imperialism and took upon himself the task of putting into practice policies that had been evolved in London. To draw a rigid line between one interest and another was a marked feature of his bureaucratic propensity. He could slide from one type of work into another with great ease. But his personal interests were kept strictly divorced from his official duties. He held court three days a week, heard the natives' cases and dispensed justice even-handedly, strictly in conformity with the Indian Penal Code. His flexiblity as an administrator did not impinge upon his probity as a judge. And that was why he had remained immune from any sort of mental conflict. His personal prejudices and values had no place in the policies which guided the affairs of administration. The thought that a person's conduct should be guided by his own beliefs was considered juvenile idealism which a person was supposed to throw overboard on joining the Indian Civil Service. The quality of a member of the Indian Civil Service lay in his shrewdness and penetrating insight in assessing a particular situation and alertness in forestalling any moves inimical to the imperialistic designs of the British ruling classes.

Their arms around each other, they went into the dining room. Of all the rooms of the bungalow, this was the one which Liza liked most. It spoke of Richard's quiet taste. Liza knew that if she had to live with Richard she must learn to conform to his tastes.

Richard lingered in the door for a while and then going into the room, settled down to breakfast.

'What are you thinking about?' Liza asked.

'I was just making up my mind where to begin'.

'Begin what?'

'To tell you about the local people, their problems, their situation.'

'Oh, Richard, I am not interested in those things. I only want to know when you will come back from the office'.

She caressed Richard's chest.

She felt that a cloud had appeared on the horizon which would soon start growing and cover the entire sky.

Richard took her in his arms, though he knew that such affection was divorced of true feeling. He did it just to mask his uncertainty. As he caressed her hair he felt that the body which he held in his arms at night was now nothing more than a lump of flesh.

The *khansama* standing in the shadows behind the table stepped forward and his red cummerbund shone in the arc of light. He pottered about, arranging breakfast on the table.

Previously, when Richard and Liza were in each other's arms with the door open, if a servant happened to pass by, Liza would struggle to disengage herself. He would hold on to her. By and by she realized that the servant was only a native and a domestic at that, and therefore, beneath her notice.

'Liza, you must take an interest in some activity or the other.'

'For instance?'

'There are so many things. The Deputy Commissioner's wife is regarded as the first lady of the district. You've only to take up something and the women will immediately flock round you.'

'I know, I know. Such as collecting funds for the Red Cross Society, holding flower shows, arranging fetes for children, collecting shoes and clothes for ex-army-men. Am I right?'

'I'm thinking of establishing an institution to look after animals. Stray dogs freely roam the roads of the cantonment and often turn rabid and bite people. And then there are people who make old and lame horses pull carriages.'

'What are you going to do with them?'

'They should be destroyed. It is downright cruel to put them to work. Stray dogs spread epidemics. You select any work you like.'

'You mean I should go about killing dogs while you rule over the district. How am I concerned? Richard, you are joking. You're always joking with me.'

'No, no. I'm not joking. I'm serious. I want you to take an interest in some social activity or the other.'

'Of course, I take an interest. You tell me more of what you were telling me in the morning. I mean about the people of India, these Hindustanis.'

Richard smiled. 'Then listen,' he said. 'The Indians are an irascible lot and highly volatile and individualistic, ready to shed blood in the name of religion. And...and...they love the white woman without exception.'

Liza looked fixedly at Richard upon hearing the last sentence. She felt he was joking with her. She regarded Richard as a highly learned and efficient man and suspected that he had a poor opinion of her, that he regarded her as ignorant and stupid. She thought his sentences often had a touch of sarcasm.

'You're never serious with me,' she said annoyed.

'It is no fun being serious,' Richard said in a disinterested voice. 'Listen, Liza, we may some have trouble here.'

'What kind of trouble?' Liza gave him a searching look. 'Is there another war in the offing?'

'Tension between the Hindus and the Muslims is mounting. There could be rioting and bloodshed.'

'You mean these people will fight among themselves? When we were in London you told me that they were fighting against us.'

'They are doing both—fighting against us and also fighting among themselves.'

'What do you mean. You're not joking again, are you?'

'They fight against one another in the name of religion and they fight against us in the name of their country,' Richard smiled.

'Richard, you make me laugh. I know everything. They fight against you for the sake of their country and you make them fight against one another in the name of religion. Tell me, am I right?'

'It's not we that make them fight, Liza. They fight of their own accord.'

'Why can't you stop them from fighting? Originally, they belonged to the same stock, didn't they? They are one nation at heart.'

Richard liked Liza for her simplicity. He leaned over and kissed her cheek.

'Darling, the rulers don't look for similarities among the ruled. They are only interested in finding out what can keep them apart.'

The *khansama* came in carrying a tray.

'Is he a Hindu or a Muslim?' Liza asked.

'You tell me.'

Liza looked intently at the *khansama*, who having put down the tray on the table, was now standing stock-still.

'A Hindu, I think,' Liza said.

'Wrong!' Richard laughed.

'Why wrong?'

'Look again—more carefully.'

'He must be a Sikh then. He has a beard and there is a turban on his head.'

Richard again laughed. The *khansama* was still standing motionless. Not a muscle on his face moved.

'He has trimmed his beard,' Richard said. 'Sikhs don't trim their beards. It's against their religion.'

'You never told me that,' Liza said.

'I haven't told you many things.'

'For instance...'

'For instance, the Sikhs have five distinguishing marks. Four more besides the hair. The Hindus generally have a tuft on their heads. The Muslims too have their distinguishing marks. Even in their food habits. The Hindus don't eat beef and the Muslims don't eat pork. The Sikhs eat *jhatka*(meat of goats killed with a single stroke) meat and the Muslims, *halal*(meat from goats where the blood is let out slowly).'

'You don't want me to learn. How can I remember so many things at a time?' She looked at the *khansama*. 'If I know all these things will I be able to know at a glance whether a person is a Hindu or a Muslim? How can one tell without seeing the distinguishing marks?' She laughed, highly amused. 'I bet they themselves don't know for certain who's a Hindu among them and who a Muslim. And Richard, you're lying. You yourself, don't know. *Khansama*, you Muslim?' She suddenly turned to the *khansama*.

'Mussalman, Mem Saheb.'

'Will you kill a Hindu?'

The *khansama* gave her a confused look. Then he turned to the Saheb and smiled. He stepped forward and held a plate out to the Saheb on which lay a folded piece of paper. As the Saheb picked up the piece of paper, the *khansama* stepped back into the shadows.

Richard unfolded the paper, read it and put it back on the tray.

'What's it, Richard?'

'The City Report, Liza,' Richard said thoughtfully.

'What's a City Report, Richard?'

'It's about the situation in the city. You know, every day I receive reports from various departments. From the Superintendent of Police, the Health Officer, the Civil Supplies Officer. Excuse me...' Richard hurriedly walked out of the room.

For sometime Liza sat silent, lost in thought. Richard had not drunk his coffee. She didn't know whether to wait for him or to finish her breakfast. Richard soon returned.

'Whose report is it, Richard?'

'The Police Chief's. But there's nothing to worry about,' Richard said in a reassuring tone. 'Only a routine report.'

Liza knew that Richard was keeping something from her.

'Richard, you're hiding something from me,' she said eventually.

'There's nothing to hide. Anyway, not from you. How are you and I concerned with their civic affairs?'

'But there must be something. What does the SP say in his report?'

'The usual routine stuff. He says that there's some tension in the city. Between the Hindus and the Muslims. But that is nothing new. You find this all over the country.'

'What are you going to do about it, Richard?'

'What am I supposed to do? I can only administer. I'll rule, what else?'

Liza raised her eyes. 'Richard, you are at it again. Why do you keep joking with me?'

'No, I'm not joking. If there's tension between the Hindus and the Muslim where do I come into the picture?'

'You can bring about a settlement between them.'

Richard smiled. He took a sip of coffee and then said in an easy voice: 'I'll tell them that their religious affairs are their own concern and they must sort them out among themselves. Of course, the government is always there to help.'

'You must also tell them that they come from the same social stock and as such it does not behove them to fight among themselves. That's what you told me.'

'Most certainly, yes. I'll tell them, Liza.' Liza did not miss the sarcasm in Richard's voice.

They drank their coffee in silence. Suuddenly Liza looked up at her husband and said in a tense voice, 'I hope you are not in any sort of danger, Richard.'

'No, Liza. When the people fight among themselves the ruler is safe.'

As the implications of Richard's remark sank into her mind he rose still higher in her esteem.

'You're right, Richard,' she said. 'You know everything. My fears are baseless. Mrs Jackson told me that once, some time ago, Jackson, with just a revolver in his hand, chased a mob away single-handed. She was standing on the balcony, watching her husband facing the crowd, and quaking with fear. Just think of it, Richard. On one side there was Jackson alone and on the other a huge mob. Yes, anything could have happened.'

'There's nothing to worry about, darling.'

Richard rose from his chair. He patted Liza's cheek and left the room.

Chapter 5

The veil of darkness had started lifting, when, wending its way through the labyrinth of tortuous lanes, the singing party reached Imamdin's *mohalla*. On the way they had collected pans, spades and brooms from Sher Khan's house. In the morning light one could clearly see their pale, tired faces. Except for Mehta they looked dirty and tired. The Gandhi cap on Bakshiji's head was askew. Shanker, Master Ram Das and Aziz carried broomsticks on their shoulders. Desraj and Sher Khan were carrying the pans to carry dirt and the General a long bamboo pole. Master Ram Das squirmed as he looked at the broomsticks on his shoulders.

'See, what times have come to!' he muttered. 'Brahmins carrying broomsticks! Mysterious indeed are Mahatma Gandhi's ways.' He laughed under his breath and hid the broomsticks behind his back. Getting no response to his remarks from the others, he turned to Bakshiji.

'I'll not clean the drain,' he said. 'I'm telling you in advance.'

'Why not? Are you someone special? The bird of paradise?'

'You don't expect me to clean drains at my age?'

'If Gandhiji can clean his lavatory, why can't you clean a drain?'

'I tell you, I'm speaking the truth. I can't bend properly. If I bend, my back starts aching. I've a stone in my kidney.'

'You prepare cattle feed for your cow—you don't have a stone in your kidney then. The trouble comes only when you have to do community work.'

Shanker turned round and said, 'Masterji, we have only to put up a show. Who the hell is going to clean the drains? You collect the filth in the pan and throw it away.'

The party entered the lane.

'Where are you going?' Gosain shouted from behind.

Desraj who was walking ahead of the party had turned into a

lane to their right and the party had followed him.

'Stop them! Stop them!' Bakshiji shouted in alarm. 'It's time for their *namaz*. We must keep clear of the mosque. Oh Kashmiri!', he cried. 'Wake up! Who asked you to lead the party towards the mosque? You never listen.'

Kashmirilal stopped in his tracks. 'Desraj and Sher Khan turned into this lane by mistake,' he said. 'We also followed them. There's no harm done, Bakshiji. We'll stop singing when we get near the mosque.'

'No, no! You must be careful. Can't you smell it in the air? Please come back. We shall go to the *chowk* through the other lane. From there we can walk across and enter Imamdin's *mohalla*.'

The singing party turned back, and crossing the narrow lane on the left, made for Imamdin's *mohalla*. This route was new to the singing party. Usually, the Congress did not venture into the new settlements on the outskirts of the city. Imamdin's *mohalla* lay across the Committee Maidan at the far end of the city.

They stopped near a public cattle trough. Kashmirilal, who was holding aloft the tri-colour raised the slogan: 'Inquilab!'

There was a loud response: 'Zindabad!'

'Bharat Mata ki Jai!'

The children of the *mohalla* came running out of their houses. The women peeped from behind the tarpaulin curtains. A red-crested cock jumped onto a mud wall and, flapping its wings, crowed with all its might, as if in response to the slogan raised by the singing party.

'Kashmiri, this cock knows its job better than you,' Sher Khan said. 'Did you hear how loudly it crowed?'

'Kashmiri is not one to be outdone by anyone,' Shanker quipped. 'Kashmiri is the cock of the Congress.'

'Kashmiri, you also put a red crest on your head. Bakshiji, get him a red crest. He will pass for a real cock!'

'Can't he look a real cock without a crest? He's a female 'cock.' A Kashmiri hen!'

The exchange was typical of the town's humour.

'Let's start!' Bakshiji said, placing his lantern on the edge of the trough.

Most of the houses in the lane were unpretentious—low and squat tenements with tarpaulin curtains hanging on their doors.

In front of the lane lay a big *maidan* across which ran two parallel *kuchcha* lanes — one of them had unpaved drains and the other did not have drains at all. Cattle were tied in the lane. Carrying earthen pitchers on their heads, women walked to the municipal tap to fetch water. A child collected dung from under a buffalo. Nearby, two children sat beside the trough, facing each other, relieving themselves.

'Why is your shit so thin?'

'Because I drink goat's milk. What do you drink?'

The Congress group looked around. They felt as if they had come to a village.

'Pick up the spades and get going,' Bakshiji said.

Lifting a pan each Mehta and Ram Das went towards the open yard while Kashmirilal and Shanker took charge of the spades and started cleaning the drains. Sher Khan, Desraj and Bakshiji got down to clearing the yard.

The people around them watched idly, somewhat puzzled by the spectacle.

A *tonga* driver came out of his house, and squatting down on his feet, watched Bakshiji sweeping the ground. After some time he got up and walked up to Bakshiji.

'Babuji, why are you embarrassing us?' he asked. 'It's not your job to clean our houses. Here, give me your broomstick.'

'No, no. It's as much our job,' Bakshiji said.

'No, *banda parwar*, I'll not allow it. Your're educated people, belonging to well-to-do families. How can we allow you to sweep our houses. God forbid. Here, give me the broomstick. Surely, you don't want us to burn in hell-fire!'

Bakshiji was pleased with the man's attitude. It showed that Congress propaganda was bearing results. That was what social reconstruction was really meant for.

Kashmirilal and Shanker were removing slush and filth from the drains. After the channels had been constructed, water had started stagnating in them and in course of time had become thick, blue scum. So long as the scum was not disturbed, the stench remained suppressed. But when Kashmirilal and Shanker started heaping the scum alongside the drain a terrible odour arose. Thick swarms of mosquitoes, disturbed from their breeding ground, buzzed about the Congressmen.

'What's going on here?' an old man, his beard dyed red, suddenly cried from his roof-top. 'You'll scatter the filth and go away. Who will remove it from here? It will spread disease. In the drains the scum was accumulating at one point. Now you have scattered it all over the place and made things worse.'

Bakshiji was watching the proceedings, from a distance. Straightening his back, he stood stiffly erect and angrily watched Kashmirilal and Shanker. 'Reconstruction does not mean that you really start cleaning up the drains. There are ways and ways of doing things. Our main purpose is to make them conscious of public sanitation and then mould their minds for the struggle that lies ahead of us.'

The old man had disappeared after expressing his disapproval. Bakshiji began working again.

A man clad in white emerged from the opposite lane. He was holding a rosary in one hand. White *salwar*, white *kurta*, a waist-coat of the latest style and a *mushaddi* turban on his head, he looked a man of religion. He stopped as he saw the men sweeping the ground.

'So, you people have come to crush us under the weight of your obligations?' He looked at Ram Das who stood there covered with dust. 'God bless you! You've a good heart. *Wah! Wah!*' He kept shaking his head approvingly and repeating, '*Wah! Wah!*'

Bakshiji, while working, came closer to the old patriarch. 'We are nobodies,' he said in a self-effacing tone. 'We are only doing some social work.'

'Laudable work!' the old man said. 'It's not just sweeping and clearing the lane. It's the spirit behind your work that shines.'

The man went away, his head swaying. Bakshiji was pleased. His objectives, it seemed, had already been realized.

'Look at Mehtaji and Aziz,' Sher Khan laughed. 'They haven't even touched their brooms.' Mehtaji was diligently arranging pieces of stone in his pan. He would lift each piece with meticulous care, between his thumb and index finger and drop it into the pan. His hands were clean. Not far from him, Ram Das was working furiously, his moustache white with the dust that had settled on it.

The General who had been standing by the side of the trough, holding a long bamboo pole, walked up to the people cleaning the drains.

'Are the drains clogged?' he asked. 'May I help you with the pole?' He spoke with military abruptness. The people standing around started laughing.

'This reconstruction work is a real nuisance.' Shanker said straightening his back. 'Cleaning the drains is not going to bring *swaraj*(freedom) any nearer.'

Kashmirilal and Shanker were drenched in perspiration. They had heaped up the mud and the scum in three places.

'Shanker, you must learn to watch your tongue.' Bakshiji admonished Shanker. He was standing in the middle of the lane, holding a broomstick. 'You seem to have more brains than the others. Is Bapu a fool to ask us to ply the spinning wheel and do reconstruction work?'

'I'm already doing it. What else am I doing? But I must confess, it does not make much sense to me.'

Bakshiji did not want to fall foul of Shanker, specially in the morning. He was a blunt, foul-mouthed man. Nevertheless Bakshiji felt he should remonstrate with him. 'Shanker, you must know it is one way of expressing our sense of patriotism. This is the least we can do. We must descend to the level of the poor and get behind their minds. If you go to work among the poor, will you go dressed in a coat and pantaloons? If you go to them wearing khadi and holding a broomstick, they will think you are one of them.'

'Ever since you took up reconstruction work the freedom movement has come to a stop,' Shanker retorted. 'Sweep the lanes and ply the spinning wheel—that's all we seem to be capable of.' He angrily threw a spadeful of mud on the heap.

'You're a traitor!' the General shouted. 'I know you to your very core. You're a Communist!'

'Stop it, General!' Bakshiji cried. He feared that if the General started talking he would only add to the trouble.

'And you Shanker! You must know when to talk and what to talk.'

They saw a man come running from the direction of the Committee *Maidan*. Running past Sher Khan he stopped abruptly before a group of people belonging to the *mohalla* and started talking to them in whispers. He wore a black vest and looked very excited. People do run when in a hurry, but there was something unusual in the way this youth had come up. The singing party was still watching, when the small group of people that had been standing around melted away. Only the children remained. Then the women also disappeared from behind the tarpaulin curtains. A woman rushed out of her house and grabbing one of the children who was defecating, dragged him back to her house.

The atmosphere was suddenly tense. The members of the singing party did not know what to make of the situation.

They saw the old man with the rosary walking towards them. Mehtaji and Bakshiji were standing together trying to gauge the situation and ascertain the cause of the sudden commotion in the lane, when the old man stopped in front of them.

'If you don't want trouble you had better disappear from here,' the old man warned them. Suddenly his chin trembled and his face went pale.

All the members of the party quickly gathered round the old man.

'Go away from here!' the old man again warned them. 'You've already done sufficient mischief. Are you listening? I say, go away.' He gave them a threatening look and walked away.

A hush fell over the singing party. Mehta and Bakshi looked at each other.

A small stone came flying through the air and fell near Bakshiji's feet. Kashmirilal and Shanker looked at Bakshiji, astounded.

'What's happening?' Master Ram Das edged closer to Bakshiji.

'Let's go away!' Bakshiji said. 'I sense trouble. We made a mistake in coming here. Where's Desraj? It's he who led us here.'

But Desraj was nowhere to be seen. He had slipped away, unobserved.

Then more stones came flying through the air. One of them hit Ram Das on his shoulder.

'Let's go away. There's no point in staying over here.'

The party rushed towards the end of the lane.

Holding his bamboo pole aloft the General cried, 'You're all cowards! I know you, one and all. I'm not leaving till I've done my job.'

Bakshiji thundered at him: 'General, take charge of the flag! Where's the flag?'

The General at once stood to attention and then, dragging his *chappaled* feet, walked towards the trough to pick up the flag.

Two more stones flew through the air. One fell near the trough and the other near the General. Three men emerged from the lane in front, and stationed themselves at its mouth.

The members of the singing party quickened their pace. Kashmirilal took the flag from the General. Mehta upturned the pan in which he had been collecting stones and, lifting the empty pan started crossing the *maidan*. The lantern swung from Bakshiji's hand. His head was bowed.

'Shall we leave the pan and the spades in Sher Khan's house?' Master Ram Das asked Bakshiji.

'We must move on,' Bakshiji said. 'It's not safe to stay here.'

Kashmirilal looked back. At the end of the lane there were now five people instead of three and he could see more people standing at the other end of the *maidan*. They seemed to be watching every move of the party. As the party entered Qutabdin's lane they saw a similar scene in front of the baker's shop. Three people standing there followed the party with their gaze, without uttering a word.

'There's something happening somewhere,' Mehtaji said to Bakshiji.

'Kashmirilal or Shanker might have teased some *mohalla* girls. You've allowed loafers to infiltrate the Congress party,' Mehtaji added in a whisper.

'How you talk, Mehtaji!' Bakshi said. 'Kashmiri was busy all the time cleaning the drains. There must be some other reason.'

As they approached the lane of the Mohiyals they saw a couple of people standing at the mouth of the lane.

'Where are you going, Bakshiji? Don't go in that direction.' A tall Mohiyal stepped forward and warned Bakshiji.

'Something wrong?'

'I've told you. Don't go in that direction.'

'But tell me. Has anything happened?'

Kashmiri, the General and Master Ram Das caught up with Bakshiji.

'Look outside the lane.'

Bakshiji looked around. His eyes came to rest on a mosque popularly known as Kailon ki Masjid.

'What's there?'

'Can't you see? Just look at the steps of the mosque.'

They saw something black lying on the steps of the mosque.

'Someone has killed a pig and thrown it there.'

Bakshiji gave Mehtaji a knowing look, as if he wanted to say:

'See, didn't I tell you that something unusual had happened?'

A dark gunny bag lay on the steps of the mosque from which two legs stuck out. The green gate of the mosque was closed.

'*Akh thoo*!' Kashmirilal looked in the direction of the mosque and turned his face away.

'Bakshiji, let's go back,' Ram Das said again, 'There's a Muslim *mohalla* further up.'

'This is deliberate mischief,' Mehtaji muttered. 'But are you sure it's a pig? It could be some other animal.'

'If it were some other animal the Muslims would not have felt so excited,' Bakshiji said testily.

The General was standing by their side, his small eyes trained on the mosque.

'It's the Englishmen's doing!' he exclaimed, his nostrils flaring. 'They have done it. I know them.'

'Yes, we know it. The Englishmen have done it.' Bakshiji gave the General a beseeching look. 'But for Heaven's sake keep your mouth shut!'

'Let's go by the other lane.' Ram Das said. But before he could utter another word the General interrupted angrily.

'You're a coward!' the General cried. 'The Englishmen have played a dirty trick on us. I'm going to expose them. No, I won't spare them.'

'Why did you bring this lunatic with you?' Mehtaji whispered in Bakshiji's ear. 'He's going to land us in trouble. Expel him from the party.'

A *tonga* passed them, driven at great speed. Soon after they heard the sound of running feet by the side of the mosque. Across the road, the man in the meatshop covered the goat carcasses hanging from hooks, with a piece of cloth, and rolled down the shutters of his shop. In the lane of the Mohiyals, people hurriedly started closing their doors.

Bakshiji turned to look and saw that Master Ram Das had broken away from their group and was now briskly walking away towards a narrow lane, Sher Khan and Aziz following him at some distance.

'Bakshiji, you must go away at once,' a Mohiyal friend advised him. 'Your presence here will cause further provocation.'

Bakshiji gave the man a suspicious look and quickly turned to Kashmirilal. 'You must remove the flag from the pole,' he said.

'Fold the flag carefully.' Then he turned to his Mohiyal friend, 'You just watch, we are going to remove the pig's carcass from the· mosque. As long as the carcass remains there the agitation will mount.'

The Mohiyal friend looked at Bakshiji in surprise. 'Who'll remove the carcass? You?' he asked. 'I think it will be stupid to do such a thing.'

'I agree with you,' Mehtaji said. 'We shouldn't get involved in this affair. It'll only worsen the situation.'

'If we turn our face against them won't that aggravate the situation? Do you expect the Muslims to remove the carcass? They won't even touch it.'

'They can entrust the job to a sweeper or a *jamadar*,' Mehtaji said Bakshiji earnestly. 'Under no circumstances should we get ourselves involved in this affair.'

Bakshiji placed his lantern on the plinth of a house. 'Mehtaji,' he said, raising his finger at him. 'I really don't understand you. You want us to slip away from here? Won't that only make matters worse? If I had not seen the thing it would have been a different matter. You come with me!' he said to Kashmirilal and the General.

Stepping out of the lane he went towards the mosque.

Kashmirilal was in a fix—whether to go with Bakshiji or to give him the slip. He had been hit by a stone in Imamdin's *mohalla*. A worse fate could be awaiting him at the mosque. Sweat broke out on his forehead. He leaned the flagpole against the wall and stood by it·as if rooted to the ground. His legs shook. Bakshiji and the General had crossed the road. Kashmirilal watched them for some time and then followed them.

The Mohiyal friend was gone, leaving Mehtaji standing in the· lane which was now deserted. There were a couple of shops on the left side of the lane but they were all closed. There was another row of shops near the well. These too were closed. Some people standing in a bunch near the well were looking towards the mosque and there were more people standing on the balconies of their houses watching the goings-on in the lane. The doors of all the houses were closed.

'The first thing, we must remove the carcass from here,' Kashmirilal heard Bakshiji saying.

It was a black pig. Someone had thrown a gunnybag over it but part of its belly, legs and snout were still visible. Bakshiji and the General caught hold of the pig by its legs and pulled it off the mosque's steps. Then they dragged it across the road and hid it behind a pile of bricks.

'Let it remain here for the time being,' Bakshiji said. 'When the door of the mosque opens we shall wash the steps. There are a few houses of sweepers behind this lane,' he said turning to Kashmirilal. 'The municipal scavengers also live there. If you can persuade them to come with their pushcart we can remove the carcass easily.'

They heard the sound of running feet and swiftly turned round to look. A cow was stampeding in their direction, a man brandishing a *lathi* in hot pursuit. The man's shirt was open at the neck through which one could see a dangling talisman.

It was a brown cow with a soft hide, big surprised eyes, its tail lifted in fright. It looked as though it had lost its way. The man's face was half covered. Goading the cow on he passed along the road and then turned into one of the lanes.

Bakshiji stood stock-still watching the scene. 'Soon vultures will fly over the city,' he said, shaking his head. 'The signs are ominous.'

His face was pale and he looked nervous.

Chapter 6

To mark the end of the weekly meeting, the revered Vanprasthiji, as was his practice, started chanting *mantras* in a guttural tone —what he called the last 'invocation' of the meeting. He maintained that these carefully selected *mantras* represented the quintessence of the Aryan culture. After years of labour, Vanprasthiji had succeeded in making all the members of the congregation learn them by heart. Sitting stiffly erect on a raised seat, eyes closed, his hands joined together, his head bowed in supplication, Vanprasthiji intoned the *mantras* in, what he professed was, the pure Vedic style.

In the entire congregation he was the only man who knew Sanskrit. He had studied all the Vedas and therefore nobody could dare find fault with his pronunciation. He intoned each word with such sharp, chiselled, rhythmic precision that it seemed to be coming from some inner depth of his being. After reciting one *shloka* from an Upanishad he would recite two *shlokas* from the Gita.

The congregation would mumble the *shlokas* after him. Some people would lag behind and their voices would float in the air long after Vanprasthiji had ceased chanting.

The meeting came to an end with *Shanti path*, the invocation to peace, and the atmosphere in the room was such that it appeared that peace was pervading the atmosphere, reaching out to every household and enveloping it in its tranquillity.

The invocation was followed by a hymn, seeking peace on earth for the animate and the inanimate world alike.

Vanprasthiji sang, keeping time with his hands:
Shower your benediction on everyone:
O, Lord!
Be merciful to everyone,

O, Lord!

At the instance of Vanprasthiji they had demoted the traditional arti from its honoured position, for he had taken exception to some passages in it in the same way he had had earlier objections to a devotional song by one Khannaji.

The weekly service over, the meeting was expected to terminate but the members of the congregation continued to sit for they knew that the Secretary had to make an important announcement. Looking very grave the Secretary rose and requested the members of the Executive Committee to stay back for an important matter had to be discussed . The audience had already an inkling of what the subject of discussion was going to be for, in his sermon, the revered Vanprasthiji had referred to it obliquely. He had chanted, for instance, this couplet:

Horrible have been the sins of the Muslims in the land
Even the sky has refused us its favour and the earth its bounty.

After the Secretary's announcement the meeting started dispersing. The people spilled through the seven doors of the hall, searching for their shoes on the verandah. Before entering the hall some people had left their right shoe outside the third door and the left shoe outside the first door to guard against anyone decamping with their shoes. There was a flurry of activity in the verandah, everyone having crowded round one focal point. Even otherwise, it was a practice with the dispersing audience to huddle together in small bunches and exchange views. Today, however, they had a readymade topic: the highly charged communal tension in the city. With the termination of the meeting, Vanprasthiji had not climbed down from his seat; he was still sitting there, looking very tense.

Some newcomers arrived. The people who had lingered behind knew who they were. They were prominent leaders representing other Hindu religious institutions. Close on their heels came half-a-dozen prosperous looking Sikhs who were special invitees from the main gurdwara.

The meeting of the Executive Committee started. The Secretary, a thin, highly irascible man, gave a brief account of the deteriorating communal situation in the city. In passing, he mentioned sinister rumours that were floating about. He also spoke about the carcass of a pig found lying in front of a mosque. He said that for several days the Muslims had been collecting *lathis*, spears and such other lethal weapons in the Jama Masjid. Concluding his speech he requested the members to give the matter serious thought and suggest how the impending crisis was to be faced.

'This is not the right place for the meeting.' Vanprasthiji waved his hand in the air. 'Come, we'll shift to some other place.'

He got down from the platform, and waving to the others to follow him, strode towards the back of the building. Climbing up the back stairs he entered a narrow room, cluttered with knick-knacks, its walls lined with chairs and wooden benches.

After all the members had sat down, Vanprasthiji began in a grave voice: 'The first and foremost thing is to decide how best we can protect ourselves. All the members should make it a point to have a canister of mustard oil and a sack of charcoal ready at hand. Boiling mustard oil can be poured over the enemies from housetops and burning charcoal can also be used in the same way.'

The members heard Vanprasthiji out in grim silence. He had certainly a point there but the majority of the audience consisted of traders and old men. Only one or two among them were professionals or belonged to the salaried class. They looked worried, no doubt, but none of them was excited like Vanprasthiji. They were reluctant to believe that the situation in the city had become so explosive that they needed to resort to such measures as the use of boiling oil. They thought that after one or two stray incidents, the government would immediately bring the situation under control.

One of the members pointing his finger towards the audience in general said: 'The activities of the Youth Samaj, I find, have almost come to a stand-still. Shri Devbrat is busy with other things. I strongly feel that all the young men should forthwith be trained to use the *lathi*. To make a good start, you should right now place an order for two hundred *lathis* and distribute them among the youth.'

At this the President of the Committee, a prominent business man of the city called Lala Lakshmi Narain, stood up. 'I'll bear the cost of the *lathis*,' he said, 'You may place an order for two hundred *lathis* today and put it on my account.'

'*Wah! Wah!*' the audience exclaimed, applauding the munificence of the President.

A member of the Committee got up and said: 'It's a great weakness of the Hindus that we begin to dig a well only when we are thirsty. Today when the situation has deteriorated and the Muslims have piled up weapons in mosques we are still thinking over the proposal of buying *lathis*.'

'There's no need to place this suggestion before the Committee for discussion,' the Secretary said. 'The Youth Samaj is within its right to buy *lathis*. We have studied the matter closely. Vanprasthiji is taking a personal interest in it. He has put his heart and soul into it, if I may say so. Besides propagating religion and doing *havans* he is actively engaged in welding the different sections of our community together. But I heartily welcome our President's suggestion. It's due to his generosity that we have been able to put many of our schemes through. We must strive hard to keep ourselves in readiness to meet any eventuality. Our preparations should go on unabated. We must not be caught on the wrong foot when the time for action comes.'

An old man, who had come with the visitors and had been attentively listening to the proceedings, his chin resting on the head of his walking stick and his legs drawn up onto the seat of his chair, said in a thin, piping voice: 'Brothers, your suggestion is all right as far as it goes. But that is not enough. I suggest that we should call on the Deputy Commissioner. Yes, we must all go and call on the DC. That is important. The trouble is not going to end here. You must meet the Deputy Commissioner and make it clear to him that the lives of the Hindus and their properties are in danger.'

'Of course, you're right, Lalaji,' Vanprasthiji said, nodding his head to add conviction to what he was saying. 'Of course, we must meet the Deputy Commissioner. I don't deny its importance. But no one will come to our rescue unless we learn to stand on our own. We must devise ways and means to protect ourselves with our own hands.'

'O, Maharaj, by all means teach the children to wield the *lathi*,' the old man said, 'Teach them to use the sword. Teach them to handle the spear. Make them brave. But you must meet the Deputy Commissioner first. Tell him that there should be no rioting in the city. He wields authority. Not a sparrow can flutter its wings against his orders.'

'Today being a Sunday, the Deputy Commissioner will not grant us an interview,' the Secretary said.

'I say meet him we must!' the old man said. 'Meet him at his bungalow. Now is the time. We can straightaway go to him from here.'

'I hear one deputation has already gone to meet him,' one of the audience said.

'Whose deputation?'

'There are some Congressmen and Muslim Leaguers. And a few others.'

A hush fell on the room.

'What good is that deputation?' The old man at last broke the silence.

'The Hindus and the Sikhs should go together and meet him. We must apprise him of the doings of the Muslims. If the Muslims are also in the deputation we can't speak against them. These Congress people have made a mess of the whole thing. They are always pampering the Muslims.'

'The situation is fast deteriorating. There is no doubt about it,' one of the Sikhs said. 'I hear a cow has also been slaughtered. Its parts were thrown outside the Mai Sati Dharamsala. I don't know how far this is true. But I've heard people talking about it.'

Vanprasthiji's face tingled. But he suppressed his anger and watched silently. 'If they dare slaughter a cow, rivers of blood will flow in the city,' the Secretary said in an impassioned voice.

They were all silent for a while. 'If what the Sikh gentleman has said is true, there seems to be a deep conspiracy behind the whole thing. The Muslims could be up to anything.'

'The situation demands that the Hindus and the Sikhs should put their heads together and devise some way to protect their lives and property by acting in concert.'

'What about the *Mohalla* Committees?' one of the members asked. 'How are they shaping?'

'Forming *Mohalla* Committees is not at all an easy job. The Muslims have infiltrated into all the *mohallas*. It's a funny city. Every *mohalla* is a hopeless mix-up of Hindus and Muslims. How can you ever form *Mohalla* Committees? The Muslims will pry into all our secrets. Nothing will remain hidden from them. After the communal riots of 1926, the Hindus formed some exclusive *mohallas* such as the Naya *Mohalla* and Rajpura where they built houses. They are exclusively Hindu and Sikh *mohallas*. But in all the others there are Muslims as well.'

Then followed a lengthy discussion on the *Mohalla* Committees. A sub-Committee was formed with a mandate to establish immediate contact with all the *Mohalla* Committees and then consider how this liaison was to be maintained in times of trouble.

An old man came up with the suggestion that they should have the temple bell thoroughly tested.

'What's wrong with the bell?' 'Nothing's wrong with it. I am suggesting this only as a precaution. If you have to give a danger signal at night the bell should be in good working order. Not that you pull the rope and it snaps without warning. How will the bell toll in that case?'

In the middle of the city they had an old temple situated on the top of a mound. It was popularly known as the Shivalaya. In course of time, shops had sprung up round the temple. Long ago they had installed a bell in the temple.

The old man said, lapsing into a reminiscent mood. 'If I remember right the bell was fixed in 1927, may be even earlier.'

'May the bell never toll!' Another old man suddenly blurted out, 'May God save us from that ordeal!'

'There you are' Vanprasthiji said in a sharp voice. 'It's feelings such as these that have made cowards of us all. We see danger stalking us everywhere. That's why our enemies make fun of us. They call our youth 'sloppy shopkeepers'.'

They again fell silent. They were all thinking in the same vein. Only they lacked Vanprasthiji's barbed tongue. They knew the Muslims were bent upon creating trouble but they did not want to provoke them in any manner. They feared that once the trouble broke out the Hindus and Sikhs would have the worst of it.

For a long time they weighed the relative merits and demerits of various measures put forward to shield them against the impending trouble. It was suggested that they should strengthen the *Mohalla* Committees and form volunteer corps which in turn would maintain active liaison between the Hindus and the Sikhs of the city. Besides mustard oil, they felt they also should arrange for sand and water.

In between these suggestions, the old man's voice rose and fell regularly: 'Brothers, you must meet the Deputy Commissioner first. You must go to him directly from here. I'm willing to accompany you.'

Finally the meeting broke up, but not until a number of decisions were taken. It was decided that the Secretary would stay back and send the peon out on an important errand. He would go from house to house urging the people to buy coal and *lathis* and keep them ready at hand. The Secretary would also establish contact with other sympathetic organizations and ask them to engage more Gorkhas as *chowkidars*. The Secretary of the Sanatan Dharam Sabha would be approached. The Youth Sabha would be told to hold itself in readiness. Most immediately, however, all the members of the Executive Committee would go *en masse* in *tongas* to the Deputy Commissioner's bungalow, the only exception being Vanprasthiji. He was a spiritual man and did not feel it was his place to get involved in mundane affairs and hobnob with householders.

*

Ranvir, the son of the President of the Committee, followed Master Devbrat, the instructor of the gymnasium-cum-wrestling pit, the sound of Devbrat's boots echoing in the cobbled lane. The fifteen-year-old Ranvir was bursting with excitement. Today he would undergo the test and if he made it, he would be taken into the fold.

No lane of the city ran straight. A lane would run straight for a few yards and would then be joined by another tortuous lane. The houses flanking the lanes almost seemed to topple over one another so packed together were they. The sound of Devbrat's heavy boots, was a familiar one in the lanes of the town.

Ranvir was still very young and his eyes had not lost their child-like curiosity. They even lacked that earnestness, so necessary when undergoing a supreme test. But in place of earnestness he had a sense of bravado, a blind determination to do or die at the behest of his mentor.

When Ranvir was very young, Master Devbrat would entertain him with stories of heroes of Indian history. There was an episode from Rana Pratap's life, for instance, when the cat had stolen his food, leaving him famished and making him acutely aware of his total helplessness. Ranvir would have visions of Chetak, Rana Pratap's favourite horse, as it went tramping over the hills overlooking the city. He would even see in his mind Shivaji watching a horde of approaching Muslims from the top of some hill. He also recalled the dramatic episode in Shivaji's life when he had caught a Muslim ruler in a fatal embrace. Masterji had taught Ranvir the basic principles of knot tying and wall climbing. He had explained the characteristics of the 'fire' and the 'rain' producing arrows depicted in the ancient Hindu epics.

Ranvir was told by Masterji that the vedas were the repository of all knowledge and held the secret of making the bomb and flying machines. Masterji talks of the marvels of yogic power had held Ranvir spellbound. 'One having yogic power can achieve the impossible,' Masterji would repeatedly impress upon Ranvir.

'You know the story of that yogi, don't you?' he would ask his pupil, and then repeat a story he had often narrated. 'A yogi had gone into a trance at the foot of the Himalayas. He achieved great occult powers. One day, when he had gone into meditation, a Muslim, an unclean man, came there with the mischievous intention of disrupting his meditation. You know these unclean people. The don't bathe, nor do they wash their hands after shitting. They have no compunction in sharing each other's spittled food. This 'unclean' person stood there glaring at the sadhu. As his polluted shadow fell over the sadhu, he opened his eyes. A gleam shot out of his eyes and singed the polluted man to death.'

These 'unclean' people would often revolve before Ranvir's eyes. In his neighbourhood, the cobbler who sat by the roadside, mending shoes, was said to be an 'unclean' man. So was the *tonga* driver who lived in front of their house. Hamid, who studied with him at school in the same class, was also 'unclean'. All the members of the family living next door were also considered to be 'unclean' and polluted. It must be some such person who had gone to the foot of the Himalayas to disrupt the sadhu's meditation. Today, out of the eight boys he instructed, Master Devbrat had singled out Ranvir for the test. The boys were scared of Masterji. He wore khaki shorts and heavy black boots and spoke in a voice like thunder. His wrath was unpredictable and could fall on anybody without warning. The test which Ranvir was to undergo was secret and esoteric. Only the initiates knew what it was.

The lanes looked desolate. At one place Ranvir felt as if they were walking along a thick web of darkness. As they drew nearer they discovered that the wall of a house had crumbled down and the darkness was seeping out of its debris.

Suddenly Devbrat stopped in his tracks. Although the desolate look of the lane had given Ranvir an eerie feeling, it had not been able to curb his exuberance. There was a narrow door framed against a long wall. Devbrat pushed it open. They stepped into a big courtyard at the end of which they saw the door of a narrow room across which hung a tarpaulin curtain. In the left corner of the courtyard lay two big heaps of rubble. The place looked deserted.

Walking across the courtyard, Master Devbrat pounded on the door. Ranvir heard the sound of coughing, followed by the shuffling of feet.

'It's I, Devbrat.'

The door was flung open. The old Gorkha *chowkidar* of the school stood in the door, peering at the visitors. He folded his hands in salutation and bowed his head.

It was dark inside the room. To one side lay a *charpoy* covered with a dirty bedsheet. A *lathi* stood against the right wall and by its side a *chelum* lay upside down. Over a wooden peg hung the *chowkidar*'s woollen overcoat and a long sword sheathed in a black scabbard.

Ranvir heard the cackling of hens and turned to look. About half-a-dozen white hens lay tied in a big basket in a corner of the room.

Holding Ranvir by the arm Master Devbrat led him into another courtyard, much smaller than the first and abruptly ending against the high wall of a neighbouring house. The Gorkha *chowkidar* followed them holding a hen in one hand and a knife in the other.

'Ranvir, kill the hen,' Master Devbrat said. The *chowkidar* handed Devbrat the knife. 'Before you're initiated into our fold you must prove that you possess a stout heart.'

Devbrat pushed Ranvir forward. 'An Aryan youth must be strong in faith, resolute at heart, and determined in action. Take the knife and go and sit there!' He gave Ranvir another shove forward.

Ranvir felt the place had suddenly turned sinister. He saw feathers of hens lying scattered all over. Near some rubble rested a slab of stone turned black with blood.

'Sit down and put one leg of the hen under your right foot.' Devbrat pressed the hen's wings and twisted one wing under the other.

The hen cackled furiously. But its wings having been firmly tied together it could only struggle futilely. It did this for a while then lay still.

'Hold it!' Master Devbrat sat down by Ranvir's side. 'Go ahead. Let the knife do its job!'

Sweat broke out on Ranvir's forehead and his face turned pale. Master Devbrat knew that the boy was feeling queasy.

'Ranvir!' he cried and slapped him hard on his cheek. Ranvir fell down in a heap on the ground. He felt like crying. The Gorkha standing behind him, watched him, a glitter of excitement in his eyes. Ranvir was still feeling unequal to the task but the slap seemed to have driven away his nausea.

'Get up, Ranvir!' Master Devbrat cried.

Ranvir slowly rose to his feet and looked at his mentor with heavy, dazed eyes.

'There's nothing difficult about it,' Master Devbrat said. 'Watch, I'll show you how.'

He pressed one of the hen's feet under his boot. The bird's eyes became glazed and then slowly closed. He held the hen's neck in his right hand and slit it. Blood spurted from the neck, some drops falling on Devbrat's hand. But he did not let the hen go even though its head had been cut off. He firmly held the wind pipe down till it turned white. The hen's headless body kept quivering and then became still and its wings drenched with blood became limp. All that Ranvir saw was a handful of white feathers spattered with blood lying before him. Master Devbrat flung the remains of the dead bird to one side and got up.

'Bring another hen!' he told the Gorkha.

As he turned towards Ranvir, he saw that he had vomited on the ground and was sitting there, holding his head between his hands, and breathing heavily. Master Devbrat felt like slapping again but he controlled himself and just stood there watching him in disgust.

'I'm going to give you one more chance,' he said at last. 'A youth who can't kill a hen — how can one expect him to deal with an enemy?'

Soon Ranvir's breathing became normal and his stomach, which had knotted gradually loosened up.

'I'll give you five more minutes,' Devbrat said. 'If you fail to kill the hen this time it's all over with you . No initiation, no nothing.' He turned on his heel and walked out of the courtyard.

When he returned after five minutes, he saw a hen writhing under the wall, drops of blood .flying from it in all directions. Ranvir was sitting by the side of the bird, his right arm held between his knees. Devbrat guessed how things must have gone. While Ranvir was struggling with the hen, it must have pecked at his hand and he had only succeeded in wounding the bird instead of killing it outright.

Writhing in agony the bird kept jumping in the air and falling heavily on the ground, leaving more and more blood stains on the ground. Blood fountained from its neck.

'Get up, Ranvir!' Master Devbrat patted him on his back. Ranvir slowly rose to his feet. He had succeeded in the test.

'*Shabash*!' Master Devbrat said. 'You've determination, you have will power. Though your arm still lacks strength, you've made the grade and won your reward.' He bent to the ground and dipping his finger in the blood spattered on the stone slab, made a blood mark on Ranvir's forehead.

*

They had arranged for everything else. Only one thing was missing. An iron cauldron big enough to boil mustard oil. The young men of the *mohalla* had not been able to lay their hands on a cauldron of the required size. On the window-sill they had placed three long knives, a dagger and a kirpan. In a corner lay two *lathis* with polished brass heads and iron spikes at the other ends. Along one wall they had arranged bows and arrows in a row. Bodhraj could shoot an arrow lying down. He could aim an arrow to the sound of the human voice and tick off a dangling string by looking at its reflection in a mirror. He had brought some arrows, their ends tipped with metal, and stood there explaining their special characteristics.

'If you rub arsenic on the tip of an arrow it'll become a poisoned arrow,' he explained. 'And if you put a piece of camphor on its tip it'll become a 'fire' arrow and ignite any surface that it hits. If you tip it with sulphite of copper it will produce poisonous gas wherever it strikes.'

Dharamdev had been able to lay his hands on an empty bandoleer and he had carefully hung it on the wall to create a proper atmosphere. To complete the picture, Ranvir had inscribed 'Arsenal' in bold letters over one of the doors of the room.

But until now they had not been able to give a practical shape to Vanprasthiji's order regarding the cauldron. None of the representatives of the Youth Committee had a cauldron in his house big enough to boil one canister of mustard oil in it. True, a canister of mustard oil had already been procured. All the young men had contributed four annas each towards the cost of the oil, with a promise to make up the shortfall soon. But a big cauldron was not available even in the temple where there was community eating on a regular basis.

Bodhraj, the leader of the Youth Group, had a sudden brain wave. 'Why not get a cauldron from the sweetmeat shop?'

'But the shop is locked.'

'Where does the sweetmeat seller live?'

'In the New *Mohalla*.'

'Does anyone know his house?'

Bodhraj himself knew where the sweetmeat seller lived but he considered it beneath his high position as the President of the Youth Group to do such a mean errand.

'We can break open his shop,' Ranvir said stepping forward.

A bold suggestion indeed, but rather indiscreet, considering the occasion.

Bodhraj stood there gazing at the ceiling. To lead his group was no easy job. The young man deputed to break the lock of the shop should not get caught. Nobody should even see him doing it. Bodhraj who was studying in the first year in the local college was the son of Mastram who worked in the Commissariat. In the group he was the only youth who had the distinction of wearing an army shirt with two pockets.

'Yes, you may break the lock,'he said at last, after giving the matter some thought. 'But you must be careful. Nobody should know who has done it. Who's going to break the lock?'

'I'll do it,' Ranvir said.

Bodhraj surveyed Ranvir from head to foot and then shook his head.

'You're too small for the job,'he said. 'If the lock is fixed on the upper part of the door your hand won't reach up to it.'

'No,the lock is fixed on the lower part of the door. I've seen it several times while passing that side.'

Ranvir was talking in an over-confident, bragging tone. Bodhraj did not like it. But though raw, the boy looked smart and agile.

Bodhraj knew that the boy would see the job through. But at the same time he feared that the boy's recklessness could get the Group in trouble .

'You and Dharamdev should tackle the job together.' Bodhraj said in a decisive tone. 'But nobody should know what you're doing. And you must select a time when the road is deserted. One thing more. Don't go together. Go separately.'

The sweetmeat shop was situated just near the big *nullah*, past the crossing. Ranvir saw something moving behind the shop. It was the end of the sweetmeat seller's turban fluttering in the air. So he had come to open his shop for the day! But to his surprise, the man kept standing behind his shop. Was he really the owner of the shop? Ranvir watched intently. It was the confectioner all right. He was bending down to unlock the back door of his shop.

The road was empty. It was generally empty at this time of the day. There was traffic on it only towards the afternoon.

The youths crossed the road, one following the other.

'You engage the man in talk.' Ranvir told his companion. 'Then I'll quietly enter and take away the cauldron.'

'There will be no need for it. He is a Hindu brother. He'll gladly part with the cauldron for us.'

'I'll ask for it, not you.'

'Get gone, you midget! Who do you think you are?'

The youths went towards the back of the shop. Its door was ajar. The shopkeeper was inside.

Though situated on the edge of the road, it was dark inside the shop. The wooden planks were smeared with ghee and oil and flies were buzzing over them. The shop smelled of stale *samosas.* Ranvir peeped in.

'What do you want?' a voice said from inside. 'The shop is closed.'

Both the youths entered the shop and stopped a little distance from the shopkeeper. He was pouring *maida* (refined flour) from a tin into a bag. Seeing two unfamiliar faces, he stopped his work.

'Come in, come in,' he said in a hearty voice. 'Today I don't have anything fresh to offer you. I had come to fetch some quantity of *maida* for myself. Son, you must stay indoors. The times are bad. This is no time to stir out.'

'Go, and pick up that cauldron!' Ranvir said to Dharamdev in a commanding voice.

There were a number of cauldrons resting against the back wall of the shop. Dharamdev walked towards them.

'We'll take away one of the cauldrons,' Ranvir said. 'We want it for the cause of the community. We'll restore it to you as soon as the danger is over.'

The confectioner could not understand what Ranvir was saying.

'What's the matter? Who are you? What do you want the cauldron for? Is there a marriage in the family?'

They ignored his questions.

'Take the one lying in the middle,' Ranvir said to his companion. 'It should serve our purpose. Take it and go!'

'Wait, wait!' the confectioner said, getting annoyed. 'You can't take it away just like that. First tell me what it's for.

'We'll tell you later,' Ranvir told the confectioner and then turned dramatically to Dharamdev, 'Lift the cauldron and go!'

'That's no way of doing things. How can you remove the cauldron without my permission? First tell me who you are.'

Ranvir put his hand into the pocket of his *kurta*. 'Do you refuse to give us the cauldron?' The confectioner stepped back startled.

Before he could utter another word he found a streak of blood etched on his right cheek. Wailing the confectioner covered his face with his hands and sat down on the floor. Blood started dripping from his cheek to the floor.

'Don't talk to anyone about it, or I'll murder you!' Ranvir said in a threatening tone.

After lingering for a moment, Ranvir followed Dharamdev who, carrying the cauldron, had already crossed the *nullah*.

So, it's not difficult to kill, Ranvir thought. He could have killed that man with no compunction. He only had to raise his hand and it was done. It would be over in no time. To fight was, of course, something quite different, specially when the other man put up resistance. But even so it would be quite easy to plunge a knife into a man's body.

Dharamdev stopped outside Ranvir's house.

'Why did you hurt the man?' he asked Ranvir.

'Because he was trying to be difficult.'

Dharamdev's throat was parched and his tongue seemed to have turned brittle.

'And if someone had seen us?' he asked , swallowing hard. 'If the fellow had raised an alarm?'

'I'm not afraid of anyone,' Ranvir replied. 'I just don't don't care. Let them do their worst. And you too can do your worst, for all I care!'

He started climbing the stairs of his house with a swagger.

Chapter 7

'Since you have taken the trouble to visit me at home and not at the office, I know it must be something urgent,' Richard smiled.

His peon lifted the *chik*(bamboo curtain), letting in the members of the Citizen's Committee deputation, one by one. Standing at the door, Richard pointed towards the chairs, while his gaze roved over each man as he entered. Then, briskly walking to the end of the room, he sat down behind his table. There were four people wearing turbans, one in a Rumi cap and two in Gandhi caps. One glance at them and Richard knew it would not be difficult to deal with them.

'What can I do for you gentlemen?' he asked .

The members of the deputation were pleased. Richard was so polite, so courteous. His predecessor was always grumpy and curt. And so inaccessible.

Richard quickly sized up all the members of the deputation. He knew the political leanings of each one of them from the police reports that were regularly submitted to him. That man dressed in loose clothes, wearing a Gandhi cap, must be Bakshi. He had spent sixteen years in jail. And that man sitting in the corner must be Hayat Baksh, the spokesman of the Muslim League. Mr Herbert, Principal of the Mission College, was present. So was Professor Raghunath who must have been dragged along for the simple reason that Richard had always been nice to him. The others must be the representatives of various other bodies.

Richard turned to Bakshiji. 'Reports have reached me that there is tension in the city,'he said

'That's what brought us here,' Bakshiji replied. He looked tense and distraught. Nothing had gone right since the morning. First he had gone to the house of the President of the Muslim League. Finding him unbending, he had decided to go in a deputation to

71

the Deputy Commissioner. He had personally called on each person, inviting them to join the deputation. It was hard going though everyone agreed that there was no harm in meeting the Deputy Commissioner.

'The Government should take effective steps to bring the situation under control,' Bakshiji said. 'Or ... or, vultures will fly over the city.' This sentence had been worrying at his mind all morning.

The other members of the deputation looked equally worried, though they were not as excited as Bakshiji.

Professor Raghunath's and Richard's eyes met. Professor Raghunath was the only man with whom Richard could talk without any reserve. Both were fond of English literature and were interested in Indian history. Richard had found in Raghunath a highly sensitive and sophisticated man. They seemed to say to each other:

'What have we got to do with these mundane matters? Our world is quite different from theirs.'

Richard tapped the table with a pencil he held. 'The government has earned a bad name,' he said. 'I'm a British officer. You've no faith in the British government. It means nothing to you. You won't care to act on its advice.'

They could easily discern the note of sarcasm in his voice.

'But the power lies in the hands of the British government and you represent the British government.' Bakshiji said. 'It's your responsibility to protect the city.' Bakshiji's chin trembled and his face went pale with excitement.

'No, the power rests in Pandit Nehru's hands,' Richard said with a smile. Then he looked at Bakshiji. 'When you're against the British government it is the fault of the British government and if you fight among yourselves even then the British government is held responsible for it.' The smile lingered on Richard's lips. He continued with a pause, 'Of course, we must put our heads together to solve this problem'.

'Nothing will happen if the police is vigilant,' Hayat Baksh said. 'You know what was found in front of the mosque. The Hindus undeniably had a hand in it.'

'What makes you say that the Hindus are at the back of this mischief?' Lakshmi Narain, the President of the Committee who was nick-named 'the Philanthropist', jumped in his seat, his voice rising.

To Richard's great satisfaction, the discussion was shaping as he wanted it.

'There's no point in blaming one another,' he said. 'I take it you've come to me to find a solution to this problem.'

'Of course,' Hayat Baksh said in a hearty voice. 'We are the last persons to create any trouble in the city. We want peace. We don't want any bloodshed here.'

Lakshmi Narain felt isolated. He was angry at his co-religionists. Instead of standing by him they had left him to face the Muslims alone. They should have told the Deputy Commissioner that the Muslims were piling up arms in the mosque, that they had publicly slaughtered a cow. To speak to the Deputy Commissioner in the presence of a Muslim was to make an ass of oneself. The Hindus and the Sikhs should have met the Deputy Commissioner in a separate deputation. That would have given them the opportunity to tell the truth without mincing words.

Bakshiji held Richard with his gaze and said: 'If the police force goes round the city and the military is posted at strategic points, it will nip the trouble in the bud. The situation will not get out of hand.'

Richard shook his head and smiled.

'I'm only a Deputy Commissioner,' he said. 'I've no control over the army. We do have a military cantonment here but that does not mean that the army takes orders from me.'

'The army belongs to the British and so does the civil administration,' Bakshiji rejoined. 'If you've the army deployed the situation will be saved.'

Richard again shook his head, 'Oh no I've nothing to do with the army,' he said. 'Let us be very clear about that. I can't give it orders. You know it. It lies beyond the Deputy Commissioner's jurisdiction to order the army.'

'If you can't bring in the army you can at least impose a curfew on the city. You can post police pickets.'

'Imposing curfew over trifles will only aggravate trouble. It will create more tension. What do you think?'

Richard said this as though he was genuinely interested in their opinion. Picking up a sheet of paper from the table he jotted down something on it with his pencil and then looked at his watch.

'You'll not find the Government lagging behind,' he said in a reassuring voice. 'The Government will definitely take all the necessary steps. But you people are the leaders of the city. People will listen to you. You should make a joint appeal to the people to maintain the peace.'

Some people nodded their heads in approval. How right the Saheb was!

Richard continued: 'The leaders of the Congress and the Muslim League are present here. Let Sardarji also join hands with you in forming a Peace Committee. You begin the good work. The government will help you in every possible way.'

'We are prepared to do all that,' Bakshiji said in an agitated voice. 'But the present situation is rather delicate. Once the trouble starts there's no knowing where it will end. If an aeroplane flies over the city it will restore people's confidence. They will feel reassured that the government has taken notice of the situation. This by itself will be sufficient to prevent trouble from breaking out.'

Richard again shook his head. He jotted down something on the piece of paper lying before him and then looked up.

'The Air Force is not under my command either,' he smiled.

'Everything is under you, Saheb. If only you have a mind to...'

The man is getting too big for his shoes, Richard thought. 'In fact, you made a mistake by coming to me with your complaint,' he said to Bakshiji. 'You should have, instead, gone to Pandit Nehru or the Defence Minister, Sardar Baldev Singh. It's they who hold the reins of the government.' He laughed.

Seeing the Deputy Commissioner's attitude, the others lapsed into silence but there was no stopping Bakshiji. He said in an excited voice, 'We have news that only an hour ago your British Police Officer Robert Saheb forcibly ejected a Muslim family from their house. It inflamed passions because the Muslim family was the tenant of a Hindu landlord. I feel that in view of the explosive situation in the city such action should have been deferred.'

Richard knew about the incident. In fact, the Police Officer had acted in consultation with him. Richard had told him that as executing a court order was a normal procedure there was no point in postponing it. But he was careful not to give any indication that he was aware of the incident. He made a note and said that he would enquire about it. He looked at his watch again.

Reverend Herbert, the American clergyman, who was the Principal of the local Mission College, said in a soft voice: 'The protection of the city should be above all political considerations; it should have no political overtones. There are some questions which are above party politics. They involve every inhabitant of the city. And the government has an important role to play in this. We must all make a concerted move to save the situation from deteriorating further. We should go round the city and appeal to the people not to quarrel among themselves.'

Readily agreeing with this suggestion, Richard went one step further, trying to give it practical garb.

'I suggest we hire a bus and fit it with a loudspeaker. All of you must go round the city in the bus and convey your message to the people.'

He had just stopped speaking when they heard troubled voices outside.

'A Hindu has been murdered on the bridge,' an agitated voice said to the Deputy Commissioner's peon who was sitting outside the room. 'All the bazaars have closed.'

The members of the delegation perked up their ears. The Deputy Commissioner's bungalow was quite far from the city. If the rioting had started they would not be able to make it to their houses. Then they heard the sound of a *tonga* speeding past the bungalow. And then of running feet on the road.

'I fear the trouble has already started,' Lakshmi Narain said in an anxious voice and abruptly got up.

'We'll do whatever we can,' Richard said. 'It's too bad. Too bad!'

They all got up, one after the other, and lifting the *chik* left the room. The Deputy Commissioner walked them to the door.

'First let me make arrangements for your safety,' he said to all of them in general. 'A few constables will accompany you to your houses.' Richard turned to the telephone lying on a side table.

'You need not worry about us, Saheb.' Bakshiji said. 'But kindly see to it that there's no trouble in the city. There is still time. You must impose a curfew.'

The Saheb smiled and shook his head.

The members of the delegation left the bungalow, upset and confused. As soon as they walked through the gate they stopped talking to one another. They walked some distance in silence and then Lakshmi Narain and the Sardarji crossed the road together.

The road dipped to the right and joined a bridge which separated the cantonment from the city.

Reverend Herbert had come to the meeting on his bicycle. He slowly pedalled down the slope. He wanted to ask when and where they proposed holding a meeting of the Peace Committee but everyone looked so panicky that he immediately gave up the idea. If trouble had already broken out, they probably couldn't hold a meeting anyway.

Hayat Baksh was walking fast, looking back every now and then.

'There's nothing to worry about,' he kept telling himself. 'It's a Muslim locality.'

Crossing the road at a brisk pace the Sardarji had left Hayat Baksh behind. Lakshmi Narain was about ten paces behind him. Being heavily built, he could not walk fast and had often to slow down to wipe the perspiration from his neck with a handkerchief.

Bakshiji and Mehta stood at the gate for a while and then started walking down the slope.

'Let's engage a *tonga*,' Mehtaji said. 'It'll take a long time to walk home.'

Bakshiji stopped and looked back. A *tonga* was approaching them from behind. Mehta quickly stepped to one side of the road and signalled the *tonga* to stop.

'Where do you want to go?' The driver who was a swarthy young man pulled in the reins of this horse.

'Up to the *tonga* stand in the city.'

'Two rupees.'

'What, two rupees? Two rupees is no joke!' Bakshiji said, unable to get over his habit of haggling. The *tongawalla* made as though to drive off.

'Get in, get in, Bakshiji,' Mehta said testily. 'Let the fellow have his way. This is no time to bargain.' He hastily climbed into the *tonga* and sat down on the back seat. 'Hurry, take us to the city without delay.'

Seeing Mehtaji getting into the *tonga*, Lakshmi Narain also walked in his direction. But the *tonga* had already started off. Lakshmi Narain stood in the middle of the road helplessly watching the *tonga* driving away.

'Only a Hindu will treat another Hindu in this shabby manner!' he muttered to himself. 'This is how it has been through the ages. These Hindus!'

Angrily tapping his walking stick on the road he walked on.

The other three persons, walking apart, were swiftly descending the slope. Abdul Ghani, who was an old worker of the Congress and was one of its office bearers, was now a little ahead of Lakshmi Narain and the Sardarji. Hayat Baksh had taken the lead, and was now followed by the Sardarji, both walking some distance from each other. Hayat Baksh had removed his coat and clung it over his shoulder.

'Shall we ask some of them to join us?' Bakshiji asked, as he ensconced himself in his seat.

'No, Bakshiji, leave them alone,' Mehta said. 'We had better take the road to our left. It's safer. Let them fend for themselves. We can't offer seats to all of them,' he added, justifying his stand. 'You can't pick and choose in such cases either.'

Bakshiji felt that he had made a blunder by getting into the *tonga*. He felt angry with Mehtaji and with himself. It was unbecoming of him to have acted on Mehtaji's advice. They had all come together and they should have gone back together. Nevertheless, he showed no sign of getting down from the *tonga*.

As the *tonga* passed Hayat Baksh, he looked at them and laughed. 'So you are running away, you infidels!' he cried. 'First you rake the fires and then you show your backs!' He playfully waved a clenched fist in the air.

They had all lived in the same city since childhood and were free with each other, never missing an opportunity to exchange banter, though they belonged to radically opposed political parties.

Hayat Baksh turned to look at the others behind him. Sardar Bishan Singh was the closest.

'So Bakshiji has fled!' Hayat Baksh said, 'Such are your leaders!'

Sardar Bishan Singh made no comment. He kept walking with his head bowed as before.

Lakshmi Narain who had been left far behind was anxious to catch up with Hayat Baksh. He was now passing through a Muslim locality and it would be safe to cross it in the company of a Muslim. They all knew Hayat Baksh.

'Please wait,' Lakshmi Narain called after Hayat Baksh. 'Where's the hurry?'

Sardar Bishan Singh and the others stopped. But tapping his walking stick, Lakshmi Narain walked past them and caught up with Hayat Baksh.

'It'll indeed be bad if there's trouble in the city.' he said as he walked alongside Hayat Baksh, who immediately guessed why Lakshmi Narain wanted to keep company with him. For that matter, he also stood to gain by this arrangement. Across the bridge lay the Hindu locality, and to reach his house, which was still some distance away , he would have to pass through that area. Hayat Baksh did not feel he was in any danger. He knew most of the people of the locality, all respectable householders. But one must always play safe.

Bakshiji fell unhappy as he went jolting along in the *tonga*. Whenever confronted with an unpleasant situation, his thinking would become confused and he would become a bundle of nerves.

'Mehtaji, kites and vultures will fly over the city,' he repeated the sentence for emphasis and looked around.

'We shall face it when the trouble comes,' Mehtaji replied. 'We must first reach the city.'

'What difference will it make whether we reach the city or not? The trouble is already upon us.'

Mehta was worried but he was not as agitated as Bakshiji.

'It's some consolation that the Deputy Commissioner gave us a patient hearing,' Mehtaji said. 'The previous Deputy Commissioner was a swollen-headed devil.'

'What good is this man to us?' asked Bakshiji testily. 'He is not prepared to wiggle even his little finger for us.'

'Nobody can trust anybody,' Mehtaji said.

'If you can't trust a Muslim can you trust a Hindu for that matter?' Bakshiji said with an edge to his voice.

'Look, Bakshiji, it is a small thing but it certainly shows the way the wind is blowing. Mubarak Ali is a member of the District Congress Committee. He wears khadi *kurta* and khadi *salwar*. Still he wears a Peshawari cap, not a Gandhi cap. Except for Muzaffar, no Muslim wears a Gandhi cap.'

Bakshiji took out a handkerchief from his pocket and wiped the perspiration from his face. He placed his turban on his lap.

'The Hindu Sabha people have formed a *Mohalla* Committee but we haven't been able to do even that,' Mehtaji said. 'We should have at least formed Peace Committees in all the *Mohalla*s if nothing more.' Mehtaji wiped his neck.

'Mehtaji, you would do well to drown yourself in a handful of water!' Bakshiji said flaring up.

'Why, what have I done? Why should I drown myself?'

'It doesn't behove a man to put his legs in two boats. But you have been doing just that all your life. One leg in the Congress boat and the other in the Hindu Mahasabha boat. You think people don't know about it? Of course they do.'

'If trouble breaks out, will you come to my rescue? The area across the *nullah* is inhabited by the Muslims and my house is just at the head of the *nullah*. If trouble comes will you save me? Or will Bapuji come to my help? I can only lean on the Hindus of the *Mohalla*. The man who comes to plunge a knife into my body will not first ask whether I belong to the Congress or the Hindu Mahasabha. Why don't you answer?'

'Go and drown yourself, Mehtaji. Drown yourself! It's in troubled times like these that man's integrity is tested. You've amassed a lot of wealth and your head has become thick. If your house is in a Muslim locality, is mine in a Hindu locality?'

'It hardly makes any difference to you. You are like a recluse—no wife, no family. Who would care to soil his hands with your blood?' Mehta was getting worked up. 'I asked you to turn out Latif from the Congress office. But you never listened to me. I can give it to you in writing that he belongs to the secret police and regularly reports to the government against us. You know it. So do I. And yet you are nursing that snake. As for Mubarak Ali he's conspiring with the Muslim League against us. He makes money from you and also from the Muslim League. He has constructed a house of *pucca* bricks. They are a bad lot. You see everything and yet pretend to see nothing.'

'Only a handful of Muslims are with us. How can I turn them out? If Latif is bad it does not mean that all Muslims are bad. Hakimji started working for the Congress much before you joined it. And Aziz Ahmed...'

The *tonga* had negotiated the slope and now turned towards the bridge. There was very little traffic on the road. A few people stood huddled together in front of the Islamia School. An occasional *tonga* or a cycle passed along the road at long intervals.

Those who were walking were still going down the slope when Hayat Baksh ran into Maula Dad opposite the electricity office —Maula Dad, the man with the thick beard who worked as a clerk in the electric supply office, and was an active member of the Muslim League.

'You had gone to meet the Deputy Commissioner, hadn't you?' he asked Hayat Baksh. 'What happened?'

'We have had a meeting with him. That's all. We were still there when there was an uproar outside his bungalow. We thought that the trouble had started and the meeting came to an end. I'm coming from there. What's the news in the city?'

'There's tension and it is mounting. I hear there has been some trouble near Ratta. How are things over there?'

'It's quiet there.'

Soon Hakim Abdul Ghani and Sardar Bishan Singh also arrived. They had covered some distance separately and had then walked together. Hakimji was a Congress Muslim and Sardar Bishan Singh had no compunction in walking with him.

'There should be no trouble,' Lakshmi Narain said. 'It will be too bad if anything untoward happens.'

Maula Dad gave Lakshmi Narain a sharp look. 'If you people could have your way you would be the first to create trouble,' he said. 'It's we who are showing such patience.' Then his eyes fell on Hakim Abdul Ghani and his anger mounted. 'Did this dog of the Hindus also accompany you to the Deputy Commissioner?' he asked. 'Whom did he represent?'

All the three fell silent. Ignoring Maula Dad's remark Hakimji looked in the direction of the bridge. Maula Dad's anger did not abate.

'The real enemy of the Muslim is not a Hindu but a Muslim who follows the Hindu, wagging his tail and living on his crumbs.'

'Look, Maula Dad Saheb,' Hakimji said with a show of great patience. 'You may brand me a dog and tarnish me in any manner you like. What matters most is the country's freedom. To snatch power from the British. The main question is not that of the Hindus and the Muslims.'

'Keep quiet, you dog!' Maula Dad cried. His eyes had become bloodshot and his lips were trembling.

'Let it be, Maula Dad. It's no time to fight.' For an instant Lakshmi Narain was terrified. What if they fought? His legs became soft like jelly. 'There's no point in your waiting here,' he said to Hakimji, 'Your patrons have escaped in a *tonga*, leaving you to your fate.'

Hakimji slowly edged away. Sardarji fell in step with him. But Lakshmi Narain remained where he stood.

'Going home ?' Maula Dad asked Hayat Baksh, 'Care to drop in at the League office?'

'You go. I'll join you later.'

Maula Dad understood. He immediately realized why Hayat Baksh was standing with Lakshmi Narain.

'Lalaji, you need have no fear as long as my body and soul are together,' Hayat Baksh said. 'Let's go.'

Hayat Baksh and Lakshmi Narain resumed their walk together.

*

At about twelve, Liza slowly walked up to the door which opened onto the verandah, and parting the curtains, peered out. Her eyes were dazzled by the glare of the midday sun beating down on the garden. Unable to stand the heat she drew the curtains. Her eyes fell on an image resting in the middle of the mantelpiece. It was a pot bellied Hindu god with red and white lines drawn across its forehead and a broad grin on its face. Its queer expression filled her with revulsion and she turned her face away. Where had Richard picked up that monstrosity?

She came into the hall where her eyes were again greeted by the sight of figurines and stone statuettes all over the place. When she watched them alone she felt as if they were the heads of dead Buddhas and it sent a shiver through her body. She felt stifled in this big house, crammed to bursting with books and images in stone. The images seemed to be watching her from the corners of their eyes. When Richard was gone she preferred to stay away from these images.

She stopped in front of an image of the Buddha and switched on the lamp. Yes, there was a hint of a smile on the Buddha's face, making it look beatific. She switched off the light. The smile was gone. She switched on the light. The smile came on. But this time the Buddha also seemed to be scowling at her from the corner of his eye.

Quickly switching off the light, she went back to her room. As she stepped in she heard a faint, tinkling sound. A small metal bell was hung behind her bedstead, in front of the window. It tinkled in the breeze that wafted in through the window-a soft, faint, far-off sound that pervaded the room throughout the day. Richard had fixed the bell while she was away in England. It was a small present for her amusement.

There was a loud thud. Liza turned round to look. At first she noticed nothing. Then her gaze travelled to her dressing table. A lizard was lying upon it on its back, writhing wildly. It had fallen from the wall. A chill ran through Liza's body. Soon it stopped struggling. It was dead. The heat was increasing as the month advanced, killing more lizards every day. Although it had count-less rooms, the bungalow was old, dating back to the times when the British had first entrenched themselves in the Punjab.

Two years ago they had discovered a two-yard-long snake in the servant's quarters. It would slip under a *charpoy* and then crawl up along the verandah wall. After this incident she found it impossible to be calm in the bungalow. For days she didn't dare open her wardrobe lest some snake should be lying coiled inside. At last when it became too much for her she had returned to England.

*

When Liza first came to India her head had been full of exciting ideas. She'd thought she would collect various samples of Indian craft, go round the country, do a good deal of sketching, have herself photographed perched on the back of a tiger, wear a sari. In fact, her head swarmed with such exotic schemes. But all that she'd encountered was the blazing sun, incarceration in a huge bungalow, the never-ending day, the images of the Buddha and snakes and lizards. Even outside the bungalow life was devoid of interest — the club, the wives of the English officers, among them the Commissioner's wife who thought herself to be even superior to her husband. No less officious was the Brigadier's wife who treated every woman in accordance with her husband's status (at that time Richard was comparatively a junior in the official hie-rarchy). On Saturday nights there was usually a dance at the club and there was an unending round of parties on the other days. Even then the days seemed to be inordinately long for Liza's lik-ing. It was then that she took to drinking beer to cut the tedium of the long days. She would keep her glass filled and would keep emptying it throughout the day.

'There must be German blood running in your veins,' Richard would laugh. 'That is why you are so fond of beer.' But there was no stopping Liza. She had turned into an alcoholic. In the afternoon when Richard came for lunch he would find Liza lying on the sofa, her eyes glazed with drink. In the midst of embraces, kisses and hiccups she would promise that she would severely cut down on her drinking but the next day she would forget her promise as the day dragged on.

This time she had returned from England with a laudable resolve: she would not only take an interest in things dear to her husband's heart but she would also help with the performance of his administrative duties, and social work. For instance, she would associate herself with the Society for Prevention of Cruelty to Animals. Exactly along what lines? Suddenly she felt a strong urge to ask the bearer to get her a glass of beer. It was a new *khansama* and he did not know about her addiction to beer... Well, would she run from one lane to the next, from one road to another, singling out useless horses or pariah dogs to be destroyed? What odd work! Or, was it that being the first lady of the district she would just need to be decorative while the others did the dirty work for her?

Liza's mind was in a quandary. On the one hand was her fear of boredom and on the other pride in being called the first lady of the district, scores of servants, a huge bungalow. While the latter aggravated her sense of loneliness, it also enhanced her prestige.

'Mem Saab!'

The *khansama* was standing before her.

'A lizard is lying dead on my dressing table. Remove it from there. Go.'

'*Hazoor!*' The *khansama* bowed to her and was gone.

Liza came up and stood at the window in the verandah. As she raised the curtain, the summer heat again hit her face. A clerk from Richard's office was sitting at a small table on the verandah, sorting out the mail. A dark complexioned young man with gleaming white teeth, he prefaced every sentence he spoke to Richard with a 'Yes Sir!' and swayed his head from left to right. Liza smiled. The clerk knew English but she always found his accent and the manner in which he intoned his sentences very amusing. She came out onto the verandah through the dining

83

room.

'Babu!' Taking her cue from Richard, she thought it appropriate to address him as such. She sat down on a chair by the door.

A little flustered, a file clutched in his hand, the clerk hurried up and stood before Liza.

'Yes, Sir...Yes, Madam!' His face was swarthy and his teeth pearly white. Each of his limbs seemed to have been joined to his torso with screws. As he stood before her, each of his limbs seemed to have gone askew, turn by turn. Now the left shoulder, now the right knee! But his mouth lay open all the time. She could see his gleaming teeth.

'You Hindu, Babu?'

'Yes, Madam.' the clerk replied, looking a little embarrassed. Liza was pleased at having guessed right. 'See, I've guessed correctly!' she said triumphantly.

'Yes, Madam!'

Then she realized she didn't know why she had guessed as she did. What made her think the young man was a Hindu? He was wearing pants, coat and tie. What were those special features that identified a Hindu? She got up suddenly and ran her fingers through his hair, as if searching for something. The clerk looked on, discomfited. About thirty years old, he had worked as a steno in the Deputy Commissioner's office for the last ten years. This was the first time the wife of a Deputy Commissioner had cared to talk to him with such informality. The wives of the previous Deputy Commissioners had spoken to him with a studied aloofness and superciliousness.

Standing at the far end of the verandah, the *khansama*, the gardener and the cook cast amused glances at Liza.

'No, it's not there!' Liza said, withdrawing her hand from the clerk's head. The clerk's lips trembled in an awkward smile.

'You are no Hindu. You lied.'

'No Madam, I'm a Hindu, a Brahmin Hindu.'

'Oh no! Then where's your tuft?'

The clerk was cautious. A riot was threatening in the city and he had only managed to reach his office with considerable difficulty. He felt a bit relieved at Liza's question. His teeth gleamed.

'I've no tuft, Madam,' he replied.

'Then you're no Hindu.' Liza pointed her little finger at him and laughed good-humouredly. 'You've told me a lie.'

'No, Madam, I'm a Hindu.'

'Take off your coat, Babu.' Liza said.

'Oh, Madam!' The suggestion caused him renewed embarrassment.

'Take it off! Take off your coat. Hurry!'

The clerk smiled nervously and took off his coat.

'Very good. Now unbutton your shirt.'

'What, Madam?'

'Don't say, what Madam. Say, I beg your pardon, Madam. All right, unbutton your shirt.'

The clerk stood before Liza, undecided. Then putting his fingers under his necktie, he opened up three buttons of his shirt.

'Show me your thread!'

'What, Madam?'

'Your thread! Show me your thread.'

The clerk suddenly realized what the Deputy Commissioner's wife was after. But he wore no sacred thread. After passing his Matriculation, when he entered college, he had had his tuft cut off and two years later, while still in college, he had discarded his sacred thread.

'I've no thread, Madam.' He smiled awkwardly.

'No thread? Then you're no Hindu!'

'I'm a Hindu, Madam. I swear by God, I'm a Hindu.' He was getting jittery.

'No, you're no Hindu,' Liza insisted. 'You told a lie. I shall tell your boss.'

The clerk's face turned pale. He buttoned up his shirt and while putting on his coat, said in a trembling voice: 'I tell you sincerely, Madam. I'm a Hindu. My name is Roshanlal.'

'Roshanlal? My cook's name is Roshandin, and he's a Musalman.'

'Yes, Madam,' the clerk said. It had become difficult for him to explain. 'He's Roshandin, true. I'm Roshanlal. He's a Muslim. I'm a Hindu.'

'No, Richard told me you people have different names.' She raised her finger at him in mock anger and continued, 'No, Babu, you lied to me. I shall tell your boss.

The clerk's throat was getting parched and his heart had started beating hard. Was she asking him this question in the context of the impending trouble in the city? What did she really want of him?

Liza got up from her chair. 'Well Babu! I shall let your boss know.'

The clerk picked up his file from the floor and turned to go. He had walked up to the other end of the verandah when Liza called him back.

'Babu!'

The clerk returned.

'Come here!'

'Where's your boss?' She had suddenly turned very grave.

'In the office, Madam. He's very busy, Madam.'

'All right, go. You and your boss, go. Get out of here!' She cried.

'Yes, Madam!'

After the Babu was gone Liza felt nauseous. Her gay mood had turned. As she saw the clerk going away with stooped shoulders, she felt he was a slithery jelly on the move. How could Richard put up with these creatures the whole day long? She sighed and disappeared into the bungalow.

Chapter 8

In the city there was a clear-cut demarcation of work. The Hindus owned most of the cloth shops, the Muslims, the footwear stores The transport business was in the hands of the Muslims whereas the Hindus had a monopoly of the grain trade. As for the petty trade, it was evenly distributed between the Hindus and the Muslims.

That day the Temple Bazaar glowed like the face of a bride, busy as on all other days, giving no hint of the pervading tension in the city. The jewellers' shops were crowded with *burqa*-clad women from the villages who had come to buy silver ornaments. In front of Hakim Labhu Ram's shop, two Kashmiri Muslims, their noses and mouths covered with cloth, pounded medicines in a pestle. The hunch-backed sweetmeat seller's shop was crowded as on other days. The hawker, Sant Ram, slowly pushed his hand-cart through the goldsmiths' lane and planted himself at his usual spot in the Temple bazaar at one o'clock on the dot. Following standing instructions, the first thing he did was to dole out half a *chhatak halwa* each on three leaf plates for the master tailor, Khuda Baksh, and his two brothers.

The tension caused by the morning's episode had long since subsided. There was a flurry of activity on the roads. In front of Khuda Baksh's tailoring shop, at the end of the lane, the municipal lamp-lighter had climbed up a wooden ladder to the top of a lamp-post and was shining the lamp fixed in the wall. Here, the entire bazaar worked to an unheard rhythm. As Ibrahim, the perfume-seller, trudged from one lane to the next, phials of perfumes hanging from his shoulders, his feet kept pace to this subtle rhythm of the city. So did the women who walked through the lanes, carrying pitchers, to fill them with water from the tap. The wheels of the *tonga*s revolved to a set rhythm, the children trudging to their schools, planted their feet to a subdued rhythm.

The entire range of activities was orchestrated to a certain rhythm — the rhythm of the city. It seemed that even if one link broke, all the strings of the instrument would snap, throwing the activities of the city out of gear, and breaking the rhythm. The multifarious activities of the people, like the measured tones of a symphony, were attuned to the heart-beat of the city. People grew from childhood to this unheard music and declined into old age to the same music. One generation merged into the next to the same tune. Call it music or give it the name of a delicate equilibrium in which people's mutual relationships and those of the various communities, constituting the totality of humanity, were precariously poised.

Not that there were no tidal waves in the otherwise placid life of the city and that it lived by its orchestrated rhythms alone. When the Congress movement started, it created ripples, disturbing the even tenor of the city. Every year when the Sikhs took out a procession on the birthday of the Guru, it gave anxious moments to the people. They watched with bated breath to see whether the procession would abstain from playing music as it passed along the Jama Masjid, or whether stones would be hurled at the procession out of wanton provocation. A similar situation arose when the Muslims took out the *'tazias'* and went through the streets beating their breasts and yelling 'Ya Hussain!' On such occasions the fear of communal clashes became real. But soon after, the tension would ease and people would lapse into their normal routine.

At Khuda Baksh's tailoring shop, Hakim Singh's wife was having it out with him: 'O, Baksha, will the auspicious moment ever arrive? What have you done with my clothes? Or do you just want me to make futile rounds of your shop?'

Khuda Baksh smiled. All the Hindu and Sikh women of the city, most of them belonging to well-to-do families, had their clothes stitched by him. Popularly known as Baksha, he was the leading tailor of the city.

'*Bibi*, when I asked you to get me the cloth you never cared to deliver it on time. The winter is gone and it is bound to take time. I don't have sixteen hands.'

'Who says the winter is gone?'

'Just try to recall. Didn't you betroth your daughter fifteen days after Shiv Ram's son's marriage? What month was that? Just tell me.'

Hakim Singh's wife started laughing. 'You forget nothing,' she said. 'Now come to the point. When will you deliver my daughter's dresses?'

'When is the marriage?'

'Now don't tease me. You remember the date of my daughter's betrothal. But you can't keep the date of her wedding in your head?'

'It's on the 25th, isn't it? What date is today? The 5th? The clothes will be ready.'

'But when? I know you well, don't think I don't? You will make me run to your shop on the day of the wedding. You did the same for Vidya's marriage. The marriage party was at our door and I had to send my man to you to fetch the brocade suit. Now tell me, precisely on what date will you deliver the dresses?'

She was still nagging him about the date, when another woman flung a bundle of cloth into Baksha's basket from behind, a green piece of silk cloth and a length of brocade border.

'Baksha, measure the cloth first. Later if it falls short of your requirements you can get some more from Budh Singh's shop. Just mention my name and tell him it's on my account.'

Baksha wet one end of the cloth with spittle and then, pulling a pencil from behind his ear, made a mark on it and put it away in an *almirah*. The *almirah* was crammed with piece-lengths, waiting to be stitched for weddings.

'I'll deliver them. I'll give them on time. I'll personally bring them to your house,'

'Huh! Just empty talk! If you fail me this time I'll not step into your shop again,' Hakim Singh's wife laboriously climbed down the steps of the tailor's shop and went away.

When the woman was gone, Khuda Baksh's eyes casually travelled to the wall of the temple on the opposite side of the road. A man had climbed up the wall. Khuda Baksh intently looked at him. It was the Gorkha *chowkidar*. What was he doing there? Behind the wall stood the oldest temple of the city. There was a big bell fixed to the temple wall. The Gorkha was busy cleaning the bell.

'What's going on there?' Khuda Baksh asked one of his assistants.

'The bell is being mended,' the assistant said.

'Ya Allah!' the words escaped Khuda Baksh's lips.

'They fear trouble in the city.'

The bell had been installed following a riot in 1926. Since then it had lost a lot of its shine. Because of the sun and rain, plaster had peeled off from the walls around it. At the time of the first communal riot, Khuda Baksh was a young man of twenty-two, or so, fond of physical exercise and just being initiated into his father's business. Now he was past middle age and there was hardly any wedding in the city for which he had not stitched the bridal clothes. The bell had been installed when Rambali, the *chowkidar*, who was still on the same job, had just been appointed. His body had now lost its firmness, wrinkles had appeared on his face and the hair on his temples had grayed, but even now he performed his duty with the same zeal as he did when he was first appointed.

The bell tinkled faintly, once more drawing Khuda Baksh's attention. The Gorkha was tying a new rope to the bell. He had already oiled the grooves and burnished the bell.

'Its sound sends a shiver through my body,' Khuda Baksh said. 'When it tolled during the first riot the grain market was set on fire and its flames covered half the sky over the city.'

The Gorkha was still at his job with great earnestness as if an important festival was in the offing. The bell now shone like a new brass vessel. The new rope hung from it.

Drifting from the bell, Khuda Baksh's gaze stopped at the nearby goldsmith's shop where a middle-aged man and his wife and daughter, apparently from a village, were arguing over the purchase of a pair of ear-rings.

'Why don't you have them if you like them so much? Hurry up. We have many more things to buy and we need to return to the village before it gets too late.'

The girl's eyes shone. Time and again she would hold the earrings against her ears and look shyly at her mother. 'How do they look, Mother?' She would ask with a smile.

Khuda Baksh again looked towards the temple. The *chowkidar* was climbing down from the wall. The rope dangled over it.

'*Ya Allah!*' Said Khuda Baksh.

*

People had collected outside Fazaldin, the *nanbai's* baker's shop. As the afternoon declined and business slackened, people from the adjoining shops also collected at the shop for a brief gossip session. As the hookah went round, the talk became livelier.

The gossip centred round the incident which had already become the talk of the town. And then, one thing leading to another, old Karim Khan brought up the subject of the rulers. The rulers, he maintained, looked far ahead of the others and every action of their's had deep meaning behind it, whose significance others failed to gauge at that time.

'Moses, one day, said to Khizr,' Karim Khan said, 'Make me your disciple. Listen, Jilani, just listen to me. It's a very instructive story.'

'Moses was young and he was fired by the ambition of becoming a prophet,' Karim Khan continued. 'He was in no way near his objective but he secretly lived with the idea in his heart. Khizr, as you know, was already a prophet. You get my point, don't you? And he was much older to him in age. Everyone held him in high regard. He was almost worshipped by them.' Karim Khan's small, beady eyes seemed to be smiling all the time and when he broke into a laugh, he would thump his thigh.

'So one day Moses requested Khizr to make him his disciple. Khizr had no objection. "Only on one condition," he added. "What's that condition?" Moses asked. "The only condition that I wish to impose upon you is that you'll not be critical of my actions. You'll ask no questions and just keep your mouth shut." Moses said that he would gladly abide by this condition and Khizr took Moses under his tutelage.'

'Of course, Khizr wanted to teach Moses a lesson. What lesson? That the God Almighty sees everything whereas we mortals are blind to what goes on around us. We just rack our brains to establish cause and effect. It is an exercise in futility for we get nothing for our pains. Because it's God who sees everything. He is the All-Seeing. So Khizr told Moses to watch without any comment, what he did or said. "You must keep your mouth shut!" he warned Moses.'

Karim Khan passed on the hookah to Jilani Mian, sitting next to him. Jilani pulled hard at the hookah. The water carrier had sprinkled water in front of the shop and a faint earth smell rose from the lane and spread in the air. The traffic had thinned. Only a few stragglers passed by, on their way to Jama Masjid for the afternoon *namaz*.

'One day Khizr was on his way to a nearby village. Moses followed close on his heels. Later Moses became a renowned prophet but at that time he was only a disciple of Khizr. Are you listening, Jilani? Listen carefully, keeping both your ears open. It's a very instructive story. So both of them set off to the neighbouring village. On the way they had to cross a small river. There was only one boat, tied at the bank, to take them across the river. They sat down in the boat and the boatman picked up his oars to row them across. To his horror, Moses saw that Khizr was drilling a hole in the bottom of the boat. It was a brand new boat and looked as though it had been constructed only that day and put out on the river. After making one hole Khizr proceeded to make another. And then a third. Moses wailed: "What are you doing? the boat will sink. We'll be drowned!"'

'Khizr put a finger to his lips, signing to Moses to keep quiet. Even though Moses was highly agitated, for water had started filling the boat, he held his peace, for he had given his word to Khizr.'

'After some time Khizr plugged the holes but serious damage had already been caused to the boat. Somehow they managed to cross the river without any mishap.'

'When they resumed their journey they came across a small boy, sitting on the ground, playing. Khizr lifted the child, and before Moses could intervene, he twisted the child's neck.'

'"What have you done?" Moses cried. "You've killed an innocent boy!" But Khizr was silent. He only put his finger to his lips, warning Moses not to speak.'

'"Oh God! How can you stop me from speaking?" Moses protested, "You've wrung the neck of an innocent child. You don't even know him. You've not set foot in this village before. What grudge did you have against this child to have taken his life?" Moses was deeply hurt as you can see. A very sensitive soul, for he was a prophet in the making.' Karim Khan swayed his head while narrating the story. 'May God have mercy on them.'

'They continued their journey. When they reached the outskirts of the village they were heading for, they saw a tumble-down wall skirting the village. Moses jumped over the wall in one bound. When he looked back he saw that Khizr was still on the other side, busy placing one brick upon the other in order to repair the breaches in the wall. Moses jumped back over the wall and joined Khizr. "Revered Mentor," he said. "You had no compunction in killing that child who had not even started his life, whereas now you are taking great pains to repair a wall which has remained neglected for years. I don't understand your ways at all!"'

'Khizr again warned him not to speak.'

'They walked on and reached a garden where a stream was flowing under shady trees. Both washed their hands and feet and sat down under a tree. Then Khizr spoke: "Listen, son," he said. "The administrator of the region through which that river flows is a very cruel person. He snatches away poor people's boats for pleasure. I thought if I drilled holes in that boat the administrator's people would not take it away and the boatman could continue to make a living." Moses listened to this, and after a pause, asked, "But why did you throttle that child?"'

"'Listen, I was going to tell you about that also. If you must know, that child was a bastard, not a legitimate child, as you must have presumed. The child's father is a very cruel person and extremely wicked. The child, when he grew up, would have also turned into a cruel and wicked man like his father. And like his father he would have also done great harm to innocent people. So I thought I would kill the child and save the people from his evil ways. Now tell me, did I do any wrong by killing him?"'

'It set Moses thinking,' Karim Khan continued. 'For some time he sat there with bowed head and then asked Khizr: "Why did you take the trouble of repairing that tumble-down wall? What good did that do anybody?"'

"'I'll explain why I did that too," Khizr said. "The wall that I repaired has a treasure buried under it. But the village people know nothing about it. As these people are extremely poor and needy, I would like help to them. Now that I've repaired the wall when they plough their fields they will find the wall an obstruction when they get to it. In their anger, they will demolish the wall and throw away the bricks. And then, lo and behold, they will discover a treasure buried under the wall and become rich overnight. They will have clothes to cover their bodies and food to eat. Tell me, did I do any wrong repairing the wall?"'

After finishing the story Karim Khan looked at his listeners, one by one. 'What I mean to say is that what the ruler can see, the common man, I mean you and I, may fail to see. The Britishers have all seeing eyes. Nothing escapes their notice. Otherwise, how can a handful of *feringhi*, coming from across the seven seas, rule over such a vast country? The Englishmen are very shrewd and far-sighted.'

'Of course! Of course!' the listeners said in unison, nodding their heads lively.

Nathu was also sitting in the shop, a little apart from the group, a cup of tea in front of him and a piece of rusk in one hand. He would dip the rusk into the tea, take a bite at it, without taking his eyes off Karim Khan's face. He was listening attentively. The story set at rest the doubts that had plagued him ever since he had killed the pig. Everywhere he went in the city people had been talking about the pig. This had disturbed him a lot. But Karim Khan's story he found reassuring. People were probably talking about some other pig. In any case if trouble did not break out soon, the slaughter of the pig would pass off as an event of no consequence. If the rulers, as Karim Khan had said, were all-seeing nothing untoward would happen.

Once again Nathu felt his pocket. The note crackled. He felt very happy, it had been really good of Murad Ali to have given him the entire amount in one lot. If he had fobbed him off with an eight anna coin, promising to pay the rest later he couldn't have done a thing about it, except wait hopefully. Somewhat guiltily he thought that since Murad Ali had been so honourable about the whole business it had been unbecoming of him to have slipped away from the room where the pig lay after telling him that he would wait for him there. But the fact was that he had felt so suffocated that he could not wait in that room a moment longer. And the more he had wandered about town the more difficult it had become to return to where the pig had been killed or even to contact Murad Ali. Everyone seemed to be talking about the pig.

Though he tried to hide his feelings he was getting more and more apprehensive as time passed. The more he thought about the matter the more confused he became. Who could he talk to? And what would he say? He had been duped. They had, indeed, played a nasty trick on him. Murad Ali had told him that the pig was meant for the veterinary doctor and had then thrown the pig's dead carcass in front of a mosque. But no, it probably was some other pig. He had stolen a glance at the pig lying in front of the mosque. It did look like some other pig. But that was no consolation. His restlessness increased. What if it was the same pig? He felt like running away from the shop, going to his room and bolting it from inside. Then he thought it would be safer to keep wandering about the city. When night fell he could probably go to a prostitute. If she demanded one rupee, he'd offer her five and stay with her the whole night. But then he also longed for his wife's company. If he had been at home now he would have been sitting with the other cobblers, sharing a *chelum* and gossiping. Yes, he must go home, have a bath, change his shirt, and talk to his wife. He would put his arms around her as he entered his room. He wouldn't tell her anything about Murad Ali though. Why should be trouble her mind with such hideous stories? He would just rest his head on her breast. Ah! what heaven. If he went to a prostitute, she would talk coarsely to him, demand money. But his wife was so sweet and undemanding. Instead of giving two rupees to Motia, the prostitute, he would spend the money on sweets for his wife. It would make her feel so happy. Of course, she would tell him that there was no need for the sweets for when he was with her she didn't feel the need for anything else. She was such a patient woman. And so full of love.

The shop was filled with smoke. Outside the shop there were two wooden benches. Two labourers sat on one of them eating from tin plates. A bowl of *dal* lay in front of them. They broke chunks from their *nan*, dipped them in the *dal*, and swallowed in a regular rhythm. The water carrier had again sprinkled water in front of the shop.

There was the sound of drums in the distance. The two labourers sitting outside the shop stopped eating, and craned their necks to look in the direction of the sound. The people inside the shop stopped talking as the sound of the drums drew nearer.

'What's happening?' someone asked.

'It's the town crier,' another man replied. 'We shall soon know. He's coming in our direction.'

A *tonga*, flying the Congress tri-colour stopped in front of the *nanbai's* shop. A man, sitting on the back seat of the *tonga*, was beating a drum. Another man on the front seat stood up and the drum stopped beating. The man who had got up, said in a sing-song voice:

Think of your country. Even the sky forebodes a holocaust!

Friends, today there will be a public meeting in Ganj Mandi at 6 p.m. under the auspices of the district Congress Committee. There will be sensational revelations. The meeting will expose the government's machinations in frustrating our struggle for independence. The meeting will also launch an appeal before the citizens to maintain peace in the city. Please turn up in large numbers and make the meeting a thumping success.

The General, who was the man sitting on the backseat with the drum, began beating on it again. Shanker, who was the announcer resumed his seat and the *tonga* started. The flag fluttered in the breeze.

When the *tonga* had receded into the distance one labourer said to the other: 'I was carrying a *babu's* luggage from Ganj Mandi when the *babu* said that independence was just round the corner. I laughed and said: "Independence has no meaning for us. Independence or no independence we will continue to carry loads."' The labourer laughed loudly showing his red gums.

'Yes, we were born to be beasts of burden,' the other labourer agreed with the first one. 'We carry loads now and we shall carry loads forever.' He laughed.

A bearded man, middle-aged, sitting in the shop wanted to know if the man who had polluted the mosque had been caught 'May his body be infested with worms!' he added.

'A most heinous act!' another man muttered.

Nathu shook from head to foot.

'I hear a cow has also been killed,' said another man, 'Its carcass was found near the main sewer.'

'Too bad! It's too bad!'

At this the beady-eyed Karim Khan launched forth into another sermon:'It's said in the Koran that man's crops grow through His benediction. Every man acts at his command. If He does not will it even the ripe crop will stop swaying and wither away. The country will be deluged with floods, bringing disaster to one city after another.' Karim Khan paused for effect and then continued. 'It's all in His hands. Nothing rests with man. All actions are ordained by the Almighty. Things happen at His command.'

The people sitting around swayed their heads in approval. The hookah went round.

Outside, one of the labourer's sang in a lusty voice: 'Why do you cast lustful looks on the fold of my *salwar*?' Nathu envied him his uncomplicated life.

There was a sudden flurry of activity on the road. People stopped and looked in the direction of the mosque.

'Pir Saheb has graced the occasion with his presence,' someone said. 'The Pir of Golra Shareef.' The *nanbai* quickly got up from his seat. The people in the shop spilled out onto the road, excited at the appearance of the Pir.

A well-built man, with a flowing beard and dressed in a long black shirt, passed the shop. He wore three or four bead necklaces round his neck. A mop of thick hair escaped from under his turban and fell down his back. The saint held a rosary in one hand and his face was suffused with what the awed onlookers thought looked like a divine glow. The Pir was surrounded by his disciples and followers.

The *nanbai* came forward, and resting his hands on his thighs, bowed low as the holy man passed. The holy man extended his hand. Taking it reverentially, the *nanbai* placed it on his eyes, covered his heart with his right hand and bowed even further. The Pir withdrew his hand and walked on without slackening his pace. All those standing on the road bowed to him, one by one, and received his blessings.

'He's a great seer,' the *nanbai* said returning to his shop, 'How radiant his face looks! How divine!'

'He's a great seer,' the *nanbai* repeated. 'He can even read your mind. Once I went on a pilgrimage to Golra Shareef. The Pir was sitting on a wooden plank. There was a heap of wheat lying in front of him. "Pick up some grains," he said. When I hesitated, he said, "What are you waiting for? Go ahead, pick up some grains and put them on your palm." I bent down and picked up some grains from the heap. "Only one hundred and seventy grains!" he said. "Take some more."'

'Astounded, I started counting the grains. There were exactly one hundred and seventy grains.'

'He can cure people,' Karim Khan said. 'God has bestowed this great boon on him. You know my grandson. He's a hefty youth now but when he was a child he got mumps. Both his cheeks had puffed out, so swollen were they. Someone told me to take him to Golra Shareef. The Pir told me to lay the child flat before him. I did so. Then picking up a big knife that was lying by his side he touched its blade against the child's cheek. He spat out some saliva onto his palm and rubbed that on the child's cheeks as well. That was all he did. I kissed his feet and took the child home. By the time I reached home the swelling had subsided and his fever was gone.'

'The Pirs have great curative powers,' Karim Khan said. 'I know of a Baba Roda who sits near Masiyari. He also performs similar miracles.'

'But the Pir Saheb does not touch *kafirs*,' the *nanbai* said. 'He hates them, in fact. In the beginning everybody had access to him. If it was a *kafir* he would place the end of his stick on his pulse and put the other end to his ear and then listen to the pulse. But now he does not allow any *kafir* near him.'

'He avoids coming to the city in summer. It's after a long time that he's visiting us during the summer.'

'Summer and winter have no meaning for him.'

'Maybe he knows what's coming. He must have known that the mosque was polluted.'

'Yes, his type have an uncanny knack of knowing everything. He learns through intuition. He knew and he came.'

'We must keep these Pirs in good humour. If a fakir or a Pir is annoyed, city after city is razed to the ground.'

'You're right'.

'Will he preach?'

'He may, if he stays here till Friday.'

'Now that he has come he's sure to stay here till Friday. And he must give a sermon. If only to sanctify the city, to save it from further pollution.'

*

When Nathu came out of the shop it was afternoon. He felt much more relaxed. The vague sense of fear that had been nagging him since the morning had disappeared. The city had seemed to have regained its usual gaiety. The episode of the pig seemed to have lost its gravity. People were already joking about it. If no one was upset, why should I worry, Nathu asked himself. Besides nobody even knew he was the culprit. Only Murad Ali knew but as he was a Muslim, he would be the last person to reveal that he'd instigated the deed. Nathu looked about him at the small events of the city. Standing in front of a shop, a villager was selecting a pair of shoes for his wife. 'Go ahead. Take this one!' he said to the woman. 'I tell you, this is just the thing for you. The ones you're wearing are completely worn out.'

His wife, who sat by his side, clad in a *burqa* shook her head. 'I don't need it,' she said in a soft, musical voice, 'The ones I'm wearing are good enough for me. In fact you need new shoes more than I do. Buy a good pair. You've to do a lot of walking every day.'

Nathu moved on. Crossing the road, he turned to his right. Another row of *nanbai's* shops came up. There were big *nans* heaped outside the shops and the smell of spices rose from big cauldrons filled with mutton curry. All the shops were crowded with people, most of them labourers or villagers on a visit to the city with their families. After a day's work, they were gorging themselves with food. After eating, they would get into their carts and take the long country roads back to their villages.

Behind the *nanbai's* shops rose the imposing Jama Masjid. In the declining afternoon sun the mosque looked clean and white. Beggars sat on the steps lower down and further up labourers lay sprawling. Worshippers cautiously picked their way through the people sitting or lying on the steps. All of them carried their shoes in their hands. Nathu watched them fascinated. Normally people flocked to the mosque in such large numbers only on Id day. Then suddenly it occurred to him that the crowds could be there because of the Pir of Golra Shareef. He must have come to preach. Nathu was suddenly afraid. Had these people assembled to condemn his evil deed?

He walked on quickly. A big sewer marked the place where the wall of the mosque ended. The filth and the dirty water of the entire city was flushed out through this sewer. Nathu stopped by the end of the sewer, and leaning against the railing, looked down. A dark-skinned man lay naked on the platform running along the sewer, a talisman round his neck and his thick matted hair standing out like spikes. Just above him, a tin hung from a nail on the sewer wall. It was a narrow platform, so narrow that the man would fall into the sewer if he turned on his side. Could he be one of those seers, Nathu wondered, keeping his eyes on him. Abruptly the man sat up and stared fixedly at Nathu. Then like a holy man he swayed from side to side, as if he was in a trance. Nathu looked away. After a short while when he looked down again he saw that the man had stopped swaying and was now beckoning to him. Nathu felt afraid. The man could cast a spell on him or put him under a curse. He took a one anna coin from his pocket, and threw it to the man. The man picked up the coin and flung it into the sewer. He looked at Nathu again and furiously beckoned to him. Even more frightened Nathu quickly moved away.

The Burra Bazaar bustled with activity. Nathu liked this part of the city most. The two aerated water shops in the bazaar had rows and rows of coloured bottles ranged in front of the shop-keepers. The vendors wearing spotlessly white clothes, briskly filled up glasses of *nimbu pani* and handed them to the crowds milling around their shops. The garland sellers had already appeared on the footpaths and the *seekh kabab* sellers had stationed themselves next to the aerated water shops. Not far away he could see the liquor shops and prostitutes who smiled lasciviously at passersby.

There were many *tongas* lined up in front of the shops, their horses brightly caparisoned.

As always Nathu found the bazaar scene diverting. His worries faded as he watched the energy and good humour of the people around him. As the evening advanced people's sprits rose even higher. Nathu caught up in the mood of the crowd headed for a *seekh kabab* shop where he bought eight annas worth of *kababs*. He then deposited himself on a bench in front of a liquor shop.

As the dusk deepened, the bazaar lit up. The water carriers came around sprinkling water and a faint smell of earth leapt up mixing with the smell of flower garlands. Nathu felt pleasantly heady. He didn't know when he bought a garland and put it around his neck. Nor did he remember when he crossed the open space of Raja Bazaar and entered the lane where the prostitutes had their rooms. As he staggered down the lane, he saw Murad Ali coming from the opposite direction. Short, stocky, thick black moustache, long coat ending at the knees, long thin stick in hand. Was it really Murad Ali or was Nathu imagining things? Murad Ali's figure moved before Nathu's eyes like a ghost. Nathu blinked to clear his eyes. Yes, it was Murad Ali all right, coming from the direction of the grain market. Had Nathu not been drunk he would have hidden. But having imbibed two bowls of raw liquor he was in high spirits, though he wasn't yet too badly drunk; two bowls of liquor were not enough to get a *chamar* drunk. But still he wasn't sober either. He felt he should let Murad Ali know how he had done the job entrusted to him.

'*Salaam hazoor*!' Nathu stepped forward, laughed and then stood stiffly erect.

Murad Ali stopped momentarily. He glanced at Nathu and quietly took stock of the situation. Then he walked on ignoring Nathu's greeting.

'*Salaam hazoor*. I'm Nathu. Don't you recognize me?'

Murad Ali kept walking. Nonplussed, Nathu stared after him.

'*Hazoor*, Murad Ali Saheb!' he shouted.

Murad Ali did not stop.

A doubt crossed Nathu's mind. Murad Ali was probably under the impression that he, Nathu, had been loafing in the bazaar, without attending to his job. He must tell him that he was mistaken.

He went stumbling after Murad Ali. The lane ahead of him was dark but he could see Murad Ali faintly in the distance. He broke into a run. He must tell Murad Ali that he had not failed him.

He was closing in on the other man. Then he saw that Murad Ali had deliberately slowed down.

'*Hazoor*, I forgot to tell you. I've done the job. The cartman had come...'

Murad Ali stopped abruptly. He raised his stick. They stood there staring at each other.

'I have done your job, *hazoor*,' Nathu repeated. 'I did it promptly.'

He realized vaguely through his drunkeness that Murad Ali had resumed walking. Nathu peered after him. Murad Ali had gone quite far. Emerging from the lane he was climbing the steep incline leading to the temple. Like a ghost in the dark, he kept receding without being lost to view.

*

Nathu's wife opened the door at his knock. She seemed greatly relieved to see him. Then before he knew what has happening tears came to her eyes. She went and sat on the cot.

'It's so thoughtless of you,' she said tearfully. 'I was worried to death, imagining the worst. This is no way to treat a wife.'

She wiped her tears with the end of her sari. Then she looked at Nathu and smiled. 'Look at the shape you're in! There's a garland hanging from your ear. Whom have you been visiting?'

Wordlessly, Nathu sat down on the cot.

'If you're drunk you must sing and laugh. Earlier when you were drunk you used to come home in a boisterous mood.'

It must be said here that Nathu's wife was patience incarnate. If he got into a temper and abused her she would endure everything without a word. She would say simply :'Go on, take it out on me. It'll lighten your heart!' Or, she would quietly stand in a corner.

It is fun sticking a thorn in living flesh and watching it wince, but what good is it sticking the thorn in a lump of earth?

Because of her extreme forbearance Nathu tended to avoid scenes with his wife. There were about twenty *chamar* families in the colony and Nathu's wife was friendly with the women of all the families. She was a contented God-fearing woman, always happy, because she did not expect much from life.

'Why don't you speak?' she asked. 'You've been away from home the whole night.'

Nathu raised his head and looked at his wife. 'To hell with Murad Ali. And the pig be damned!' he shouted suddenly. 'Thank God I'm home. Did the neighbours ask about me?'

'Yes, they did. In a casual way.'

'What did you tell them?'

'I told them that you had gone to work and were expected any time.'

'Did they want to know where I was?'

'Oh, no. Don't people go to work? In the evening, when my neighbour asked me, I told her you had gone out to skin a horse.'

Nathu smiled thinly.

'But where were you all this time?'

'I'll tell you some other time.'

Nathu's wife looked at him questioningly. He had never concealed anything from her. She did not ask him a second time. She knew some day he would tell her on his own.

'I won't ask you if you don't feel like telling me,' she said. 'Come, have your food. It won't take me a minute to prepare *cha-*

102

patis for you. Hot *chapatis.* Have them with tea.'

She got up from the cot. Impulsively Nathu pulled her down to his side.

'Have you eaten?' he asked, caressing her hair.

'Yes, I have.' She thought her husband's behaviour was rather odd.

'You're lying. I know you haven't eaten?' His wife looked at him and smiled. 'I cooked the food, all right. But I was in no mood to eat.'

'Did you eat in the morning?'

'Yes, I did,'

'There, lying again! Tell me, did you eat?'

She again looked at her husband and smiled. 'No, I didn't eat. I just kept waiting for you. How could I eat without you?'

'And if I had failed to turn up tonight?'

'How could that be? I knew you would come.'

Nathu was still afraid of what he had done earlier. He heard a sound outside his door and jumped. Could that be Murad Ali scraping at the door with his stick? 'No,' he said to himself, reassuringly. 'Murad Ali could not have recognized me in that state. Otherwise, he would have stopped to have a word with me.' He probably took Nathu for a drunkard who was chasing him for fun.

'You have something on your mind,' his wife said 'You don't look happy. You make me worry about you.'

Nathu looked at his wife. She looked back concernedly. 'People have been fearing trouble in the city,' she said. 'Somebody killed a pig and threw it in front of a mosque. I was worried. If trouble had broken out, where could I have gone to look for you?'

Nathu looked at his wife sharply. 'What kind of pig?' he asked. 'Whose pig?'

'Don't you know what a pig looks like?' Nathu's wife laughed. She was relieved Nathu was back.

'I mean was it black or white?' Nathu asked. He looked intently at his wife, anxiously awaiting the answer.

'What difference does it make?'

'Did you see the pig?'

'How could I? Besides, it's none of my business to wander around looking at pigs.'

'Did our neighbours see it?'

'What are you saying! Have our neighbours nothing better to do than go about inspecting pigs? They told me what they had heard from others.'

The night advanced. The voices from the neighbouring hovels slowly ceased.

'Would you like to sleep outside or inside?' Nathu's wife asked.

'Why?'

'One can never trust you. If you're sleeping outside you suddenly take it into your head to shift inside and drag me along. I thought I would ask you in advance.It's very humid inside.' She untied her hair. 'You haven't told me yet whether you'd like to eat or not. Why are you sitting silent? I felt so lonely when you were not at home yesterday.'

As he watched his wife untying her hair, a surge of passion rushed through Nathu and he took her in his arms. He felt more and more aroused as he lost himself in his wife's lush body.

'Today I cried thrice', she said. 'I stood outside for hours waiting for you. Then I went in and cried. I was afraid you would never return.'

Nathu hugged his wife harder, stilling her words, kissing her lips, her eyes, her hair.

Suddenly they heard dogs barking loudly on the *maidan* and then, far, far away, the sound of subdued voices. Nathu in his ecstacy ignored everything but his wife's gaze travelled to the wall near the ceiling. A dim light trembled there as of a red shadowy figure dancing.

'What's that?' she said, pointing towards the light. 'What's that light? Looks like a fire. Have they set something on fire? And what's that noise?'

Nathu raised his head and a groan escaped his lips. The barking of the dogs had become louder and the noise in the distance had also increased — it sounded like an advancing army.

'A fire has broken out somewhere in the city,' he said, grumpily, and sat up. Then he heard the sound of a bell above the other noise. He had often heard the sound of the tower clock in the Sheikh's garden. About the time his wife finished her chores and came to bed the clock would start chiming and she would count the chimes — ten, sometimes, eleven. But what they heard now was not the sound of the Sheikh's clock. It was the tolling of a bell which Nathu had never heard before. The bell kept tolling without a break. Sometimes the sound would be drowned in the rising noise and then they would hear it again, floating in on the breeze.

People came out of their hovels to find out what has going on.

'It's the grain market!' a man cried,' They have set it on fire!'

Then another sound rose clear of the background noise '*Allah-o-Akbar!*'

Nathu stared at the ceiling with wide open eyes. He felt paralysed.

'Let's get out!' said his wife in a whisper. 'Let's ask the people in the compound what's going on. I feel scared in here.'

Nathu did not move. He sat on the cot, still and inert, holding his wife's arm.

Then another call came: '*Har, Har, Mahadev!*' The last word was long and drawn out.

In the pervading noise the calls, interspersed with the tolling of the bell, rose with great passion as if in celebration of some special occasions.

At last, Nathu's wife could not bear it any more. Slipping out of Nathu's arms, she opened the door and rushed out. Nathu did not attempt to stop her but continued to lie down and stare at the ceiling.

*

The noise, like a muted symphony, carried far out of the city and struck the walls of Richard's bungalow. Floating over the noise came the sound of the temple bell. Richard kept sleeping through the disturbance, but Liza came awake. At first she thought the sound came from the little bell in her room but when she had shaken off her sleepiness, she realized that this was not so. Sometimes the sound would disappear as if it had been carried away by the breeze and then it would come floating back. Still sleep-sodden, Liza imagined a ship, tossing in a storm, struggling to find its way to safety.

Rising on her elbows she looked at Richard. He snored softly. One good thing about Richard was that he slid into sleep the moment his head hit the pillow.

The darkness in the room unnerved Liza. She could hear the staccato sound of the night watchman's heavy boots as he walked towards the gate.

'Richard, what's the noise?' Liza said shaking him awake.

'Eh? What's it?' Richard woke up.

'What's that noise?'

'It's nothing. Go to sleep.' Richard turned on his side.

Liza put her arm on his neck. 'I can hear a bell tolling somewhere. Like a church bell.'

Richard came fully awake. He lay listening for a while, then sat up.

'The church bell rings deeper,' he said. 'It sounds like the temple bell. A Hindu temple.'

'Why are they ringing it at this time of the night? Are they celebrating some festival? Listening to this bell makes me think of a storm at sea and ships' alarm bells.'

Richard was silent.

The noise coming from city was getting louder.

Sometimes a voice would rise above the hubbub before being swept back into the ocean of noise.

'*Allah-o-Akbar.*'

Richard's body suddenly became taut and then just as suddenly relaxed.

'What's that sound? What's its meaning?'

'It means that God is great.'

'Why are they raising this now. It must be a religious festival.'

Richard laughed to himself. 'It's not a religious festival, Liza,' he said. 'I think riots have just broken out in the city between the Hindus and the Muslims.'

'You mean rioting goes on even when you're in charge?'

Richard was annoyed. Why did the woman ask such silly question ? She should know better.

'We don't interfere with their religious affairs. Of course you know that, Liza.'

For an instant Liza felt she was surrounded on all sides by a jungle and that the sounds that she was hearing were animal sounds — the sounds of jackals and foxes.

'You should have stopped it, Richard. I feel frightened.'

Richard was silent. He rested on his elbows while his mind raced over the various options open to him. How was he to interpret the government policy in a time like this?

Liza put her arms around him. 'If these people fight, your life is also in danger, Richard.' To her, the slim, slightly built Richard was alone and in danger among barbarians. It was no easy task to rule over such people.

Out of the plateau of darkness outside rose the sonorous sound of the temple bell.

'It isn't nice that they should fight among themselves.' Liza said.

Richard laughed, a sharp nervous laugh.

'Will it be nice if they joined hands and fought against me? Spilled my blood, butchered me?' He sprawled on the bed and ruffled Liza's hair. 'How would you like it if these people were creating this racket outside my bungalow and aiming their spears at my bed?'

Liza shuddered and drew closer to Richard. Didn't human values mean anything any more?

'There's trouble in the city,' he said. 'You don't bother your head about these things. Just go to sleep. I'll find out what's going on.'

Just then the telephone bell rang.

Chapter 9

'What chaos!' Lala Lakshmi Narain fumed. 'One has to ransack the whole house to find anything.'

He was searching frantically in an *almirah* for a small axe he had hidden there. Oh hell! There was trouble in the city and he couldn't find his axe. He had gone out twice to ask his wife if she knew anything about it and both times she had languidly shaken her head.

Look, do I use· twigs for brushing my teeth that I should require an axe to pare wood for tooth-sticks?' she asked. 'I don't chop wood tor fuel either.·How should I know where the axe is?'

'Is it a sin to ask you about the axe?' Lala Lakshmi Narain said. 'Tell me, whom I should ask, if not you?'

'If I were you, I'd forget about it,' his wife said. 'There's God above. You must have faith in Him. What good is a small axe, anyway? How many of us can you protect with it?'

It was indeed a very small axe with yellow and green carvings on its wooden handle. A long time back Lalaji had taken his children to a fair. There he had seen and taken a fancy to the axe which he had bought. For some time he had carried it with him on his morning walks for it was useful for cutting twigs from *kikar* trees and whittling them into toothsticks. He required only one stick to brush his teeth every morning, but he would return home with an armload and spill them in the courtyard. His wife would threaten to throw the discarded tooth-sticks in the garbage bin but he would remonstrate. 'Why waste them?' he would mutter. 'See how fresh they are! The garbage heap is not the place for them.'

'Fresh or stale, they are of no use to us. What do you want to preserve them for?'

'You must use a tooth-stick in place of a tooth brush.'

'And ruin my teeth—what remains of them! They have already become loose. Your blasted tooth-sticks have done it. In the beginning my teeth were firm and strong like iron.'

'My good woman, let them remain there for another day. Throw them away when they have dried up. Nobody ever throws away fresh tooth-sticks.'

He was really missing the axe. To know that it was there and within easy reach gave him a sense of security. Without it he felt so defenceless. There was nothing else in the house that could be used as a weapon. Perhaps the the kitchen knife or the mosquito net rods. There was only one small phial of mustard oil in the house and as for coal, there was not a chunk of it to be had. In spite of Vanprasthiji's advice he had not been able to lay in a stock of these things. He was confident that the government would not allow any rioting in the city. And even if a riot broke out it would be a long time before it engulfed him.

The axe was now in the Yuvak Sangh's arsenal. It was lying on the window-sill, alongside the bows and arrows which Ranvir had amassed.

'Oh, what chaos!' Lalaji groaned. 'I wish there was something I could do about it.' He called out to his servant Nanku, 'Have you seen my axe?'

'It was somewhere in the house. But I haven't seen it lately.' 'If it was somewhere in the house, has it grown wings and flown away? Stop fooling around with me! It's your business to know where things are.'

'I don't know,' the servant replied. Lalaji thought about the Executive Committee meeting and how he had given money to buy five hundred lathis. Inspired by this offer the committee had been able to collect two-and-a-half-thousand rupees on the spot for further arms purchases. Lalaji said that he was prepared to fight the enemy. As a fight with the enemy at that time had appeared a very remote possibility he had felt safe being aggressive. A further thought had comforted him. As he was a wealthy man he had felt he could never come to any harm. True, his house was situated in a Muslim locality. But the Muslims around his house were poor and depended on him for their business. Besides, he was always on good terms with them. Last night's fire had, however, completely altered the situation and now he was living in fear.

'I think your worthy son has donated the axe to the Yuvak Samaj,' Lalaji said to his wife .

'It's your and your son's affair. I don't want to poke my nose in your affairs.'

'Did he tell you about it?'

'Who?'

'What do you mean, who? Ranvir, who else?'

'No, he didn't tell me anything. You preach and he listens. How do I know where he's gone? Just imagine, the city is on fire and he's not at home.'

Lalaji threw up his hands in exasperation and went towards the storeroom hoping against hope that the axe would be there. It was not. He picked up a couple of mosquito-net-rods and came out. He handed one rod to his servant, Nanku, and asked him to go down and guard the main door. He stood the other rod by the wall next to which his wife and daughter were sitting on a *charpoy*. The third rod he kept. For sometime he stood there holding the rod and then feeling rather silly he stood the rod next to the other one and went up the stairs to the roof.

There was a lavatory on the roof and Lalaji went inside to relieve himself. The previous time too rioting had broken out in the city they had set the grain market on fire. There had been no bloodshed that time but now things looked different. The only similarity was that this time too the rioters had, set the market on fire.

The fire spread, turning the north-westerly sky over the city red. The flames licked upward like the red fangs of a mighty snake gradually spreading towards the north. The scene was reminiscent of the burning Lanka on the Dussehra Day. The flames grew thicker with every minute that passed. They would roll on like a tornado unclenching itself, get bloated like an inflated bag and then leap towards the sky, which had turned a ghastly red. Sometimes a cloud of red dust would billow up into the sky and dissipate itself. The stars seemed to have lost their glitter. In the distance the horizon was a deep red that became sable as one looked higher.

Emerging from the lavatory, Lalaji stationed himself behind a abutment of his roof from where he could see numerous human figures silhouetted against the sky, watching the fire. Far into the distance the outlines of other houses and *bastis*, sharply etched against the sky, made a fantastic mosaic.

Lalaji's godown was in a narrow lane, adjacent to the main shopping centre, known as the Burra Bazaar, not far from the grain market. He was greatly relieved to note that that part of the city was still plunged in darkness; the fire, it appeared, had not spread that far.

Lalaji saw there were three people standing on the adjoining roof,watching the fire. They were Fatehdin, his brother and their old father. As Fatehdin's gaze swept upwards, scanning the sky, it came to rest on Lalaji.

'What a fire, Babuji!' he said. 'It's like hell let loose upon the city.'

Lalaji made no reply.

'Don't worry, Lalaji,' Fatehdin said in a reassuring tone. 'No one dare cast an evil eye on your house. It's first us and then you. We'll bear the brunt before anyone touches you.'

'I know, I know,' Lalaji said in a hearty voice. 'Neighbours are like limbs of the same body. And then good neighbours like you...'

'Have no fear. Only mischief-mongers create trouble. They harass good people. We have to live in the same city. There's no quarrel between us. Don't you agree, Babuji?'

'Of course, of course!'

Lalaji wished he could believe Fatehdin. Although Fatehdin's words seemed sincere there was still some doubt in Lalaji's mind. He had been living among these people for the last twenty years and they had hardly ever given him a chance to complain. But they were Muslims, all the same, even though there was nothing to fear from them. If they tried to burn down his house, their houses, in fact, most of the houses in that locality—would go up in flames. In the morning, Hayat Baksh, who was the President of the local Muslim League, had assured him that as long as he was alive, no Muslim would dare touch him. Lalaji did not worry too much about his godown, either. The entire contents of the godown were insured.

But things could take an ugly turn any moment. No one could trust these wretched Muslims. Lalaji was also worried about Ranvir not being home yet. Volatile by nature and prone to acting thoughtlessly, Lalaji hoped that Master Devbrat was keeping him in control. In the evening one of Ranvir's friends had dropped in to say that all the boys were with Master Devbrat. But one could never be sure of Ranvir. He was capable of giving Masterji the slip. He might have gone to the grain market and started something.

Then he heard the temple bell. He felt pleased. It was he who had put forward the suggestion at the meeting of the Executive Committee. So they had acted on his advice and put the bell in working order. But the next moment the tolling of the bell in the midst of the raging fire sounded meaningless to him.

The bell tolled, the fire spread through the grain market, devouring the fortunes of the Hindus. Lalaji muttered under his breath as he paced up and down on the roof of his house, his hands locked behind his back. His heart sank. He had a young daughter living in the house. If trouble came how would he protect her? And where was Ranvir?

'What a foolish boy!' he said to himself. 'He doesn't listen to anyone. Service to the community! Huh! It has become an obsession with him. A boy who does not care for his parents—of what good can he be to the community?'

He was sure that Ranvir had gone to the grain market. The thought sent a shiver through his body.

Others' sons too were members of the Youth Squad. They also knew how to manipulate the *lathi*, but they were not so foolish as to come into the open at the first sign of danger. And this fellow—he thought he was the only hero around! As Lalaji thought over the matter he blamed himself for it. He was the only one who had bragged at the meeting while others had kept quiet. They had made him shell out five hundred rupees whereas they had got away with one hundred rupees each. If anything happened to him would anyone of them come to his rescue? No, no one would dare enter a Muslim *mohalla*.

Lalaji looked down into his house. It was dark inside. Near the railing, his daughter sat on the edge of a *charpoy* next to her mother.

'Take the name of Hari,' his wife was telling her daughter. 'Take Hari's name and chant the *Gayatri Mantra*.'

The daughter immediately joined her palms together and started reciting the *Gayatri Mantra*.

'Has Ranvir returned?' Lalaji asked in a loud voice, looking down from the roof top. 'Ranvir's mother, has Ranvir returned?'

'No, not yet. I don't see him around.'

'Not so loud! Can't you speak in a low voice?'

Lalaji started pacing once again. 'If any one tries to set fire to my house his own house will also burn down,' he said in an effort to reassure himself. Then he climbed down the stairs.

'Ranvir's mother, why are you looking glum?' he asked in an attempt at bravado. 'There's nothing to worry about take heart!'

His wife was silent. Like her husband, she had also been thinking of Ranvir.

'Fancy you telling me?' she mumbled after a pause. 'And you've yourself been thrice to the latrine.' Lalaji went to his room.

A little later, his wife said to her daughter 'Vidya, go and find out what your father is doing.'

Lalaji had removed his *dhoti* and was putting on his pyjamas. Vidya returned looking very worried. 'I think he's going out!' She said anxiously.

'Hey Bhagwan! I never know what he's up to!' Lalaji's wife exclaimed and made for Lalaji's room.

'Look here!' she said, in a voice trembling with annoyance, 'May you see my dead face if you step out of this house now.'

'What do you want me to do? Keep sitting at home? Don't you want me to go and find out what has happened to him?'

'How can you leave me alone with a young daughter? And at a time like this?' his wife said excitedly.

'Talk sense. My son is in danger. Do you want me to wear bangles and stay put in the house?'

'He's as much my son as he is yours. Where will you search for him? The school must have closed long ago and the temple must be deserted. Where will you search for him? He must have taken shelter somewhere. He's quite clever that way. In the evening his friend came and told me that all the boys were with Masterji. Didn't I tell you that there was no need to make a brave Arya out of him? This is the time for him to study, eat and have some fun. But, no, you wouldn't listen to me. You drove him out every day to learn the drill, handle the *lathi* and God knows what else. It's a Muslim city and we have to live among Muslims all our lives. If one has to live in the sea one does not make enemies of the crocodiles. And now you'll rue the consequences.'

'Will you stop sermonizing! What's wrong if he has joined the Youth Squad? One must serve one's country and the community.'

'Then go ahead. Serve your country and suffer! But I won't let you go out now. Come what may. I won't allow you to go out.'

Lalaji dropped the idea of going out. He had never imagined that the fire would cause such havoc and that his wife would be so forceful.

'There are people who make it a point to cultivate government officials,' Lalaji's wife said. 'They are friendly with their neighbours, Hindus and Muslims alike. Take the case of your own counterparts. They hob-nob with Muslims all the time. But you've neither made friends with officials nor with Muslims.'

It was true, of course. His opposite numbers in his in-law's family were very friendly with Shahnawaz, who was influential among the Muslims. He ran a big transport business and he also had a share in a petrol business. Now Lalaji thought it might be a good idea to go to the city with Shahnawaz's help till things quietened down. He would do well to shift, for the time being, to Sunder Bazaar with his wife and daughter. But how?

He heard loud slogans in the distance, '*Allah-o-Akbar!*'

The refrain was picked up from many nearby roofs. Hindu slogans were also being shouted from the vicinity of the temple. But they were heard at long intervals and were much less vociferous. Besides, to Lalaji's great chagrin, nobody was responding to them from the nearby houses.

'Listen, Ranvir's mother. Send Nanku to me.'

'Why, what's the matter?'

'Don't preface your answers with why's all the time. Just send him up. I want him to carry a letter for me.'

Lalaji's wife stared. 'At this time? Where do you want to send him? You mean you want him to find out about Ranvir? Don't you know he's with Masterji? Why are you worrying your head over it unnecessarily. Trust in God and remain calm till the morning.'

'No, I don't want to send him after Ranvir. It's for some other purpose.'

'Look, why do you want to be so hard on the poor boy? It's hell to go out at this time.'

'Must you poke your nose in everything? I don't want to stay here with Vidya. Anything can happen anytime. I'm writing to the in-laws to pull us out of here with Shanawaz's help. Our young daughter is on our hands. I don't want to take a chance.'

'You can attend to it tomorrow morning. Is it necessary to do it

114

just now? Do you think the in-laws will rush to Shahnawaz the moment they get your letter? Sometimes you really act funny.'

But Lalaji was adamant. 'Once he takes something into his head there's no going back,' his wife muttered. 'How will this boy deliver the letter?' she asked him. 'He doesn't know the place.'

'He should know it. What have we engaged him for? It'll take him hardly two minutes to reach the in-law's place if he goes through the lanes. It's not far.'

'Once you're set on something there's no stopping you. We are not leaving just now. Why can't you wait till tomorrow?'

Lalaji was silent for a while and then he said: 'I'm thinking of going away this very night.'

'Are things that bad? Is it our neighbours that you're afraid of? I don't expect any trouble from them. You must trust in God and hold on to this place.' She saw the determination on her husband's face and fell silent.

There must be some special reason which he was hiding from her, she thought. Well, maybe Nanku should deliver the message! It would be a risky journey to the in-laws place but she had to think of her daughter's safety. Maybe it was right they should leave immediately.

'Ask him to carry a mosquito-net-rod with him,' she said.

Lalaji handed the boy a letter he had written to his in-law's and then held him up for last minute instructions which were interminable.

'Now listen carefully,' he said to the boy. 'If you sense trouble in one lane, retrace your steps and go by another lane. If you can manage it, take the temple peon along. Now go. Don't delay. And make sure you deliver the letter.'

'Can't you wait till tomorrow?' his wife said in a last appeal. 'What's the sense in sending him out so late at night? Trust in God and pass the night here. We'll know tomorrow what the situation is. He's also the son of some mother. Why do you want to push him into the fire knowingly?'

'Nothing will happen,' Lalaji said. 'I tell you nothing is going to happen. If I can go why can't he? Has he lily feet?'

They heard the sound of running feet in the back lane. The footsteps grew louder; someone was coming towards their house. Every sound that night appeared to be unusually loud and charged with danger. Lalaji stopped pacing the room as if his legs had become dead wood. His heart started pounding. Could it be Ranvir? He did not know. Could anybody recognize a man from the sound of his running feet.

And then they heard more footsteps which seemed to be chasing the first. A cry rose 'Help! Help!'

Lalaji shuddered. He could hear a medley of sounds emerging from the back lane. He looked at his wife and daughter. They were sitting glued to the *charpoy*.

'H-e-l-p!' The sound echoed through the lane—shrill and haunting, the fear-stricken cry of a hunted man. Was it his son? He wasn't sure. All terrified people cry in the same way.

Then they heard the sound of something being thrown. They could not make out whether it was a *lathi* or a stone. It could even be an axe falling on the paved lane, making a sharp sound and then skidding over the cobbled path with a grating noise.

'Catch him! Kill him!'

Had the *lathi* missed its mark? Was someone attacking Ranvir? Would there be a knock on the door?

Judging by the sound of the footsteps, the pursuers seemed to have crossed the lane. Lalaji's heart was still pounding. He waited nervously for someone to knock on his door. But no one came.

Lalaji's feet suddenly regained their mobility. He swiftly climbed the stairs to the roof in the hope of seeing something. But when he got to the roof, the road lay deserted. Men, women and children were still standing on the roofs of the *kuchcha* houses. They seemed unconcerned.

Then Lalaji saw three men walking down the lane. They held *lathis* and were still panting.

'So the Sikh has escaped!' one of them said. 'If he had not started running we wouldn't have chased him.' They disappeared.

Lalaji heaved a sigh of relief as did the servant boy who had joined him. Locking his hands behind his back, Lalaji paced up and down. Nanku picked up a mosquito rod and, climbing down the stairs squatted beside the door.

Chapter 10

It was a bright day, but the city lay in a swoon as if it had been bitten by a snake. The grain market still smouldered. The Municipal fire brigade, had long since given up a losing fight against the fire. Columns of smoke darkened the sky. Sixteen shops had been reduced to cinders.

But for a milk-and-curd-seller's-shop here and there, all the other shops along the length of the street were shuttered. People stood around in small bunches and discussed the previous night's incidents. There were rumours about rioting in other parts of the city. The people of Gwalmandi said that rioting had broken out in Ratta; the people of Ratta in turn said trouble had begun in the Committee *Mohalla.*

They had found a dead horse at the crossing of Naya *Mohalla,* and the dead body of a middle-aged man on the road leading out of the city. They had looted a shoe shop and a tailoring establishment on College Road. They had found another dead body in a graveyard at the other end of the city. It was the dead body of a middle-aged Hindu. They had found some coins and a piece of paper listing items of dowry in his pocket. And thus the news seeped from mouth to mouth.

The limits of Hindu and Muslim *mohallas* had suddenly been clearly demarcated. The Hindus and the Sikhs dared not trespass into Muslim *mohallas,* nor the Muslims into Hindu and Sikh lanes. Holding lathis and spears, people guarded the entrances to their lanes. Where Hindus and Muslims happened to live together, only one sentence was heard, uttered again and again, 'It's too bad! It's too bad!' Conversation in any case was spasmodic. Everyone seemed to know that what had happened was only the beginning What was coming next?

Everyone kept their doors closed. Business had come to a

117

stand-still. Attendance at the government offices had dropped and the schools and colleges had closed. People walked warily on the road, casting furtive glances around, afraid that eyes were following them through the crevices of closed doors or from behind the dark vestibules of houses. Most people did not stray beyond their own *mohallas*. The more prosperous of them planned to get out It was now every man for himself. Even the Social Re-construction Programme of the Congress and the morning singing parties had died premature deaths. Only the General would somehow manage to reach the Congress office every morning. Finding the office locked he would stand outside the closed door and, when no one turned up, he would climb the platform in front of the office, make a small speech and walk off in a huff.

Ranvir had failed to turn up the previous night. But Master Devbrat managed to send word to Lala Lakshmi Narain that the boy was safe with him. Lalaji was wondering how he could get away from his house to safety when of all people Shahnawaz himself descended upon the house. He came in his blue Buick, tearing through the streets at reckless speed. Soon enough Lalaji, his wife and daughter got into Shahnawaz's car and left. Nanku was told to stay behind and look after the house.

The blue Buick sped off, along deserted roads. On the way, people looked curiously at the occupants of the car—Shahnawaz, wearing a plumed turban, at the wheel, Lala Lakshmi Narain by his side and the two women in the back seat. It was dangerous to drive through that part of the city and Lalaji kept turning his face away whenever people looked at the car.

The Buick deposited Lalaji and his family at some relative's in Sadar Bazaar and turned towards Raghunath's house in the city. Shahnawaz and Raghunath were great friends. No place in the city seemed out of bounds to Shahnawaz as he went about his mission of mercy.

Past Jama Masjid, the Buick headed towards Mai Sattan's Tank. The road was flanked by small squat buildings, housing nondescript shops. Soiled tarpaulin awnings projected over their fronts and were held in place by long bamboo poles. A Muslim locality, it looked old and dilapidated. Crossing over a crumbling bridge, the car turned towards the Sayyed *Mohalla*. Here, the houses on both sides of the road looked more respectable, some of them two-storeyed and three-storeyed structures, with coloured win-

dow panes, mostly inhabited by rich Hindu lawyers and contractors with whom Shahnawaz was on the friendliest of terms. He
knew that they were probably secretly watching him from behind
their windows. Although he knew they were friendly he acceler-
ated and turned to the right as he reached Mai Sattan's Tank.

This was a mixed locality. There was a long row of Sikh
cobblers' shops—the shopkeepers had migrated here from
Hoshiarpur. Their shops were closed. Further up, there were a
few *kuchcha* houses, their walls plastered with cowdung cakes.
This part of the lane also lay deserted. This was where the scavengers lived. Shahnawaz again slowed down for here it was rela-
tively less tense. Two small children ran round and round an
electric pole, playing catch. Shahnawaz saw another small group
of children playing. They were standing in a circle. A small girl lay
in the middle of the circle, her *kurta* pulled about her waist. A
boy sat astride her, his *kurta* also pulled about his waist. The
other children stood around the pair giggling. Shahnawaz
laughed. 'What a game! How quickly they learn!'

Shahnawaz was a man who looked as though he would never
do another harm. A portly man, broad-chested, he always wore a
plumed turban upon his head, well-polished shoes, and spotless-
white, dhobi-washed, finely starched clothes. They said of him, 'If
he smiles at a girl she must smile back at him.' But his days of
chasing women were long over. Now he was a respected business
man, the owner of two petrol pumps and a fleet of trucks. One
thing, however, had not changed in him. Even in middle age, he
was still very jolly. And loyal to his friends.

Friendship was in his very blood. When trouble had started in
the city, he had come to see if his friend Raghunath was safe. He
had told the baker who lived next door: 'Look, Faqiria, let it damn
well sink into your mind, if Raghunath comes to any harm I'll
hold you responsible for it. Let no mischief-monger come close
to his house!'

The car came onto the main road. The houses here were more
ostentatious and stood in large spacious compounds. Being a
Muslim locality the car again dropped to a leisurely pace. Maula
Dad stood at the end of the road where it branched off to Bhab-
bar Khan. Shahnawaz saw five of six people sitting on the plinth
of a shop, holding *lathis* and spears at the ready. Maula Dad wore
his favourite outfit: khaki breeches and a green silk scarf. He

stepped out when he saw Shahnawaz's car approaching.

'What's the news?' Shahnawaz asked, turning off the engine of his car.

'Nothing special, Khan Saheb. Those infidels living in the back *mohalla* have done a poor Muslim to death.' Maula Dad looked enraged. It seemed to Shahnawaz that he was also trying to show his displeasure at Shahnawaz's friendship with Hindus. He could not express his displeasure openly for he knew that Shahnawaz was a man of considerable importance. He had easy access to the Deputy Commissioner and had many friends among the elite of the town whereas Maula Dad's influence reached only as far as the Municipal office.

'For that matter, I've also dispatched five *kafirs!*' Shahnawaz said. 'The fucking bastards!' he added in an angry voice which seemed to mollify Maula Dad somewhat.

Shahnawaz started his car. He had not gone far when he saw a lot of people spilling out onto the road from a lane on his left. It was a funeral procession carrying a coffin, headed by Hayat Baksh, wearing a white *salwar-kamiz* and a *kullah*. Shahnawaz knew the dead man must be the person Maula Dad had alluded to a few minutes earlier. Two small boys made up the rear of the procession—evidently, the victim's sons.

The procession passed. Shahnawaz started his car again. Passing through a big gate, Shahnawaz parked his car under a tree and, swinging his car keys, walked towards the bungalow his friend Raghunath had moved into when the rioting started. Raghunath's wife who was standing at the window saw him coming and joyfully rushed to tell her husband. 'Shahnawaz is here!' she said, knocking on the bathroom door. Finish quickly and come. I'll look after him in the drawing room.'

'*Oh, Yabu!*' Shahnawaz said, banging on the main door. 'Why don't you open the door? Has living in a bungalow gone to your head?' Then he saw Raghunath's wife. '*Salaam, Bhabhi,* where's my friend?' He walked into the drawing room.

'He'll be here in a minute.' Raghunath's wife said, sitting down next to Shahnawaz.

'How are you, *Bhabhi?*' Shahnawaz asked. 'No trouble, I hope. You did well in pulling out of there.'

'We are quite comfortable here. But you know home is home. I wonder if we'll ever be able to go back to our own house.' Tears came into her eyes.

'Don't cry, *Bhabbi*,' Shahnawaz said fervently. 'If I am still alive when all this ends I'll see to it that you go back to your own house, I promise you.'

Raghunath's wife did not veil herself with Shahnawaz. He was the only Muslim friend of her husband with whom she did not observe *purdah*. Raghunath was proud of the fact that his dearest friend was a Mussalman.

'Why haven't you brought Fatimah along?' Raghunath's wife asked. 'You always come alone.'

'There's trouble in the city, *Bhabbi*. You know that. Do you think I've come on a pleasure trip?'

'If you can come, why can't she? Doesn't she know how to sit in a car?'

Raghunath came in.

'*Oh Yabu*! Are you suffering from nervous diarrhoea? Even in this bungalow? Did you run away from home and come here just to shit?'

They hugged each other. 'If any man tries to hurt my friend I'll flay him alive!' Shahnawaz said.

Raghunath's wife got up to go.

'Where are you going, *Bhabbi*?' Shahnawaz said. 'I've not come here to eat.'

'Why not?'

'I know him,' Raghunath said. 'He always says 'no' to begin with. Let's have something to eat.'

'I know what you're going to serve—ladies' fingers. *Bhabbi*, I don't want anything.'

But Raghunath's wife had already left the room.

'I'm in a hurry to go,' Shahnawaz called after her. 'I've dropped in just for a minute.'

'Of course, you'll have tea.' Raghunath's wife had returned and was now standing in the door.

'I knew in advance you'll not give me something sumptuous to eat,' Shahnawaz laughed. 'All right, only a cup of tea, and nothing else.' He suddenly turned solemn as he looked at Raghunath's worried face.

'There's great trouble in the city,' Raghunath said gravely, 'It really hurts. Brother cutting brother's throat.'

Then he realized that he had been tactless. It could create a distance between him and Shahnawaz. Enmity between brothers was one thing but enmity between a Muslim and a Hindu had other sinister implications.

'I hear trouble has started in the villages too,' he added after a pause. But there did not seem much either of them could say about the problem for it only served to remind them of the gulf that lay between the two communities.

'*Yahu*, let us talk of something else,' Shahnawaz said at last.

'Do you know whom I met yesterday? Take a guess. Bhim, of all people.' Shahnawaz laughed.

'Which Bhim?' Raghunath asked. Then they both started laughing. Bhim was a friend from school and the son of a Deputy Assistant City Postmaster. He always introduced himself with the prefix of his father's designation. His friends always made fun of him.

'He's living here' Shanawaz said. '*The kafir*!He has been in the city for the past two years, but never cared to look us up. I recognized him the moment my eyes fell on him. "Deputy Assistant City Postmaster Saheb," I called out. He just stopped in his tracks. The rogue!'

Raghunath's wife came in with tea.

'Khanji, I've a special request to make to you,' she said, putting the tea things down on the table.

'What's it, *Bhabhi*?' Shahnawaz asked. Both men were relieved at the change of subject.

'If you don't mind.'

'Go ahead, *Bhabhi*.'

'My elder sister-in-law's and my jewel boxes are lying in our house. They must be retrieved from there. We had left the house in a hurry, carrying only a few things with us.'

'That's no problem, *Bhabhi*. Where are the boxes?'

'In the small room on the mezzanine floor.'

Shahnawaz was familiar with every nook and corner of Raghunath's house. 'But there must be a big lock on the room.' Shahnawaz said. 'A big, thick metal lock.'

'I'll give you the keys. And I'll tell you exactly where to find the boxes.'

'I'll bring the boxes. I'll bring them today.'

'Milkhi will be there. He'll unlock the door for you.'

'You mean Milkhi is still there? I'll go there as early as possible.

122

Where does he eat?'

'The entire house is in his charge. He must be cooking in the kitchen,' Raghunath said.

'There are enough rations to last him six months,' Raghunath's wife said. 'May I give you the keys?'

Shahnawaz felt proud that Raghunath's wife had such implicit trust in him that she had no hesitation in handing him the keys to a room which held jewellery,costing thousands of rupees.

'And if I filch your jewellery?' Shahnawaz said.

'Jewellery is not more precious than you, Khanji,' Raghunath's wife said. 'Even if you throw it into a well I'll not utter a word.'

Shahnawaz got up to go. Both friends came out together and walked towards the car.

'I don't have words to thank you,' Raghunath said. 'I'm greatly indebted to you.'

'Shut up, *Yabu*!' Shahnawaz said with a laugh and got into his car.

*

It was afternoon when Shahnawaz entered Raghunath's ancestral house to retrieve the jewel boxes.

Milkhi was a long time opening the door. 'Who's there?' he asked.

'Open the door. It's me, Shahnawaz.'

'Oh, I'm coming. The door is locked from inside. Just a minute I'll get the keys from the mantelpiece.'

Feroz, the hide merchant, had his godown across the road. He was standing in front of his godown, supervising some work. As Shahnawaz looked at him he stared back. Shahnawaz turned but he could feel Feroz still glaring at him. 'So you're still sucking up to the Hindus?' he seemed to be saying.

A *tonga* passed Shahnawaz and he turned to look at it. Maula Dad was sitting in the *tonga*. He was making a round of the Muslim localities. He smiled as he saw Shahnawaz.

'*Salaam-ulekam*!' he greeted Shahnawaz with exaggerated politeness.

Shahnawaz felt embarrassed. He cursed the servant for being so slow in opening the door.

Inside, the key clicked in the lock. Milkhi opened the door a little, ensured that it was indeed Shahnawaz, and bared his teeth in a smile. Shahnawaz kicked the door open and went in.

'Close the door!'

'Yes, Khanji.'

As he walked through the verandah of the house Shahnawaz saw the place was falling apart but he liked its familiar smell. Many years ago, when he used to walk along the verandah with Raghunath, his small daughter would watch him, holding her finger in her mouth and then raise her arms, asking to be picked up. Every time he came she would run up to the end of the verandah, raise her arms and smile. The young women of the house would also rush through the same verandah, towards the privacy of their rooms. But when they discovered that it was only Shahnawaz who was visiting they would stop and greet him shyly. Shahnawaz would be deeply moved. Raghunath and his family had always welcomed him. Whenever he came, Raghunath's younger brother's wife would immediately go to the kitchen to make an omelette for him. They knew that Shahnawaz was very fond of omelettes. Then all the members of the family would gather round him in the big inner yard of the house.

'Khanji, I hope all is well in your family,' Milkhi said, folding his hands together.

Shahnawaz looked at Milkhi with distaste. He had never liked his dirty eyes, whining tone and his puny body. Even now his eyes were muddy. Sometimes,when members of the family made fun of him, he would hide his face behind his arms, like a shy woman, adding to their mirth. Even Shahnawaz would feel amused though ,most of the time the fellow reminded him of a slimy lizard. Nobody knew his origins, whether he was a Punjabi Garhwali or something else. His speech was of no help either in tracing his origin for Milkhi spoke an improvised patois.

He had improvised a *chulha*(hearth) in the courtyard by putting three bricks together. The ash from the *chulha* was strewn all over the courtyard, which was further dirtied by the large number of *biri* stubs scattered over the entire place.

'Why don't you cook in the kitchen?' Shahnawaz asked.

In reply, Milkhi hung his head and gave him a sheepish smile. 'I'm alone here,' he said after a pause. 'Sahib, I cook nothing but *dal.*'

'Have you sufficient rations? Anything you require?'

'I've more than sufficient rations, Sahibji. The baker who lives next door often drops in to enquire if I require anything. You had asked him to.'

'Which baker?'

'The one who sits by the side of the big *nullah*. He often throws packets of *biri* over the wall into the yard. He's a good man.' Milkhi laughed, producing a hissing sound between his teeth.

The stairs were by the side of the kitchen. Planting his foot on the first step, Shahnawaz looked around the yard. The door of the big room opening into the yard was padlocked. He was familiar with the contents of the room. Raghunath's old mother's photograph was still resting on the mantelpiece. The room held a big bedstead and two *charpoys*. The whole place now looked forlorn. Milkhi's *chelum* lay upside down against the door and, alongside it, a soiled rag.

'What do you do all the time?' Shahnawaz asked. 'Can't you find time even to sweep the floors?'

'I don't feel like sweeping the floors, Sahibji. My good masters for whom I took all this trouble, are gone.' Milkhi again bared his teeth in a smile. Shahnawaz had felt their voices were echoing through a dome and trailing into silence no sooner the words were uttered. It was eerie.

'Where's the luggage room? It's on the mezzanine floor, if I'm not mistaken.'

'Yes, just facing the landing. That's where they have kept the big trunks.' Milkhi followed Shahnawaz as he climbed up the stairs.

There were no less than fifteen keys in the key-ring, some of them tiny brass ones. *Bhabhi* had shown Shahnawaz the key of the big lock and then the small brass key to the *almirah*. 'Khanji, this is the key. Don't forget,'she had said while handing the bunch of keys to Shahnawaz.

But Shahnawaz had forgotten and now was having a lot of difficulty in finding the correct key. 'Do you know the key of the big lock?' he asked Milkhi impatiently.

'Yes, Sahebji, I know,' Milkhi said and bent over the bunch of keys. Milkhi barely came up to Shahnawaz's elbows. From his towering height, Shahnawaz could see Milkhi's tuft peeping through his turban. It had spilled through his turban like a centipede. Shahnawaz looked at it with great loathing.

Milkhi turned the key and opened the door. The room was dark and stuffy. Quickly stepping in, Milkhi opened a window. Now the contents of the room came into bold relief. The room smelt of stale women's clothes...The women of the house in their hurry to depart had probably bundled all their clothes, whether dirty or not, into the trunks. The room was crammed with boxes and trunks.

Carefully picking his way through the trunks, Shahnawaz gained the *almirah* in which the jewel boxes lay locked.

As he looked through the open window his gaze travelled to the courtyard of the adjacent mosque. There were many people sitting near a cistern, doing their ablutions, a dead body lying in their midst. Shahnawaz was suddenly reminded of the funeral procession which he had seen from his car on the way to Raghunath's house. Shahnawaz stood for a long time at the window, watching the proceedings in the mosque.

It did not take him long to remove the jewel box from the *almirah*. It was like a woman's vanity case, covered with a blue velvet cloth. He carefully locked the *almirah*.

Then he climbed down the stairs, Milkhi preceding him, holding the bunch of keys. Shahnawaz was still on the stairs when his mind went into a crazy whirl. What had set it off? Was it the sight of Milkhi's centipede-like tuft or was it the thought of the congregation in the mosque? Or was it what he had been seeing and hearing for the past three days finally taking its toll? Taking two steps at a time he kicked Milkhi in the back. Milkhi went crashing down the stairs and struck the wall. His skull cracked open and his back broke. He lay still where he had fallen. As Shahnawaz passed him he saw that the servant's head had lolled to one side and his legs lay sprawled across the bottom steps of the stairs. 'You worm!' Shahnawaz muttered.

Coming into the yard he looked back once at Milkhi. The man's eyes were open as if they were trying to guess why the Khanji had punished him so cruelly.

That same evening an unruffled Shahnawaz handed *Bhabhi* the jewel box. Tears came into *Bhabhi*'s eyes as she took the jewel box from him. Mercifully, good men had not become extinct in this world.

'There is some bad news, *Bhabhi*,' Shahnawaz siad.

'What news?Has there been a theft in our house?'

'Milkhi fell down the stairs and is badly hurt. Maybe he has broken some bones. I wanted to call in a doctor, but you know these days doctors are not available easily...I'll make some arrangements tomorrow.'

'Poor fellow!'

'Perhaps I should bring him here as he will be alone in that house. In his place I could leave a man of my own.'

Raghunath and his wife were not too keen on Shahnawaz's proposal as they themselves were new to the house they were staying in. It would be difficult for them to look after a patient. If Shahnawaz could not find a doctor, with all the resources at his command, how could they?

'Don't worry, I'll fix up everything,' Shahnawaz said. 'I'll manage somehow.'

Bhabhi looked at Shahnawaz gratefully. It was almost as though it wasn't a man she was looking at but an angel.

Chapter 11

Having spruced himself up after his morning bath, Comrade Devdutt planted himself outside his house and stood there rubbing his hands. Whenever he rubbed his hands together or caressed his nostrils with his right hand it meant that his mind was busy working out the day's programme. He carried his diary in his hand and ticked off each item by rubbing his hands together or caressing his nostrils. 'There's no likelihood of a report from Ratta. A man must be assigned to that job.' Up went the hand to his nostrils.

'To prevent a riot from breaking out, the Congress and the Muslim League leaders must hold another joint meeting. Hayat Baksh and Bakshiji must first put their heads together and settle the preliminaries.' Yesterday Devdutt had called on many people. Raja Ram had shut his door as he saw him coming. Ram Nath had been curt with him and had sworn at Communists in general. Hayat Baksh had not turned him away. Instead, his eyes blazing with excitement, he had declared: 'We must have Pakistan!'

'Pakistan is a must for us!' Hayat Baksh had kept shouting, preventing Devdutt from speaking. He must go and call on Hayat Baksh again. Devdutt rubbed his hands together. He must send Bakshiji to Hayat and himself call on Bakshiji along with Atal, and on Hayat along with Amin.

No, that wouldn't work. He dismissed the whole plan. These leaders did nothing but create complications. He must instead assemble ten representatives each of the Congress, the Muslim League and the Singh Sabha. Yes, the idea appealed to him. He must go to the Party office and try to give it practical shape. Oh hell! he had to do so many things, all at once and single-handed. Now he was confronted with another problem. Just one volunteer was not sufficient to stem the trouble among mill workers in the industrial area. Ratta was a Muslim area. They had sent Comrade Jagdish to keep watch over that area. But just one man could not handle the job. He must also depute a couple of Comrades to the adjoining villages. The problem was that he had only a handful of Comrades to cope with a huge problem. But whatever the constraints he must do everything in his power to stop the communal violence. He ran his fingers over his nostrils and then looked at his watch. The Communist Party was to hold its meeting at ten. At this meeting various members were required to report on the conditions prevailing in the areas assigned to each of them. It was time he started for the meeting. He went back into the verandah to pick up his bicycle.

'Who's there? Devdutt?'

Leaving the cycle resting against the wall he went inside.

'Going out again?' a fragile-looking, middle-aged man was sitting on a cot. 'If you are determined to die, first kill us and then go out. Don't you know what's happening in the city?'

Devdutt stood in the door, clasping his hands and watching his father. Then his mother emerged from the kitchen, wiping her hands on her *dopatta.* 'What do you gain by tormenting us?'she asked. 'You kept us on tenterhooks all night. A fire was raging in the city and you didn't show up till the morning.'

'The entire area up to Murree Road and from there up to the Company Garden is Hindu,' Devdutt said running his finger over his nostrils. 'You have nothing to worry about.'

'Has some divine voice whispered in your ears that we are immune from danger?' his father growled.

'In this very row ten people own guns. The Youth Squad of this block has murdered three persons...'

'You stupid fool! Can't you understand? We are not thinking about ourselves. It's your safety we are worried about.'

'You need not worry about my safety,' Devdutt said, returning to the verandah and picking up his bicycle.

Throwing her *dopatta* round her neck, his mother blocked his way.

'I've spent the whole night in agony,' she said. 'Don't you realize how bad things are?'

The situation was getting out of hand. Devdutt caressed his nose, rubbed his hands and then putting his mouth to her ear said, 'Ma, I'll be back very soon. I promise.'

'Stop fooling me! You said the same thing last evening. Place your hand on my head and swear by my life that you'll return before nightfall.'

'I tell you, I'll return before nightfall. But I refuse to swear by you.' He again picked up his bicycle.

'The bastard is not going to listen to you!' his father shouted out to his mother from inside his room. 'Come back and stop wasting your breath on him. The wretch is bent upon humiliating us. The pig! He has no regard for his parents. Bastard! He thinks he can stop the rioting in the city! Bad!'

Devdutt was gone but his father kept bawling.

'No one has a good word for him,' the old man shouted.

'He has no regular work. All he does is to gather labourers and coolies around him and harangue them. The bastard! He has not one single hair on his chin by way of a beard and yet he claims to be a leader. The son of a pig!'

Devdutt reached the road-crossing.

The place was tense as though everyone was waiting for something to happen. The roads lay deserted, no shop was open. If the door of any shop was ajar it was because the shop had already been ransacked. The only people around were vigilantes from both communities who guarded their own localities. All the localities were not clearly demarcated for in some places the two-storeyed *pucca* houses belonged to the Hindus whereas the *kutcha* houses in the lanes at the back were owned by the Muslims. These places were the ones in which, Devdutt knew, people were the most insecure.

'Devdutt!' Someone called out from the lane on his left. He stopped.

'Don't go any further. A man is lying dead on the road.' A short man, holding a *lathi*, appeared on the road.

'Where?'

'Just beyond the crossing. Along the slope.'

'Who's he?'

'A Mussalman. Who else? Where are you going?'

'To my Party office.'

'A Hindu is lying dead in the compound of the graveyard,' the man said with an edge to his voice. 'You always spoke in favour of the Muslims. Go and ask them to take away their corpse and give us ours.'

'Don't go!' a man cried from the balcony of his house. 'They'll kill you.'

'He's very friendly with them. Nobody is going to kill him.'

'But he's a Hindu all the same,' the man from the balcony retorted.

A small crowd had gathered around Devdutt.

'Go and tell them that for every Hindu that they kill, we shall retaliate by killing three Muslims.'

It appeared that the man was not dead. He lay gasping for breath, his body lying slackly on one side of the road. His salt-and-pepper beard had turned red with blood. There were tin buttons on his khaki coat—cheap buttons which sell eight for a pice. His shoe laces were untied, as if he had untied them in anticipation of his last journey to the next world He appeared to be a Kashmiri. Turning his head Devdutt saw some people watching him from a distance. Devdutt recognized the man—a Kashmiri *hato* (coolie) who worked at Fatehchand's woodstall, delivering charcoal and fuel wood to his customers' houses. Fatehchand's stall was not far from where the man lay.

Devdutt caressed his nose and shook his head. It was no time to save a man or remove a dead body. Nor to have a look at the dead body of a Hindu in the compound of a graveyard. He must reach the Party office.

The Party office had only three men and a plethora of Party flags. The entire Party had a strength of eight men of whom five were out on field work. There was bad news awaiting him. A Muslim Comrade has lost faith in the Party and was thinking of leaving it. The man, his lips working with emotion, said to Devdutt, 'You keep harping on the fact that the English administrators are at the root of the mischief. But where do the rulers come into the picture? They throw a dead pig in front of a mosque and I've seen three poor Muslims being butchered to death before my own eyes. I don't want to have anything to do with the Party. It's useless.'

'Comrade, don't act in a hurry,' Devdutt said, trying to soothe the rebellious man. 'We are from the middle strata of society. The old prejudices have still a great hold on us. If we came from the working class we wouldn't have made such distinctions between Hindus and Muslims.'

It didn't work. The Muslim Comrade picked up his bag and

stormed out of the office.

'He's still half-baked so far as his convictions are concerned,' Devdutt said, looking very thoughtful. 'A Communist must not allow himself to be swayed by sentiment. He bends all his mental faculties towards understanding the evolution of society in its correct perspective.'

The meeting started. The first item on the agenda was a review of the situation in the city, the workers' settlements in particular.

'People are spreading lies that there has been trouble in Ratta. So far all workers' *bastis* have remained free from trouble. No doubt, some tension in these *bastis* is inevitable. Comrade Jagdish is working in the Muslim locality. People there still listen to him. There are twenty families of Sikh workers living there but there hasn't been a trouble there either. Comrade Jagdish has, however, reported that the situation is deteriorating. Yesterday two workers fell out among themselves. Rumours from outside are sapping their morale,' Devdutt said.

It was decided that Qurban Ali should also be assigned to the Ratta area in order to strengthen Jagdish's hands. Devdutt duly jotted down the decision in the minute book.

'Dada' had been visiting the countryside but there was no news from him. All means of communication had been disrupted. Only a dark blue car had been seen going from village to village. Nobody knew whose car it was and what it was doing in the countryside. Some people said the car belonged to Shahnawaz.

The meeting lasted a long time. The three Comrades present discussed each item with Devdutt minutely.

They came to the last item: To call a meeting of the representatives of all the political parties.

'It's not possible to hold such a meeting,' one of the Comrades said. 'The Congress office is locked up. If you try to talk with the League People they only shout Pakistani slogans in reply. They insist that the Congress represents only the Hindus and that it should accept this fact before they can sit round a table with them. And what is worse, at the present juncture, nobody dares stir out of his *mohalla*. With whom will you hold the meetings?'

Devdutt caressed his nostrils. He explained that he didn't want ten representatives from each party to attend the meeting, only the top leaders.

'Nobody will come, Comrade,' one party member said. 'And if

they come at all, it will only result in a war of words. It will lead us nowhere.'

'Comrade, if we can prevail upon them to sit together, that by itself will have a salutary effect. It will be conducive to the establishment of a Peace Committee in the city. We can propagate the idea in every *mohalla* through a town-crier. What's happening at present? There's no wholesale rioting. We have only stray cases of stabbing on both sides. It is essential that representatives of all the communities should sit together and try to resolve their differences...'

The problem was debated from every possible angle. Finally, it was decided that the meeting should be called at Hayat Baksh's house. 'I'll bring Bakshiji along,' Devdutt said. 'Comrade Aziz must bring three or four Muslims of his *Mohalla* with him and we can then go to Hayat Baksh's house.'

'Have you talked it over with Hayat Baksh?'

'No.' 'Comrade, you are living in a fool's world. Do you really mean to tell me that you propose to go to Hayat Baksh's house? You'll never be able to make it. They will get you before you reach his house.'

'Why, you'll be with me,' Devdutt said to Aziz with a smile.

'Comrade, it's a huge problem', Aziz said. 'One can't put out such a big blaze with a few drops of water.' Devdutt refused to waver.

Immediately after the meeting, he and his party set out for Hayat Baksh's house. It was a difficult journey and they encountered much hostility but they eventually got to Hayat Baksh's house and the meeting was held.

Devdutt was able to fetch Bakshiji from his house to join the deliberations. He was able to persuade him to come, where any other Congress leader would have balked. But Bakshiji was a safe bet. He had spent sixteen years of his life in British jails. Though his political acumen was questionable, Devdutt was sure of one thing: Bakshiji would be prepared to go all out to avoid bloodshed, to save the city from a bloodbath. Devdutt found Bakshiji nervous and confused. It was obvious he was finding the problem too big to handle. On the way to Hayat Baksh's house he had castigated the Communists. But Devdutt did not mind. He was pleased that Bakshiji had agreed to come and had brought two Congress workers with him.

As was expected, the meeting stalled in the very first hour. Hayat Baksh insisted for half an hour that Bakshiji accept the fact that the Congress was purely a Hindu body and represented no one but the Hindus. It therefore followed that Bakshiji was present at the meeting only as a representative of the Hindus. Devdutt tried to end that stalemate. 'Gentlemen,' he said, 'it's no time to get into arguments over side issues. There is a fire raging outside. Houses are being razed to the ground. I hear this fire is fast engulfing the countryside too. What's our duty at this time? I submit that we should try to understand this critical situation in all its sinister implications and bend all our efforts to keep the fire from spreading.'

Then he read the draft of the Peace Appeal he had prepared. This led to another round of heated arguments. Devdutt said that the League and the Congress could not be a party to the Appeal, Bakshiji and Hayat Baksh could append their signatures to the Appeal in their individual capacities. Other persons should also lend their support in a similar manner.

The wrangling went on and on till everyone was on the verge of giving up in disgust. Then Hayat Baksh's son whispered in his father's ear that to sign a Peace Appeal would make no difference to him either way; it was after all only a Peace Appeal. At this Hayat Baksh signed the Appeal. Taking his cue from him, Bakshiji did likewise. Then Hayat Baksh shouted slogans in support of Pakistan: 'Pakistan Zindabad.' The sound of the slogans still ringing in his ears, Bakshiji was putting on his shoes when news came that rioting had started in the labour colony of Ratta and two Sikh carpenters had been killed.

At first, Devdutt refused to believe the news. 'Are you sure? Have you checked it for yourself? Who has brought the news?' Though he kept asking these questions he had already realized that the trouble had got out of hand. Now even the workers had started killing each other. Signing the Peace Appeal, he thought, with a heavy heart, was like signing on water.

He decided that he would go straight to the Party office, pick up his cycle and go to Ratta. Jagdish, he feared, would not be able to handle the situation single-handed. His presence there could possibly stop things from deteriorating further.

When Devdutt reached the Party office, his father was already there, waiting for him, holding a walking stick. When Devdutt attempted to explain what he proposed to do his father exploded:

'*Harami*, if you're killed nobody will even come forward to pick up your dead body. Are you such an idiot that you do not realize what bad times we are passing through? What audacity to think that you can stop the rioting single-handed!' His father banged the door of the office shut. He felt like thrashing his son. He picked up his walking stick, but instead of hitting Devdutt, he burst into tears, 'Why are you bent upon ruining me?'he wailed, 'You're all we have. Have some sense. Your mother is worrying herself to death. If that is what you want, I'm even prepared to put my turban at your feet. Come home with me!'

Devdutt ran his fingers over his nose, rubbed his hands together. The situation was getting complicated. He must seek somebody's help to send his father home.

'I must go to Ratta,' he said. 'I can't delay this visit.But before I go I'll see to it that you are safely escorted home. Comrade Ramnath will go with you.'

*

That afternoon one more death took place. The General, eccentric that he was, set out from his house, holding his swagger stick under one arm. His boots ran on the street. Left!Right!Left! He had taken it upon himself to put a stop to the rioting. The city was in turmoil and these Congress people were sitting in their homes, unconcerned. Too bad! Too bad! They were worse than traitors.

He marched out of his house, stopping at every corner and haranguing the people: 'Gentlemen, I want to remind you that Pandit Jawaharlal Nehru had taken a pledge on the banks of the Ravi to win *Puran Swaraj*(Complete Self-government) for the country. Full of patriotic fervour, he danced on the bank of the Ravi. I too joined the dance and following his example, all of us took the pledge. Today all those who are sitting behind the walls of their houses are traitors to the country. I know each one of them, inside out. May I know what those people are doing, sitting inside their homes? They would do well to wear *burqas* and dye their hands with *henna*. Gentlemen, Gandhiji has said that the Hindus and the Muslims are like brothers. It does not behove them to fight among themselves. I beg of you, the old and the young, children, men and women alike, to stop fighting among yourselves. Fighting does great harm to our country. It gives the Englishman, the red-faced monkey, an opportunity to rule over us...'

Speechifying from one street corner to the next, he at last reached the Committee Mohalla. The day was almost over, but the General was tireless. Caught up in his cause, he scarcely even noticed whether he was addressing an audience or not. For the speech at the Committee *Mohalla*, too, he was so engrossed that he didn't notice a group of *goondas* edge up to him. 'Gentlemen. I repeat with all the emphasis at my command that the Hindus and the Muslims are like brothers. There is rioting in the city. There's arson. There's loot and pillage. Nobody is even raising his little finger to stop this carnage. The Deputy Commissioner is holding his memsaheb in his arm and enjoying himself. I say, the Englishman is our real enemy. Gandhiji says it's the Englishman who incites us to fight among ourselves. But we shouldn't fight amongst ourselves for we are brothers. Gandhiji says that Pakistan can come into being only over his dead body. I repeat, Pakistan will come into being only over my dead body. We are one. We are brothers. We shall live in amity. And...'

'You son of a...' swore one of the *goondas* standing next to the General, and swung his *lathi* with all his strength at the General. The *lathi* connected, cracking the General's skull open. His swagger stick fell from his limp hand and his torn khaki turban fell from his bloody head. The General crashed to the ground without completing his sentence.

Chapter 12

'A man must keep watch from the top room!' Ranvir said. Killing the hen had filled him with great self-confidence. He had proved to be the cleverest, smartest and the most dependable member of his squad. Even his voice had become imposingly deep.

Lathis, axes, daggers, knives, bows and arrows, catapults—in spite of these weapons, the arsenal still looked somewhat bare. Outside the room, a little away from the stairs, rested a cauldron of mustard oil. But because they still hadn't got the wood for fuel, they had deferred the boiling of the oil to the next day .

'Yes, *Sardar*,' Chajju said and swiftly climbed the stairs to the roof.

The four warriors in the squad were spoiling for action. Stationed on the roof they felt like gallant Rajputs waiting for the Muslim foe down in the Haldi Ghati.

Being rather short Ranvir liked to believe he was like that other great short-statured hero Shivaji. His fists clenched, his eyes would sweep the road below, watching for the enemy. Sometimes he wished he were wearing a long Rajput coat, a saffron turban on his head and a long sword hanging from a broad cummerbund round his waist. To take part in a fierce fight in loose pyjamas, an ill-fitting shirt and worn out *chappals*, didn't seem right; it was not the dress of a fighting man. But what he lacked in dress he tried to make up in presence. He shouted his orders in a sharp, ringing voice and kept the members of his squad under strict discipline. Slightly bent forward, as if weighed down by the responsibility he bore, his hands locked behind him, he paced thoughtfully outside his arsenal, as he imagined Shivaji would have paced outside his tent before throwing his gallant soldiers into battle against Aurangzeb.

'*Sardar*!'

Ranvir turned sharply to look. Manohar, who, a short while ago, had heaped small stones by the side of each catapult stood before him.

'We are short of fuelwood,' the boy said. 'We can't boil the oil.'

'Don't we have charcoal?'

'No, *Sardar*!'

Ranvir resumed pacing the room, his hands still held at his back. Strategy demanded that he should carefully study the situation before taking a decision. One must think, carefully before taking the plunge.

'Bring something from your house,' he said at last.

'Anything, wood or charcoal—whatever you can lay your hands upon. Whatever quantities you can get hold of readily.' 'Quickly. There's no time.'

Manohar stood there without showing any signs of moving.

'What's it now?'

'What if my mother does not allow me to take fuel?'

The *Sardar* (Chief) gaped at him, astonished. Then he thundered. 'Don't stand there like a moron. Go and bring the wood from somewhere. I don't care how you do it, just do it.'

'Yes, *Sardar*!' Manohar bowed before Ranvir and stepped back.

'Wait!' Ranvir said. 'You need not go just now.' He decided he would boil the oil some other time.

The arsenal had been set up in an attic at the top of a two storeyed house, for the simple reason that it had been unused for a long time. On the lower floor Shambhu's aged grand-parents lived. The upstairs room faced the road and a big *peepul* tree, hid it with thick foliage. The house was approached by a narrow lane overshadowed by the *peepul* tree. The lane was dark and meandering lane and would easily swallow up an intruder. While explaining the lie of the land to Ranvir, Shambhu had compared it to the *chakravyuh* of the battle of the Mahabharata. He said that for the enemy to enter the lane would be as fatal as entering the *chakravyuh* , the labyrinthine army formation designed by the Kurus in the great battle. Past the house in which the young warriors were closeted the lane turned left and went past the tumble-down tomb of a Muslim saint. In front of the tomb lived an old Muslim with his two wives. Further on, there was a water tap which did not work in the afternoon. Nobody came to the tap till four in the afternoon. From the tap started the Hindu houses, running in a series along both sides of the lane and ending in three or four dilapidated *kuchcha* houses, belonging to Muslims. One of them was occupied by Mahmud, the washerman, and another by Rehman, who ran a public *hamam*. From here still narrower lanes took off to the right and the left. The Muslims, if at all they dared to come into the lane, could be bottled up between the tap and the far end of the lane. In case of danger, one could easily take shelter in any of the Hindu houses located along the entire length of the lane.

'Are you acquainted with the Muslims who live in this lane?' Ranvir asked Shambhu.

'Yes, *Sardar*, I know them very well. Mahmud, the washerman, washes our clothes and the old man who lives in front of the saint's tomb is quite friendly with my grandfather.'

'You're not going to be assigned duties in that lane,' Ranvir said in a decisive tone.

Shambhu was taken aback. Now the squad planned to go after their first kill. The four warriors were tense with excitement. Until now they had been making their preparations in secret but now the time had come to go into action. 'Son, enter the fray and prove your mettle!' So went a patriotic song. Dharamdev was bursting with patriotic fervour but Manohar looked a little subdued. He had come away without telling his mother . And now it was almost two—the time his mother finished cooking. She would miss him and probably come looking for him. It would be disastrous if she found him here.

Ranvir assembled the three warriors in front of the arsenal and discussed his grand strategy with them: 'The time to pour boiling oil on them has not yet come. Scalding oil is poured over the enemy only when the enemy is making an assault on our citadel. Or when you find yourself besieged from all sides. Here we will require only the knife— the knife with the long handle.'

He singled out Inder, 'show us how you plan to use the knife. Go ahead. Pick up the knife from the window sill!'

Inder stepped forward with great alacrity and came back holding the knife. He planted himself in the middle of the room, legs apart knife firmly held in his hand, blade pointing inward. Then he jumped, lifted his left foot and, making an arc in the air with his arm, planted himself in front of Ranvir, his back towards him. While leaping he had swiftly thrust the knife towards Ranvir's waist.

Ranvir nodded in approval. 'Never aim the knife at the enemy's chest or back!' he said. 'One should always aim at his waist or belly. After planting the knife in the enemy, twist its curved blade around before pulling it out. The enemy's entrails will spill out of his stomach. If you attack an enemy in a crowd, don't make an effort to pull the knife out. Let it remain where it is and lose yourself in the crowd.'

Ranvir was faithfully repeating what he had learnt from Master

Devbrat.

His squad broke up in two. Inder was going to make the first attack. So, Inder, Shambhu and *Sardar* came downstairs, while Manohar remained on the roof. They had decided that the boy upstairs would keep watch from the roof while Ranvir, Inder and Shambhu would keep an eye on passers-by in the lane and identify the victim. At a signal from Ranvir, Inder would rush out of house and pounce upon the enemy. By keeping the door slightly ajar they had, a view of part of the road and the entrance into the lane. The road beyond the *peepul* tree was drenched in sunlight.

A *tonga* stopped in front of the lane. Ranvir watched through a narrow chink in the door.

'Who's there?' Inder asked in a whisper.

Ranvir was silent. The other two warriors put their eyes to the chink. 'It's Jalal Khan. Nawabzada Jalal Khan!' Shambhu said excitedly, 'He lives in the house at the end of the road. A rich and influential man. He even calls on the Deputy Commissioner.' Shambhu uttered the words in one breath.

For a fleeting moment they had a glimpse of the man's white turrah, twirled moustache and face. He disappeared from sight. They could hear the sound of his stiffy starched flowing salwar and the staccato thud of his shoes as he walked away. Before they could act Jalal Khan had disappeared into his house. The three warriors stood around sheepishly. They were also slightly scared. And what would they have done if the hulking man had turned on them?

Master Devbrat had warned Ranvir never to size up his adversary. That diminished one's confidence. Also if one looked long enough at one's adversary it aroused sympathy for him in one's mind.

In the back lane a door suddenly opened and as suddenly banged shut. The three warriors perked up. Ranvir peeped out of the door.

'Who's it this time?' Inder asked in a whisper.

'A wretched one!' Ranvir replied.

Both of them put their eyes to the chink. An aged, bearded man was walking down the lane.

'It's Mianji!' Shambhu had recognized the man. 'He is the one who lives in the house opposite the tomb. Every afternoon, at about this time, he goes to the mosque to say his *namaz*.'

'Not so loud!'

Walking along the lane, the old man came up to the *peepul* tree and then turned onto the road. He wore a black vest, a salwar and loose *chappals.* A small rosary dangled from his right hand. His back was bent with age and he walked slowly.

'Should I?' Inder asked the *Sardar*.

'No, it's too late. He has already crossed on to the road.'

'So what?'

'No, we must not attack anyone on the road,' Ranvir said.

Shambhu thought Inder was losing confidence, whereas in actual fact it was Shambhu himself who was losing his nerve .

He felt greatly relieved at the *Sardar's* answer.

They kept waiting behind the door. Minutes slowly passed. They hoped someone would come soon for at four clock the corporation released water to the tap at the end of the lane and the women would start queueing up. Traffic also tended to increase in the late afternoon.

Two people entered the lane, one after the other, one of them wearing sun glasses and pushing a bicycle.

'That's Babu Chuni Lal,' Shambhu said. 'He works in a government office. He owns a dog.'

The other was a Sikh who was carrying a bundle on his shoulder. They passed along the lane and were gone.

They heard footsteps again. Inder peeped through the crack in the door and gently touched Ranvir's elbow.

'Who's he?'

'A hawker,' Inder whispered.

'He sells perfumes,' Shambhu said. 'He lives far away from here. He makes a round of this place almost every afternoon. He's a Muslim.'

The hawker was a portly man. His moustache was dyed red with henna, and he had a goatee. A large number of cotton bags dangled from his body. He was now walking under the *peepul* tree. Beads of perspiration stood out on his forehead. His right ear was stuffed with small cotton swabs and he had stuck a couple of metal swab sticks in his turban.

Ranvir felt Inder stirring behind him. He turned round to look. Inder's hand had gone into his pocket and gripped the knife.

There was not a moment to be lost. He must decide and decide quickly. This man was a Muslim and a stranger to the place, carrying a heavy load of bags. He could neither flee nor protect himself. And he looked so tired. Everything was in favour of attacking. Ranvir's eyes met Inder and he signalled his decision. Inder leapt out of the house. Something flashed in the air and dazzled the watchers in the house. Ranvir quickly closed the door.

They heard no sound as they stood behind the door holding their breath. Greatly excited, Ranvir could not hold himself back. He opened the door and cautiously peeped out. Some distance away, he saw the perfume seller lumbering along his back slightly bent under the weight of his bags. Inder, dwarfed by the other man's size, was slowly walking behind him, his hand still in his pocket.

Ranvir almost fell out of the door in his excitement. Shambu had to pull him back. The last glimpse that they had of the pair was their disappearing round a corner.

Shambu latched the door from inside and they stood face to face, peering at each other in the dark, both breathing heavily.

At the turning of the lane, the perfume seller's eyes fell on Inder and he gave the boy a friendly smile.

'Where are you going, beta?' he asked, patting the boy on the head. Inder stopped and gazed at the man his hand still in his pocket. He noticed the man's face was puffy and he recalled what his teacher had said. According to his teacher all men with puffy cheeks were cowards. They suffered from indigestion and could not run. If they ran they were soon out of breath. Well, he thought the man was already panting.

His eyes fixed on the man, Inder waited for the right moment to strike.

The perfume seller looked at the boy. He looked so innocent, almost as if he was seeking his protection. Maybe he was afraid of something, He had noticed that these days everybody in the city looked scared.

'Where do you live?' he asked Inder. 'Come on, keep up with me. These days one should not stay out alone.' Inder said nothing and his eyes remained on the man.

'I'll go with you up to the oilmen's *mohalla*,' the perfume seller said. 'If you have to go far I'll entrust you to someone else's care. He will escort you up to your house. Today there's trouble in the city.'

Without waiting for the boy's reply, he started walking. Inder caught up with the man.

The house on both sides lay quiet and still, their fronts so dark that one could see nothing inside, even if one strained one's eyes.

'I shouldn't have come out,' the perfume seller said to Inder. 'This is no time to venture out. The whole city is still. But I thought there was no point in idling away my time at home. Even an anna or two through honest work is always welcome. If I don't work, how will I eat? Just tell me that!' He laughed good humouredly.

They were within sight of the tap. The tap was still dry and the stone slab under it — in which a small depression had formed due to the dripping of water — was lying dry. A couple of wasps circled over-the tap. When very young, Inder had amused himself catching wasps.

'If anyone buys four cotton plugs of perfume from me it fetches me four annas', the perfume seller said. He seemed to be talking to himself Maybe he was just scared like everyone else. Especially as he had ventured out of his own area.

'I'm familiar with each and every lane in this city,' the man said. 'And I know each one of my customers. A man with two wives never fails to buy my perfume. He buys it every day. And he buys a hair dye too, not to talk of collyrium. An old man having a young wife must buy my scent. Wait, I'll tell you more...' He kept talking to amuse the boy.

Inder was very composed. He kept walking steadily, his hand firmly gripping the knife in his pocket, his eyes fixed on the perfume seller's waist. Even Arjuna who had killed a bird by looking at its reflection in a receptacle of oil would have envied Inder his concentration. As they walked past the tap Inder's energy suddenly concentrated in his right hand, his mind measuring each step as they walked on together. The bag of bottles was swinging against the perfume seller's waist, exposing it to Inder's view, while his loose shoes made a flapping sound.

'In the bazaar there is greater demand for cotton swabs while in the lanes I sell more bottles of oil and perfume,' the old man said.

Suddenly Inder lunged. The old man saw the boy's left hand move swiftly. Something bright flashed in the air. Before he could stop and feel his bag to see if something had been taken, he felt a sharp agonizing pain in his stomach. Inder twisted the knife he had plunged into the man's belly as had been taught. Then leaving it where it was he ran.

The perfume seller turned and saw the boy running away.Everything had happened so suddenly that he still wasn't sure what had happened. He felt like shouting out to the boy and asking him to come back. Then he saw blood dripping down over his feet. Something sharp protruded from his waist. Dazedly he looked at the knife. Then the pain came.

'O, my good men, they have killed me! I'm dead!' he cried in a terrorstricken voice. His bag slipped from him and he crashed to the ground.

Only a moment ago he had seen Inder's running feet but now the lane was empty.

O, my men...!' he groaned, his voice ending in a long drawnout wail. His eyes turned towards a patch of the blue sky, visible over the lane, where a few vultures were flying. Their number had suddenly increased. The sky wavered before his eyes. Its blue seemed to have lost some of its lustre.

Chapter 13

Nathu looked worried. Sitting outside his room, he puffed away grimly at his *chelum*. The more he lent his ears to rumours of beastly killings in the city the more apprehensive he became. Then he consoled himself by saying that he was not omnipresent and omniscient like God. How could he see through their evil design in hiring him to kill the pig? That reassured him until another spate of doubts assailed his mind. There was no escaping from the fact that had helped spark off the trouble.

All the *chamar*s had been sitting outside their doors since the morning, smoking *biris*, and exchanging notes. Nathu would join in their talk for a while, but soon his throat would dry up, his legs would feel wobbly and he would return to his hovel. Should he tell his wife? Being an intelligent woman she would understand. And by sharing the secret with her he would lighten his own burden. Maybe if he had a pot of country liquor he could get drunk and forget all about it. But where could he get liquor at this time. He ran the whole scene through his mind again. No, he must not let his wife into his secret. It was fraught with risk. If she could not hold his secret, the police could come and take him away. Nobody would believe him if he said he had done it at the instance of Murad Ali. Murad Ali was a Muslim and it was impossible that he would allow a dead pig to be deposited in front of a mosque. Again he consoled himself by saying that it could as well have been some other pig. Couldn't there be two black pigs of the same appearance? Feeling reassured he would start jesting with his wife or go to a neighbour and talk with him about the fire that had razed the grain market to the ground. But this feeling of well-being wouldn't last long. His mind would revert again to the night he had killed the pig. That God-forsaken place, the damp room filled with stench, the stolen pig and Kalu suddenly bursting upon him with the hand cart through the darkness. His imagination would vividly recreate the whole scene. Would a Veterinary Doctor ask him to slaughter a pig and that too a pig stolen from the local piggery? 'You must wait till I come,'the words again echoed in his mind. He felt a strong urge to go to Kalu and ask him what he had done with the pig. Or better still go to Murad Ali himself. But he thought the better of it. For Murad Ali would be the last man to admit that he had had a hand in the affair. On the contrary, he would try to implicate him in the conspiracy.

Nathu picked up his *chelum*. 'To hell with Murad Ali and his pig!' What was done could not be undone. He had not done it deliberately; he had been dragged into it. And what about their own misdeeds? They were openly indulging in wanton arson and manslaughter. How did his killing a pig matter so much? If he could be damned as a criminal on that account, their crimes were much worse. They had burnt down an entire market. He had done nothing on purpose. What was done was done and he was in no way responsible for it.

Nathu thought of his father who was a God-fearing man. 'Son, keep your hands clean,' he had always advised him. 'And earn your bread with the sweat of your brow. Not through dishonest means.' Tears came into Nathu's eyes. His mind was filled with remorse.

A man walking at the other end of the *maidan* suddenly stopped to look at the *chamars' basti*. Nathu's heart started pounding. He felt the man was looking for him —the culprit who had killed the pig.

Nathu's wife came out wiping her hands. Should he tell her about that night's incident? He was aching to confide in someone.

Why not her?

Once again he looked across the *maidan*. The man was still standing there.

'Are you looking for someone?' his wife asked. 'Who's that man?' she asked, following his gaze. 'Do you know him?'

'No, I don't know him. Why should I know him? I don't know him at all.' He looked at his wife with an abstracted air. 'What are you doing, standing here?' he asked, finally. 'Go in and do your work.'

His wife gave him a puzzled look and disappeared into the

hovel.

Nathu glanced towards the road out of the corner of his eye. The man was walking away puffing on a cigarette.

'I am unnecessarily suspicious,' Nathu muttered to himself. 'Scores of people stray towards this side. Many come here on business every day.' He was sorry he had been so short with his wife.

'Listen,' he called out to her. 'Make some tea for me.'

His wife appeared at the door. There was something in her which always made Nathu feel secure. Today, more than on other days, he wanted his wife to be around him all the time. She never lost her mental poise, nor took anything to heart like him. He secretly believed that the cause of her equanimity of mind was her full body. She didn't look emaciated like him.

She stood, one hand resting on the frame of the door, a soft smile playing on her face.

'You've never asked for tea at this time of the day,' she said. 'Why do you want it now? Is it because you have taken time off from your work?'

'You mean I'm celebrating?' Nathu flared up. 'You call it a holiday? If you can't make tea for me I'll make it myself. Why all this idle talk?' He got up and walked in.

'Don't be angry. I'll make it for you. It'll take me no time at all.'

'No, you stand away from me,' Nathu said angrily 'I'll make it myself.' He squatted down next to the hearth.

'You mean you'll light the fire, while I'm around? No, that won't happen.' She took hold of his shoulders and forced him up. For an instant, Nathu glared at her and then caught her in his arms.

'What's wrong with you today?' his wife asked, giggling. Her instinct told her that there was really something the matter with him. He had been behaving so strangely since the previous evening.

'I feel scared. You have been behaving very strangely,' she said.

'Why are you scared of me?' he said, 'I've not burned anybody's house that you should be scared of me?'

She went still in Nathu's arms.

The pig's body glowed in Nathu's mind. He could see it as it lay in a pool of blood in the middle of the room, its legs pointing towards the roof. Nathu shuddered and sweat broke out on his body. His wife knew that his mind had suddenly wandered far away from her. A faint sound, resembling a sob escaped his lips and he broke off from his wife. Then he tried to embrace her again.

'No, not tonight. I'm in no mood for it,' she pleaded, knowing what he wanted. 'Can't you see what's happening outside? They have set houses on fire.'

Nathu stood before her looking dazed.

'What's the matter with you?' his wife asked in a worried voice. 'Why are you looking at me like that. Tell me the truth. Is it something serious?'

Without a word, Nathu sat down on the cot.

'Has something happened?'

'No, nothing.'

'I know. You're hiding something from me.'

'No, I'm not hiding anything.'

His wife edged closer to him and ran her fingers through his hair. 'Why don't you tell me?'

'There's nothing to tell you,' he said in a faint voice.

'May I prepare some tea for you? Wait, I'll get you some tea.'

'I don't want tea.'

'You were going to make it yourself, now you tell me you don't want any tea.'

'No, I don't want...'

'All right, then lie down on the cot,' his wife said.

'No, I won't lie down on the cot.'

'Angry? Why do you get angry with me so quickly?'

Nathu made no reply. His wife felt he was behaving like a spoilt child.

'Where were you last night?' she asked. 'You've told me nothing.' She sat down on the ground by his side.

Nathu gave her a sharp look. So she knew! They will all come to know about it sooner or later. His legs started shaking.

'If you don't tell me, I'll bang my head against the wall,' Nathu's wife said. 'You have never kept anything from me. Why are you behaving this way now?'

Nathu's eyes looked at his wife. Did she suspect anything? Finally he said:

'Do you know why the grain market was set on fire?'

'Yes, I know. Somebody had thrown a dead pig in front of a mosque. The Muslims retaliated by setting the market on fire.'

'I killed that pig.'

148

His wife's face suddenly turned ashen, 'You?...You mean you did it? Why did you do such a wicked thing?'

Haltingly, Nathu told her the whole story.

'Did you yourself deposit the pig outside the mosque?'

'No, Kalu carried it away on a pushcart.'

'Kalu is a Mussalman. How could he do it'

'Kalu is not a Mussalman. He goes to church. He's a Christian.'

His wife stared at him.

'You have done a very wicked thing,' she said at last, 'But you're not to be blamed for it. They fooled you into doing it. They laid a trap for you and you walked into it unknowingly.' She sounded as if she was talking to herself. It was obvious that what Nathu had told her had really unnerved her. It was as if an evil shadow had fallen across their house which they couldn't cast off even with the most rigorous penance.

Nathu looked so distraught, however, that despite being upset his wife's heart went out to him. She held his hand and said, 'I was wondering why you were looking so agitated all the time. Why didn't you tell me before? One shouldn't allow such things to weigh on one's mind.'

'If I had known, I would have kept away from such mischief,' Nathu said. 'They told me that the pig was for the veterinary doctor. Last night I happened to run into Murad Ali but he refused to talk to me. I ran after him but he did not so much as cast a glance in my direction.' Nathu's voice quivered and then it trailed into silence.

'How much did they pay you for killing the pig?'

'Five rupees. He paid the whole amount in advance.'

'Five rupees! It's a lot of money. What did you do with the money?'

'Nothing. I've four rupees still left with me. The money is lying in the alcove.'

'Why didn't you tell me?'

'I thought I'd give you a surprise. Buy you a pair of *dhotis*.'

'You mean I would have allowed you to buy *dhotis* with polluted money? I would have burnt the money.' Then she smiled, realizing that she had gone too far. 'It's your hard-earned money,' she said. 'It's most welcome. I'll buy whatever you want me to.'

She went to the alcove and, rising on her toes, looked at the money in the alcove, but returned without touching it. Nathu was sitting there lost in deep thought.

'Did you see the man who was standing at the far end of the *maidan*?' Nathu asked his wife.

'Yes. I did. But how are you concerned with him?'

'I think the pig belonged to him. He must have come to investigate.'

'What's gone wrong, with you? If he knows what happened, what's stopping him from coming here and asking for the pig?' she said. 'We are tanners. It's our job to kill animals and flay them. You killed a pig. Whether they throw it in front of a mosque or sell it in the bazaar is not our business. And how do you know it was the same pig? Well, I'm certainly going to buy *dhotis* with the money,' she said mischievously, in an attempt to lighten his mood.

She went to the alcove and picked up the money. But the next moment she put it back.

'You're right,' Nathu said. 'How am I concerned? It's none of my business. To hell with Murad Ali and his pig. That was exactly what I told myself yesterday...!' Having unburdened his mind, Nathu was feeling greatly relieved.

'Now I've got fifteen full rupees with me,' Nathu's wife said.

'You can also buy something for yourself.'

'I want nothing for myself,' said Nathu. He felt overwhelmed. 'When you're by my side, I've everything.' He went to start the fire and get the tea ready.

'God overlooks the lapses of those who have a clear conscience,' Nathu's wife said. 'Our conscience is clear. We have nothing to fear. But don't speak a word about it to anyone.'

Nathu's wife was pouring the tea into tumblers when they heard the sound of running feet from across the *maidan*. Nathu's wife stopped pouring the tea abruptly and looked at Nathu. They heard people talking in the yard.

'What happened, *Chacha*?'

'There has been rioting?'

'Where?'

'On the road. The Hindus and the Muslims have clashed. They say two persons have died.'

'Who was the man we saw running away?'

'I don't know. Could have been an outsider.'

A hush fell in the hovel.

'You must go out and find out what's happening,' Nathu's wife said, handing him a tumbler of tea. 'Wait, I'll also come with you.' The next moment, she didn't know why she was doing it, she fetched a broom and started sweeping the floor. She did it diligently, sweeping every inch of the floor. Perhaps she was sweeping away all the evil from her hovel. She was at it a long time. Then she washed the floor.

In the end, when she sat down on her cot, utterly exhausted, she felt that something evil had again crept back into the hovel through a crack in the door. The hovel suddenly became dark. She felt a presence in the hovel, going round and round, giving off an evil smell.

Part II

Chapter 14

Starting from Khanpur, the first bus usually reached the village at eight in the morning. That bus had not arrived. There was another bus service from Khanpur as well as one from the city but though it was now almost afternoon, there was no bus in sight from any direction.

At the tea-shop the water had been boiling from the morning but the two benches in front of the shop remained unoccupied. On other days the benches were always crowded. Every man from the village stopped for a cup of tea at Harnam Singh's tea-shop. Today, but for three pariah dogs hovering round the bus stop, the place seemed to lie in a swoon.

Women have an unfailing instinct. Since yesterday Harnam Singh's wife, Banto, had been telling him that they should leave the village and shift to Khanpur where they had friends and relatives. They were the only Sikhs in the village; all the other inhabitants were Muslims. But Harnam Singh was adamant. How could he give up such a lucrative business? People fought among themselves but business somehow always went on. People did not fold up their business and flee from the place just because some fighting was going on. Besides, he could not think of any other place to go to. The city was out of the question. There was already rioting. As for Khanpur, he wasn't certain they would be welcome there. It cost money to feed two mouths. And if the village people looted the shop in their absence they would have nothing to fall back upon. They could probably go and stay with their son. But he was living in Mirpur, twenty miles away, and he was as defenseless there as they were helpless here. All aspects considered, it was probably best for them to stay on here and hope for the best.

Sitting on his *chowki*, Harnam Singh would, every now and

again join his hands in prayer and recite: O, Master, the one on whom you place your protective hand can come to no grief!

Banto had stopped arguing in the face of his faith, but she had lost her peace of mind. When in very low spirits, she would suggest that they should go away to her sister's village. It was within manageable distance from their own village and they could take shelter in the gurdwara there. Besides, there were many Sikhs living in that village which would add to their sense of security. But even this proposal was not acceptable to Harnam Singh. Somehow he had a feeling that the Muslims of his village would not harm him.

'Listen, fortunate one!' Harnam Singh would address his wife. 'We owe nothing to anyone. We have done nobody any harm. These people too have always been nice to us. As you have seen for yourself, Karim Khan has visited our house as least a dozen times, loud in his assurance that there's nothing to worry about, that no one dare cast an evil eye on us as long as he is there, that we should stay put where we are till the riots end. In this village Karim Khan's word counts. He commands influence. There's only one Sikh house in the entire village—our house. Won't they feel ashamed of hitting two old, defenceless people?'

Banto had no desire to argue with her husband. She wanted to believe in him. His faith was so steadfast, his mind was so strong. But as the day wore on and no customer came to his teashop, Harnam Singh's strong spirit began to waver. What was going on? Even more disquieting when some strangers came by and paused as if to make sure of their man. In the afternoon he heard familiar footsteps coming from the direction of the village pond. It was Karim Khan. Harnam Simgh felt reassured for he knew Karim Khan would surely suggest some way out of this predicament. If danger threatened he might even ask Harnam Singh to shift to his own house.

Karim Khan passed Harnam Singh's shop without stopping. He did not even look in his direction. He only slowed his pace and said as if speaking to himself, 'Things are not too good, Harnam Singh. You had better go away. I know the people of my village. They will do you no harm. But what about the people from outside? I may not be able to do anything about them.'

Karim Khan went away coughing and swinging his *lathi*.

Harnam Singh's confidence wavered even more. The fact that

Karim Khan had not stopped was a clear indication of what was coming. The old man must have brought him the message at great personal risk. Harnam Singh felt more sad than apprehensive. What had the world come to?

Not five minutes had passed when Karim Khan returned. 'Don't delay, Harnam Singh,' he said, panting while climbing the path, his hand resting on his back. 'There's bad news everywhere. The rioters may be here anytime.'

Harnam Singh felt helpless. Where could he go? Karim Khan had advised him to leave. But where? Where would he find refuge? He was past sixty and, to make matters worse, he was responsible for a helpless woman. How far could they run? And in which direction?

'Don't go!' an inner voice said to him. 'Stay where you are. When the rioters come, offer them your shop. Offer them your life if it comes to that. It is better to die here than rot in an unknown place. Who is going to attack you, anyway?' However much he thought about it, he could not believe that any of the villagers would attack him or even allow outsiders to attack him.

Harnam Singh went into the back room where Banto was sitting. 'Karim Khan came by just now and asked me to go away. He fears trouble from outside.'

Banto looked at her husband aghast; her body suddenly went limp. What were they to do? The night was approaching and they had nowhere to go. Her husband standing in the dark back room looked a picture of despair. But now there was no time to think. They must leave as soon as it became dark.

'Even now I feel that we must stick to this place,' Harnam Singh said. He pointed towards his double barrelled gun, hanging from the wall. 'If it comes to the worst, I'll first kill you and then myself.'

Banto heard him out in silence. What could she say?

Harnam Singh went and sat down on the plinth of his shop. He removed the petty cash from under the tarpaulin and then went to the cup board where his savings were. He sorted out the notes and left the coins behind. He put the money in the inside pocket of his vest. Then he took the gun down from the wall and slung it across his shoulder. What else should he take? He wasn't sure. Should he take the registration document of his shop with him? But he had no time to sort out the papers. Banto was also in the same state of mind. Should she carry her ornaments with her? Should she cook some food for the journey? Say, two big, thick *chapatis*, if nothing more. For all she knew, they might not get anything to eat on the way. She must at least change her clothes. It would not look proper to go out in soiled and rumpled clothes. But, like her husband, she was also unable to make up her mind about anything.

'What should I do with my jewellery bag? May I wear the ornaments?'

'Yes, you may,' Harnam Singh replied. Then he thought for a while and said, 'If they see you with the ornaments they will kill you. We'll bury the ornaments behind the shop.'

Banto hid her jewellery bag under her shirt. She collected some other pieces of jewellery in a handkerchief and put the bundle in her trunk. Whatever remained, she buried in the vegetable patch behind the shop. In the room lay trunks, cotton coverings, durries—all the things she had collected bit by bit for her daughter's dowry. There were a lot of other things in the house which would have to be left behind.

'Wait, I'll prepare two thick *chapatis*,' she said. 'There's no knowing how long we'll have to wander all over the countryside.'

'Good woman, where's the time to prepare *chapatis*? Had we known in advance that we were leaving we would have fixed up everything in good time.'

Just then they heard beating of drums in the distance and looked at each other's face.

'The rioters! It sounds as though they are coming from the direction of Khanpur.'

The people back in the village raised the slogan: '*Ya Ali! Allah-o-Akbar!*'

'They must be Ashraf and Latif. Both of them belong to the Muslim League. They have been talking of Partition all the time', Harnam Singh said.

Though it was late evening it was not yet dark. The cries of the rioters seemed to be coming from the left, from across the canal.

Harnam Singh's eyes suddenly fell on the mynah's cage.

'Banto, take the cage behind the house and release the mynah,' he said.

Only a short while ago Banto had put birdfeed and water in the small receptacles in the cage. When she took the cage down from the rafter the mynah chirped: 'Banto, God is our saviour. He is everybody's refuge.'

Banto was deeply touched. 'Yes, mynah, he's everybody's saviour.'

The mynah had learnt these words from Harnam Singh.

The mynah's words comforted Banto. A small bird. But how much it could teach man!

Harnam Singh had a small vegetable patch at the back of his shop which he had tended with great care. He had also planted a mango tree on one side of the patch. Standing in the middle of the patch, Banto opened the door of the cage. 'Fly away, mynah. God is everyone's refuge!'

The bird refused to leave the cage.

'Fly away, fly away, mynah! Fly away, my love!' Banto's voice became strained. Leaving the cage in the patch she returned to her room.

They heard drum beats again, louder this time. The medley of sounds in the village had also increased. It sounded as if several people were marching forward in a group. There were intermittent bursts of slogan shouting.

Carrying a few belongings and his gun, Harnam Singh left his house, followed by his wife. She locked the door of the house behind her. As they stepped out of the house they felt they were walking on alien soil. They stood still, unable to decide in which direction to go. On their left lay the village. Beyond the village was a small canal, from where the voices of the rabble and the boom of drums drifted towards them. On their right stretched the *pucca* road leading to Khanpur. It was dangerous to take the road. Across the road, some distance away, flowed a *nullah*—a wide *nullah* with a high embankment. That was perhaps the safest route to take. At that time of the year the water flowed in a very thin stream on the sandy and rocky bed of the *nullah*.

Harnam Singh and his wife quickly crossed the road and descended into the *nullah*. By now the rioters were in the vicinity of the village and were moving towards the *nullah*. The air resounded with their slogans and the throb drums.

While descending into the *nullah*, Harnam Singh and Banto heard a thin piping call. 'Banto, God is your protector. He's everyone's refuge!'

The mynah had been flying over their heads and had followed

156

them into the *nullah*. It was now sitting on the branch of a tree.

The rioters were now on the top of a mound which led down to Harnam Singh's shop. Raising slogans and beating their drums they hurried down the slope.

The moon had come out and in its light it looked as though an enemy lurked under the shadow of every bush and tree. The *nullah* gleamed white under the light of the moon. Harnam Singh and his wife cautiously picked their way forward under cover of the embankment. They were panting from their exertions and their ears strained to catch every sound.

The noise came nearer and then stopped. Harnam Singh knew the rioters had stopped in front of his shop and were deciding their next move. He thanked Karim Khan wordlessly. If he had not warned them in time, they couldn't have escaped. They heard a heavy sound as if someone was battering something down. Harnam Singh guessed that it must be the door of his shop. For an instant their resolve faltered. Then holding hands to gain courage they began walking again.

'Remember *Vah Guru* and keep walking,' Harnam Singh said to his wife, dragging her after him.

They heard the barking of a dog and looked up. A big, black dog stood on the embankment, barking at them. Harnam Singh's blood froze. For which past sin of his, was God punishing him so heavily? Following the barking of the dog the rioters were sure to come this way. It would take them no time at all to pick up their trail.

'Keep walking!' Banto said. 'Don't stop!'

The dog kept barking at them. It was a black, hairy dog that Harnam singh had often seen wandering outside his teashop. After walking some distance, Banto looked back. The dog was still standing on the embankment remorselessly barking at them. They walked on.

'We must get out of here first,' Harnam Singh said. 'And then we shall leave it to God. At least that dog has stopped following us.'

'But he's still barking.'

They stopped behind a big rock and holding their breath listened to the barking of the dog.

'*Ya Ali!*' the rioters screamed as they broke open the door and rushed into Harnam Singh's shop.

'*Hai*, our shop! They are plundering our shop!'

Mercifully, no one seemed to notice the barking of the dog. Both of them now felt less panicky. The rioters, they argued, would not chase them. They had no use for their lives. It was the shop they wanted. It meant so much loot.

'It's no more our shop,' Banto said. 'What's gone is gone. Gone for good!'

The sandy expanse of the stream, studded with trees, the black, hairy dog standing on the embankment, ceaselessly barking at them—it all seemed a dream. One living moment had wrought this change. It had transformed everything. They had been living in this village for twenty years and had now become aliens in a single shattering moment. Sweat broke out on Harnam Singh's hands, making them cold and limp.

'Let's go!' he kept repeating to his wife, his voice hoarse with fright, 'Let's go! Can you make it?'

They had left the village behind. But the dog still stood on the embankment. They felt a bit reassured that it had not advanced upon them. Maybe it had lost interest in them and would soon go away. The noise in the village had subsided. The rioters, it seemed, had finished their job. Perhaps, satisfied with their loot, they would even forget about them.

They had barely walked some distance when they saw a light spread across the sky. They turned and looked. Beyond the embankment the sky had turned red.

'What's that?' Banto asked, fascinated.

'It's our shop. They have set fire to it!' Harnam Singh said. As if hypnotized he looked steadily in the direction of the village. The flames rising from one's own house are probably different from other flames. Otherwise, they wouldn't have held the fascination they did.

'It's all reduced to ashes!' he said sadly.

'And before our eyes!'

'That's how God wished it.' Harnam Singh sighed and resumed walking.

He wished there were houses they could take refuge in but here there were only sand dunes, interspersed with boulders. They could probably hide behind the boulders, but for how long? In a few hours the darkness would fade, exposing them to pitiless eyes, like a woman suddenly finding herself naked, with nowhere to hide.

Banto's mouth had gone dry and Harnam Singh's legs trembled as he walked. There were thousands of others like them who were wandering about in the countryside in search of shelter. Like them they had also heard the sound of doors crashing down and had fled without pausing to think. Harnam Singh knew they must keep walking as long as the night lasted. The dawn was dangerous.

They were feeling the strain now. But they were secure in the thought that they had got away unscathed. Their thoughts reverted to their children. Where was Iqbal Singh and how was Jasbir? They were not so much worried about Jasbir as about Iqbal Singh. Jasbir lived in a big village, among other Sikh families. The village could face the enemy collectively. Maybe they had already congregated in the village gurdwara or planned other ways of protecting themselves. But Iqbal Singh must feel utterly isolated. He had a small cloth shop in his village. They had no way of knowing whether he had got away and was roaming harried and fear-stricken like them. The whole situation was so frightening. Harnam Singh closed his eyes, joined his hands together and bowed his head in prayer, repeating God's name. 'If God's protective hand is over someone's head such a one can come to no harm.'

As dawn broke, they sat down on a boulder near a narrow stream. Harnam Singh was familiar with the area. They were near a small hamlet called Dhok Mureedpur. In a strange way, the dawn had brought with it peace to Harnam Singh. The world seemed safer. From a distance came the smell of loquats wafting over the morning breeze. Dhok Mureedpur was known for its loquat orchards. As they looked up the colour of the moon first turned orange red and then started turning pale. Around them birds chirped.

'Banto, wash your face. After that we'll recite the Japji and then resume our journey.'

'Have we anywhere to go?' Banto asked unhappily. She didn't share the peace her husband felt. 'Have we to walk the whole day again? I wish I'd baked some *chapatis* before starting. We could have stopped somewhere and eaten something.'

'We shall go to Dhok and knock on someone's door,' Harnam Singh said. 'If they have any compassion left in their hearts they will give us shelter. Or, we shall leave it to God.'

'Do you know anybody in Dhok?'

Harnam Singh smiled. 'I knew all the people back in our village, didn't I?' he said. 'But what kind of protection did they give me? They plundered my shop and then burnt it down. If the people I played with and grew up with did not help, how can I expect any help from the people of Dhok?'

As the morning haze lifted they plodded wearily towards the village. Past a grove, consisting of *sheeshum* and mulberry and rosewood trees, they came to a small graveyard, holding many graves, some big, others very small, many of them in a dilapidated state. One of them looked like the grave of a pir for a clay lamp burned dimly on it and green festoons hung from its sides. They reached the outer fields. The wheat had ripened, ready to be harvested. From here they could clearly see the squat village mud houses, with their flat terraces . Cows and buffaloes were tethered outside the huts. Chickens scurried around in search of food.

'Banto, if they are out to kill us I'll first shoot you and then shoot myself. I'll not allow you to fall into their hands while I'm alive.'

They stopped in front of the first house. Its door was closed—a discoloured door made of rough, cheap wood. They didn't know whose house it was. They did not know how fate would deal with them as the door opened. Harnam Singh lifted his hand. It remained arrested in the air for a while. Then he knocked on the door.

Chapter 15

The gurdwara was full to capacity and the congregation swayed in a religious frenzy as the worship reached a crescendo. The singers, their eyes closed, sang in a voice charged with fervour:

'I have no saviour but you ...'

Their eyes closed, their hands joined together, their heads swaying in unison the members of the congregation repeated the lines after the singers. Some clapped their hands marking time. It was the voice of sacrifice, resounding again after a lapse of centuries. Three hundred years ago they had sung the same song before going to meet the enemy. Now that another crisis was upon them, their souls had merged with those of their ancestors as they lived their glorious past once again. It was time to fight the Mussalman again. They did not know when or from which direction the enemy would attack. Every member of the congregation was on the alert, prepared to face the worst.

The light in the gurdwara came in through the two stained glass windows at the back of the building. The holy book, the Granth Saheb, rested on a wooden *chowki*, enclosed by a brass railing. The *chowki* was covered with a red silk cloth bordered with gold thread. One end of the cloth fell to the floor on which lay a white cotton sheet. A large number of one-anna and two-anna coins lay strewn in front of the *chowki*. Wheat flour was heaped to one side.

The women sat to the left of the *chowki*, their faces covered with their *dopattas*, their eyes bright with the excitement of throwing themselves into the fray and sacrificing their lives if necessary. Many women had kirpans hanging from their waists. All the people were caught up in the glorious pride that prompts martyrs to fight.

Their weapons were piled in the long verandah at the back of

161

the gurdwara and in the priest's room. Seven of the Sikhs owned double barrelled guns. There were five boxes of cartridges in all. Jathedar Kishan Singh, who had taken part in the last World War on the Burma front, was put in charge of organizing the defence. On being entrusted with the responsibility, he had rushed home and put on his khaki shirt which was embellished with three war medals and several combat ribbons. The shirt was rumpled but there was no time to have it ironed. He posted two armed men in a house to the left of the lane leading to the gurdwara and two men to the right. Three armed men were posted on the roof of the gurdwara. Kishan Singh himself kept watch there, round the clock. Apart from the weapons distributed to those keeping watch, the rest of the swords, knives, spears, *lathis* and javelins were arrayed along the back wall of the gurdwara. The swords, sheathed in various velvet coloured scabbards, were lined up against the inner wall. Sunlight glittered on the weapons. There was an assortment of shields, collected from Nihang Sikhs, two of whom guarded the roof, armed with their own spears. The Nihangs, easily distinguishable from the others because of their dress, a blue robe with a yellow sash, a blue turban supporting an iron circle which they used as a boomerang, were the fiercest of the lot. There was one at either end of the gurdwara roof, his spear on the ready, watching intently for the direction from which the enemy would mount his attack.

'Nihang Singhji, hold the end of your spear down,' Kishan Singh warned one of the men. 'It glints in the sun. The enemy may be warned.'

The Nihang *Sardar* flared up. 'No, I won't!' he replied. 'A Nihang Sikh never holds his spear down!' Holding his spear in the same position he gazed into the distance. Battles of long ago passed before his eyes. Armies marched, spears glittered in the sun, horses neighed, war drums boomed and conch shells blew.

Two Nihangs had been posted outside the entrance of the gurdwara. They stood there, spears at the ready, bristling with confidence. In days gone by, the Khalsa would go into battle dressed in yellow. In an effort to maintain his links with his great ancestors Bishan Singh, a grocer, who had been assigned to the community kitchen, had adorned his turban with a yellow hand-kerchief which he had taken from his son after Basant Panchmi, the spring festival. He had discovered the handkerchief lying in his coat and had stuck it in his turban. In the congregation some people wore yellow cummerbunds . Most of them were in *salwar-kamiz.* Even Kishan Singh was wearing pajamas below his crumpled army shirt. There had been no time to worry about dressing properly.

The atmosphere of the gurdwara was heavy like rain-laden clouds. The people swayed their heads as they sang, but their subconscious minds, attuned to the past, were saturated with the spirit of sacrifice. The only people they were oblivious to were the Britishers. Forty miles away from the village, the Britishers had the biggest cantonment of the country. But the people in the gurdwara were not thinking of the cantonment, nor of the British administrators. They were only thinking of the Khalsa and of the Muslims whose hordes were at that very moment marching upon them.

The back alley of the gurdwara was where the Sikhs were the most vulnerable. Across from the gurdwara the Sikh shops ran the length of the lane. Behind the shops the ground dipped sharply towards a narrow stream, across which lay a big loquat orchard. Considering the terrain, there was no possibility of any attack being launched on the gurdwara from the front. If anyone did attempt to attack he would immediately be picked off by Kishan Singh and his men who kept watch from the roof.

At the end of the alley were a couple of Muslim houses, and behind them the Khalsa School, at which point the fields began. To the right of the far end of the lane was a Muslim *mohalla* but the Sikhs had manned this point also.

Behind the gurdwara, two lanes away, stood Sheikh Ghulam Rasool's two-storey house. According to the news spies had brought, this house had been converted into a citadel where the bulk of the Muslims' weapons were stocked. Like the Sikhs, the Muslim inhabitants of the village—farmers, oilmen, bakers and the like—had overnight turned into crusaders and were preparing to earn merit by killing the infidels. All the doors at the back of the house were closed and so was the room at the top. The roof of the house looked deserted but the Sikhs expected the first shot to be fired from there.

It was a beautiful village. In normal times no one could fail to be impressed by the beauty of the village. Built in the shape of a horse-shoe on a bluff by the side of a small river, it was surrounded by loquat orchards. The water of the river was blue like the cerulean blue of the sky, set off by the deep red of the earth. The village stretched up to the hills flanking the plains. The hills changed colour all the time, sometimes wearing a mantle of soft blue, at other times shining like burnished copper and then rippling into luxuriant green. Small streams flowed at the foot of the hills through dense clusters of fig trees. The people of the village had been bountifully blessed by nature for generations.

Suddenly a wave of excitement ran through the gurdwara. Everyone looked towards the gate. *Sardar* Teja Singh, the headman of the village, had arrived. He knelt and touched the threshold of the gurdwara with his eyes. The fingers of both his hands, as they rested on the platform trembled.

He stayed in that position a long time, his forehead resting on the threshold,till tears flowed from his eyes.

Then he got up and, joining his hands together, his head bowed, his white beard covering his chest, he reverentially walked up to the Holy Book, the Granth Saheb, and bowed before it. His face had flushed and there were tears flowing from his eyes as he worshipped the Holy Book.

The congregation watched him with bated breath. Teja Singh rose to his feet and slowly walked up to a pillar against which a sword rested. He lifted the sword with trembling hands and walked back to the middle of the hall. The sword belonged to his maternal grand-father who had been a courtier in Maharaja Ranjit Singh's court.

'*Jo Bole So Nihal*!' Pritam Singh, a youth standing near the door shouted.

'*Sat Sri Akal*!' the congregation responded .

The gurdwara walls shook with the resounding noise of the slogans. It was unwise to shout slogans, for that would warn the Muslims, but the congregation was so charged that there was no stopping them.

As Teja Singh's aged hand raised the sword to his eyes, the whole congregation writhed in a frenzy.

'The Khalsa Panth once again asks for the blood of Sikh warriors,' *Sardar* Teja Singh said in an impassioned voice. 'It's time to test our mettle. At this time of crisis God demands only one thing: sacrifice and more sacrifice.'

'Recite the *Ardas*!' *Sardar* Teja Singh said his voice breaking with emotion, though there was no missing the note of authority in it. 'You, who are so dear to the Guru. You, valiant ones. Recite the *Ardas*.'

The congregation rose to its feet as one, its head bowed in prayer... 'The Khalsa, the pure at heart will dominate the world. The enemy will be annihilated...!'

They recited in unison, their voice floating in the air in waves. As the *Ardas* ended, the Nihang Sikh standing at the gate yelled in a sharp ringing voice:

'*Jo Bole So Nihal!*'

'*Sat Sri Akal!*'

Just then they heard the sky-piercing slogan: '*Nara-e-Takbir!... Allah-o-Akbar!*'

The Nihang Sikh standing at the entrance to the gurdwara clenched his fist and was going to shout a counterslogan when *Sardar* Teja Singh stopped him. 'That's enough!' he said. 'The enemy knows...'

'Well...we don't want the enemy to gauge our strength, nor do we want them to know that we have assembled in the gurdwara. It's a question of strategy...'

Sardar Teja added, 'We have apprised the English Deputy Commissioner of the trouble that the Mussalmans are creating in the countryside. I know Richard Saheb. He is very shrewd and fair. At the moment, the only thing that we can do is to knock on the doors of the high-ups and tell them about the deplorable state of affairs in our village. All sorts of alarming news are floating down to us. We have come to know that arms are being piled up in the house of Rahim, the oilman. We have come to know that a big dark blue car was seen coming from the direction of the city yesterday afternoon and it stopped outside our village, in front of school-master Fazal Din's house. Some things were quickly removed from the car and carried into his house. Then the car sped away. It is reported that the car stopped at many places *en route*. We have also got the disquieting news that the Muslims of this place have sent word to the Muslims of Muradpur to help them. We are trying to establish contact with Sheikh Ghulam Rasool and others to sort out the matter peacefully. But we can't trust them.'

'It's all a lie! You have made no attempt to contact them,' someone shouted angrily from the congregation. A hush fell over the hall. Who dared to make such a bold allegation before the whole congregation? The audience looked around and frowned.

A thin and lean youth stood up. 'We forget that we are being provoked and incited against the Muslims,' he said. 'Likewise efforts are being made to turn them against us. We are being fed false rumours. We must make all possible efforts to maintain amity and goodwill with the Muslims of our village. We must take every possible step to guard against trouble breaking out.'

'Sit down! Sit down!'

'A traitor to the community! Who's he?'

'I refuse to sit down. Stop me if you can. Friends, I still insist that we should try to have a meeting with Sheikh Ghulam Rasool and other well-meaning Muslims of the village. If Sheikh Ghulam Rasool does not see eye to eye with us...well...we can ignore him. There are other Muslims in the village. We can join hands with them in maintaining peace. If they are trying to get arms from Muradpur are we not trying to get help from Kahuta? Nobody wants bloodshed and arson. The Sikhs and Muslims of this village can stand together and maintain peace. This very morning I had a meeting with Ghulam Rasool and some other Muslims.'

'What business had you to go there? Are they your relatives?'

'Is Ghulam Rasool your father?' another from among the audience asked.

'Please, please, allow me to finish. The trouble makers will come from outside. We should try to ward off such trouble. I can see only one way out of this . The peace-loving Sikhs and Muslims of this village should join hands and fend off the mischief-makers. They are collecting arms because they are afraid of us. And we are collecting arms because we are afraid of them.'

'One can never trust a Mussalman. Sit down!'

'And they say one can never trust a Sikh.'

'Sit down!' An old man stood up, his lips trembling with rage. 'What right have you to disrupt our meeting? Your mother's milk has not dried on your lips and you've started talking big already. One shouldn't be cheeky before elders.'

Sikhs from different parts of the hall got up protesting.

'Do you know they have burnt down the grain market in the city?'

'It's the *angrez*'s doing,' The youth, who was called Sohan Singh, shouted. 'Our welfare lies in keeping the trouble from breaking out. Listen, friends, today no bus has come from the city. Our communications are being cut off. It's a Muslim area. If people from outside attack us how long can we fight them? Besides, how much help can you get from Kahuta?' The audience fell silent.

Sardar Teja Singh walked up to the middle of the hall. 'It pains my heart to see our own children going astray and turning against us' he declaimed. 'Tell me, do I want communal discord? I myself had a word with Sheikh Ghulam Rasool. He put his hand on his heart and assured me that there would be no trouble in the village. I had just turned my back when some ruffians attacked the Khalsa School. They killed the peon of the school who happened to be a Brahmin and carried away his wife. I did not tell you about this till now for that would have angered you further.' A wave of indignation ran through the gurdwara.

'Someone has given you wrong information,' Sohan Singh said. 'True, there was an attack on the Khalsa School. But the Muslims of our village were not in it. It was the doing of some ruffians of Dhok Ilahi Baksh. Mir Dad, our friend who had just arrived from the city, reached the scene just in time. He, along with two other young men of the village, saved the situation from deteriorating. The peon was not killed. He only got hurt. Nor was his wife carried away by the Muslim ruffians. She's very much there in the school.'

'Who's this Mir Dad?' someone asked.

'I've seen him hob-nobbing with Mir Dad at the teashop. These *Muslas* are bent upon dishonouring our womenfolk and our youths unashamedly fraternize with these very *Muslas*,' a member of the congregation said. The man turned to Sohan Singh. 'Don't try to teach us. Go and practise your art on those *Muslas*. Has any Sikh killed a Muslim or looted his house? Stop pestering us with your sermons. We don't want them.'

People were turning against the youth.

The Nihang Sikh guarding the entrance strode up to him and slapped him.

'Don't beat him! Stop it! Don't beat him!'

Some people sitting near the youth swiftly caught hold of the Nihang.

*

167

At that very moment Mir Dad found himself in trouble in another part of the village.

Some people sitting on the platforms of three butcher shops in a row, shut due to the rioting were having an altercation with Mir Dad.

'Don't give me that rubbish', one of them said. 'Has anyone seen the *angrez* doing it? I'm told scores of Muslims were butchered in the city. Their dead bodies, it is said, are still rotting in the streets. Did the *angrez* kill them? Did they throw a pig in a front of a mosque? Don't tell me it was the *angrez*'s doing?'

'I leave it to you,' Mir Dad said. 'But there's one thing to consider. If the Muslims, Hindus and the Sikhs unite it will defeat the *angrez*'s plans. If we keep quarrelling among ourselves it strengthens their position.'

The people Mir Dad was arguing with had heard the same argument several times before and were in no mood to accept it.

'First go home and rub some almond oil on your head!' a fat butcher said. 'The *angrez* has done us no wrong. It's the age-old enmity between the Hindu and the Muslim. A *kafir* is a *kafir*. As long as he does not profess the right religion he will remain our enemy. To kill a *kafir* brings merit.'

'Listen, *Chacha*,' Mir Dad said. 'Who's ruling over us?'

'The *angrez*, of course. Who else?'

'Who commands the army?'

'The *angrez* of course!' the fat butcher replied.

'If the *angrez* wants to stop us from fighting can't he do that?'

'Of course, he can stop it. But he doesn't want to interfere with our religious affairs. He believes in justice and fairplay.'

'You mean he'll allow us to cut one another's throats and just watch the fun pleading that it has to do with religion and so he has nothing to do with it. What kind of ruler does that?'

The fat butcher lost his temper. 'You, Mir Dad, listen. The fight is between the Hindu and the Muslim. Where does the *angrez* come into the picture? Stop talking rubbish. If you're your father's son, right now go to the gurdwara and tell those fellows not to collect arms. Tell them to leave all those arms behind and go back to their homes. We don't want to fight with them. We'll go back to our homes if they do. If you have any guts, go and tell them that and don't keep bothering us.'

Mir Dad always tried to defuse tensions between people

through discussion. People usually listened to him because he was literate and travelled. But this time his word did not seem to carry weight. Perhaps it was because he did not have any land of his own, or a house in the city. He lived in the city with his younger brother Allah Dad and had only come out to the village to try and bring people together against the British. He taught at the village school but his real reason for coming here was to weld the people against the British and prevent them from fighting each other. Comrade Devdutt had sent him to do this. Harbans Singh too had been sent out on a similar mission. Both worked for the Communist party.

As Mir Dad stood there disconsolate, the first incident occurred. A Sikh spy, Gopal Singh, had been hiding behind a curtain in widow Chanandei's house quietly listening to the Muslims' discussion. He had slowly edged out from behind the curtain and into the lane as the Muslims' arguments grew more heated. It was dark in the lane and most of the doors of the houses on either side were shut. The spy thought that if he there was any danger he could quickly slip back behind the curtain. But as he listened to the discussion between the butchers he failed to notice a man leaving a nearby house. He only spotted him when he was almost on him. Gopal Singh turned pale with fright. The man had his hand inside his shirt front. Was he going to whip out a knife or a pistol from under his shirt? The spy panicked and tried to run for it but he missed his footing and crashed into the man.

'O, he has killed me! He has killed me!' the man howled.

Events had moved so fast that most of Muslims were caught unawares. Then, recovering, two of them caught up spears and ran after Gopal Singh. Ashraf, the butcher, threw his *lathi* at him but it missed.

More people came rushing into the lane. 'O, it's our blind Noora!' one of them cried as he bent over the man who lay prostrate in the lane holding his pajama cord and moaning that he was being killed.

Breaking away from the crowd, Mir Dad bent over the blind Noora and lifted him. The fat butcher shouted after him, 'Mir Dad, don't you have eyes to see?' he cried. 'Who do you think has done this to old Noora? An *angrez*? Be gone from here! I don't want to see your dirty face!' People began jostling him.

'A foot-loose man! Antecedents unknown! And he has the gall

to play the role of a peace-maker!' the fat butcher shouted. 'I'm asking you! Who are you? These scoundrels. Disowned by their mothers' they try to foist themselves on us. One slap and all your teeth will jump out of your mouth! Go and lecture your father, not us!'

Gopal Singh, the spy, did not stop running till he reached the gurdwara. The congregation was shaken by the news of what had happened to him. Several people felt Gopal Singh's body all over to make sure no bones were broken. He stood there panting, still terrified by what had happened.

'That man was heading for me!' he said.

'Who was he?' *Sardar* Teja Singh asked.

'Baba Noora!' Gopal blurted out.

'You mean that old, blind Noora?'

'I'm not very sure. All I know is I saw a man coming out of Noora's house.'

'Then what happened?' 'I saw a lot of people spilling out of the butcher's lane. They hurled *lathis* at me and I ran.'

People had started collecting in the lane outside the gurdwara. An old, venerable looking Sikh tried to disperse the crowd.

'There is no cause to be alarmed.' he said. 'Our Singh Khalsa has come back safe. Please go in. All of you, go in.'

After Gopal Singh had calmed down a bit, *Sardar* Teja Singh asked him in a whisper, 'What did you hear? What's their plan?'

'Mir Dad was there, trying to force his trash down their throats. He never gave me a chance to listen. The fat butcher admonished him, telling him to go and preach to the Sikhs and his own co-religionists. If the people in the gurdwara went back to their respective homes they would also go home, the fat butcher said.'

The congregation returned to the gurdwara. By now everyone was angry. The *kirtan* was resumed.

'Did you see what happened, *Sardar?*' A man asked Sohan Singh, who had attempted to defend the Muslims. Those *Muslas* tried to kill him. It's his good luck that he escaped death. Can't you see it? And yet you try and preach to us.'

'I suggest that this man should be shut up in his house,' another man said excitedly, rising to his feet.

'He has lost our trust,' yet another one said. 'For all we know he may be a spy.'

The Nihang Sikh hit Sohan Singh.

'Stop it. Don't beat him! Don't!'

'Go and preach to those uncles of yours in whose laps you sit all day long. Get lost!'

The *kirtan* began again.

As night fell they lit two lamps over the Holy Book. *Sardar* Teja Singh sat under the lamps, his blue turban and white beard shining in their light. The men and girls in the congregation followed *Sardar* Teja Singh's movements attentively. One of the girls was Jasbir, the daughter of Harnam Singh and Banto. She was married to one of the men in the village. Deeply religious her voice rose above the chanting of the others, as she recited the *Ardas* with great devotion. A small kirpan, sheathed in black, hung from her waist. She was usually addressed as the Guru's daughter. Every morning she washed the gurdwara stairs. The silk cloth covering the Holy Book had also been embroidered by her. Now she lost herself in the chanting.

The Nihang Sikh keeping watch on the roof suddenly saw a cloud of dust on the horizon. The cloud steadily shifted closer. He informed Kishan Singh and Kishan Singh in turn peeped through the trellised window and intently watched the cloud. So they had been wrong. They had thought that the trouble would start in the village. But now it looked as though the trouble was going to come from outside the village. They heard the boom of drums. Kishan Singh decided to tell *Sardar* Teja Singh of the latest development. He told the Nihang Sikh to go down and warn *Sardar* Teja Singh. He remained on the roof to keep watch.

The Nihang rushed down the stairs and cried: 'The Turks have come! The Turks are here!'

The congregation was stunned by the news. They had never expected the attack to come from outside. *Sardar* Teja Singh had expected stray incidents from their own village's Muslims. They could have handled that easily but this was different.

The boom of the drums drew nearer. '*Ya Ali!*' the rabble yelled. Then they heard another slogan '*Allah-o-Akbar!*'

For an instant everything stopped. Then a wave of excitement ran through the gurdwara. '*Jo Bole So Nihal! Sat Sri Akal!*'

'No Sikh who is dear to the Guru should leave the gurdwara! Everyone must be at his or her post!'

'The Turks! The Turks have come!' Everyone took up the call.

'The Turks have come!' Jasbir Kaur shrieked, in a voice tense with excitement. Removing her *chunni* she put it round her neck. Then she warmly hugged the woman standing next to her.

'The Turks are here!' she repeated emotionally.

The other women had also removed their *dopattas* from their heads and thrown them round their necks.

'Everyone to his post!' someone yelled.

Some of the Sikhs had loosened their hair and had already drawn their swords.

'*Jo Bole So Nihal*!' '*Sat Sri Akal*!' the congregation roared.

Sardar Mangal Singh, the jeweller, Pritam Singh, the cloth dealer, and Bhagat Singh, the grocer, who were members of the Council of Action, rushed to the roof, where *Sardar* Teja Singh and Kishan Singh had preceded them. They attempted to work out a rough strategy to meet the attack.

The mob, beating their drums, entered the village. They fired in the air and chanted their slogans.

'*Ya Ali*!'

'*Allah-o-Akbar*!'

'*Sat Sri Akal*!' screamed the Sikhs.

Then someone said the Turks were planning to approach from the river, which meant that they could reach the Sikh houses on that side unhindered. There, only a few old Sikhs had been left behind to guard the houses. Baldev Singh suddenly remembered his old mother whom he had forgotten in the excitement and had left behind at home. She must be in great danger. There were others too who had parents in the houses that were under attack.

Letting his long hair down and stripping down to his under-wear Baldev Singh unsheathed his sword and ran from the gurd-wara to his home shouting, 'Blood for blood.'

Some people shouted after him, asking him to come back, but there was no stopping him. Yelling, 'Blood for blood!' he was gone.

People didn't know why Baldev Singh was behaving the way he did. His mother did not live in the lane that was being threatened. So he couldn't be going there. Nor had he been heading in the direction of the enemy. What was he doing?. Then they saw him return with his sword dripping with blood, his hair flying in the air. Slowly people learned what had happened. Baldev Singh had plunged his sword into the old blacksmith, Karim Buksh, who lived in a nearby lane. Thinking that the Turks had already killed his mother he had taken revenge by killing the old man. 'Blood for blood!'

Darkness fell. The slogans were much louder. They heard the crash of breaking doors. The anger in the gurdwara could not be held back much longer.

Chapter 16

Harnam Singh rattled the door chain a second time. A woman's voice said, 'There's nobody at home. All the men are at work.'

Harnam Singh took stock of the situation. Banto cautiously looked around to make sure that no one had seen them.

'Banto, you ask them to open the door. There's a woman inside the house,' Harnam Singh said.

Banto rattled the door-chain and said in a loud voice, 'Kind one, open the door. We are in trouble.'

Harnam Singh lowered his head. What had the times come to that his wife should be driven to begging for shelter in such a cringing voice.

They heard footsteps and then the rattling of the door-chain. The door opened slowly. A hefty old village woman stood there, her hands smeared with cow dung, her head bare. Behind her stood a young girl, her hair a tangled mass, her sleeves rolled up, as if she had been mixing green fodder for her buffalo or cow.

'Who are you? What do you want?' the old woman asked, although she had gauged the situation at the very first glance.

'We want your help. We have come from Dhok Ilahi Buksh where rioters turned us out of our house. Our house has been plundered. We have been walking all night.'

The woman stood there, watching them. They could see she was weighing the consequences of taking them in. Finally she flung open the door. 'Come in. Do come in,' she said.

Harnam Singh and Banto silently offered thanks to God. They walked into the courtyard of the house. The woman leaned carefully out of the door, looked to her right and then to her left and then, stepping back, latched the door.

The young woman watched the old couple, her eyes full of suspicion and disbelief.

'Akran, spread out a cot for them,' the old woman said and began to mould cow dung into cakes.

The young woman Akran spread out a folding cot which had been standing against the courtyard wall.

'May God bless you, sister,' Banto said in a grateful voice. 'We lost everything overnight.' Her eyes filled with tears.

'We spent all our lives at Dhok Ilahi,' Harnam Singh said, 'We had a shop there. And a house. In the beginning they advised us to stick to the place. We would not come to any harm, they said. Then, yesterday, Karim Khan warned us to go away from there. He was right. We had just turned our back on the village when in came the rioters. They looted our shop and set it on fire.'

Banto got up from the cot and sat down on the ground by the side of the old woman.

Akran came in. Removing the cowdung cakes from the iron trough the old woman was putting them in, she stuck them, one by one, against the courtyard wall.

'Where are the men?' Harnam Singh asked.

The old woman turned to look at Harnam Singh but ignored his question. Harnam Singh immediately guessed where the men had gone and a tremor ran through his body.

'All that we have are the clothes that we are wearing,' Banto said. 'May God bless Karim Khan who saved our lives. And may God bless you for giving us shelter.'

An eerie silence hung over the house discouraging Harnam Singh from asking further questions. The younger woman had gone inside the house. Harnam Singh felt she was glaring at them, from the gloom of the house.

The old woman got up and, after washing her hands, went to a corner of the courtyard where a heap of unwashed utensils lay. She picked up an earthen bowl and pouring some buttermilk into it came back to where Harnam Singh and his wife were sitting. Harnam Singh's gun was still slung over his shoulder. His cartridge belt had become damp with perspiration and clung to his body.

'Here, have some buttermilk,' the woman said, 'You must be tired after walking all night.'

As Harnam Singh held the bowl in his hand he burst out crying. Until yesterday he had been a prosperous shopkeeper. And he still had two hundred rupees on him. All his life he had never

175

asked for a favour, and, yet, today he was knocking on a stranger's door, seeking shelter.

'Don't cry, Sardarji,' the woman said. 'If people in the lane hear you crying they will come rushing in to find out what is happening. Stop crying and sit still.'

Harnam Singh stopped crying and wiped his eyes with the end of his turban. 'May God bless you, sister,' he said. 'We'll never be able to repay your debt.'

'No worse fate can befall a man than to be made homeless,' his wife added.

'May God not make anyone homeless,' the old woman said. 'If God is kind all will turn out well.'

The woman then went and filled a bowl with butter milk and gave it to Banto who wondered if she should accept it. She looked at her husband in some confusion. How could she accept a bowl of milk from a Muslim hand? At the same time she felt famished. The woman understood her predicament.

'If you are carrying some utensil of your own you can pour the buttermilk in it,' the woman said. 'We have a *pandit's* shop in the village. If he is still there I'll get two tumblers from him. But I'm not sure. He may not be there. You may not like to eat the food touched by our hands. But surely, you don't want to stay hungry either.'

Harnam Singh extended his hand and took the bowl from the woman.

'Any food given by you is like nectar, sister,' he said. 'We'll never forget what you've done for us.'

The sun had come out and they could hear voices in the neighbouring houses. Harnam Singh passed the bowl to Banto.

'Listen, Sardarji, I'm not going to hide anything from you,' the old woman said. 'My husband and my son are both away from the village but they'll be back very soon. My husband is a God-fearing man. He'll do you no harm. But I can't say the same thing about my son. He belongs to the Muslim League and there are others with him. I'm not sure how he will deal with you. What's good for you and what's bad, well, you must decide for yourself.'

Harnam Singh's heart sank. Only a moment ago the woman had promised to get some utensils for him and now suddenly she was saying something different.

'Where can we go at this time of the day?' Harnam Singh said, folding his hands.

'That's none of my concern. If it had been some other time, things would have been different. But now nobody cares to listen to anybody. I've told you my menfolk may be here any time. I don't know how they will treat you. If anything goes wrong don't blame me.'

Harnam Singh sat lost in thought for a long time. Then he said, 'You're right. What God wishes must happen. You took pity on us and opened your door for us. Now if you want us to go away we must abide by your wishes. Banto get up. Let's go.'

Harnam Singh picked up his gun and walked towards the door. His wife followed him. He knew they'd be in danger the moment they stepped out of the house.

The woman stood in the middle of the courtyard watching them.

As Harnam Singh lifted his hand to remove the door chain, she said suddenly, 'Don't go. Put the chain back. You've knocked at my door. You came here with hopes of safety. Come back. Whatever happens I shall face the consequences.'

Akran who had come out of the house looked at her mother-in-law surprised, 'Ma, let them go,' she said, advancing towards the old woman. 'We haven't asked our men. They may object.'

'Leave that to me,' the old woman replied. 'I know how to handle them. Go and fetch the step-ladder. Hurry up. How can I turn away a person who has knocked at my door? We have all to appear before God one day. Go, what are you gaping at my face for? Go and bring the ladder.'

Harnam Singh and his wife walked back to the woman. Harnam Singh again folded his hands and said, 'Sister, may the Almighty preserve you. We'll do what you tell us to do.'

The morning advanced. Women came out of their houses. Some called on neighbours. Everyone talked about the riots. In this village too, the men had gone round raising slogans, brandishing spears and beating drums. Then they had gone *en masse* in an easterly direction. Nobody knew where they had gone and what they had been doing the whole night. Now that it was morning the women awaited their return.

Akran brought the ladder. Her mother-in-law took it from her and put it against the wall. The ladder led up to a small attic.

'Come here,' the old woman signalled to Harnam Singh and his wife. 'You go up and hide in the attic. Mind you, make no noise. Nobody should know you're in this house. The rest is in God's hands.'

Harnam Singh found it difficult climbing up the ladder. He was heavily built and the gun which dangled between his legs obstructed his movements. Panting heavily with the exertion, he managed finally to heave himself into the attic. His wife followed. The attic was very small and cluttered up with junk. They could just about squat. When Harnam Singh closed the trapdoor the attic was plunged into darkness. They sat in the dark, their minds gone blank, their tongues dry.

Harnam Singh got his breath back finally. The attic was stuffy and very dark and they felt suffocated. After some time Harnam Singh opened the trapdoor slightly to let some air in. Now he could see a part of the courtyard and the door that opened into the lane. He couldn't see the young woman and her mother-in-law.

'Banto, if something untoward happens I'll shoot you first with my own hands and then...' Harnam Singh whispered to his wife for the third time. 'If we are found out and caught, this is how things are going to end. There's no other way.'

Banto made no reply. She was counting every minute, dreading the worst. She couldn't think clearly; her mind seemed to be paralysed.

Down below, in the back room, the old woman and her daughter-in-law were quarreling in subdued tones.

'You've not done the right thing by helping *kafirs*,' the daughter-in-law said. 'My husband will be angry. Will you be able to deal with him?'

The old woman sat there unperturbed. 'Now stop babbling!' she said at last, 'I can't push out those unfortunate people.'

'You don't know them. Do they mean anything to us? Abba and Ramzan will be really angry. They are nicely entrenched in the attic and *Sikhra* is armed with a gun. What if he fires at our men? It was foolish of you to trust them.'

The old woman stared at Akran. The girl had a point there. If her men tried to evict the Sikh and there was a scuffle the Sikh would probably shoot them. What made matters worse was that Ramzan was very volatile by nature and could easily lose his head. Anything could happen. It was one thing to give shelter to a helpless person and quite another to wantonly expose her husband and son to danger. She should have given the matter some careful thought.

She came out of the back room and stopped under the attic.

'Listen, *Sardarji*,' she said quietly.

Harnam Singh opened the trap door a little and peered out, 'What's the matter, sister?' he asked.

'Hand me your gun. You lower it from the window and I'll catch it.'

Harnam Singh was silent for a while, 'Sister, how can I trust you with my gun?' he asked finally.

'You must give me your gun. You can't sit in the attic armed with a gun.'

Harnam Singh and Banto looked at each other. If he gave the gun away it was almost as though he was mortgaging their lives to her. But if he refused to part with the gun she could create trouble and turn them out. And come to think of it, if a Sikh carried a gun in broad daylight in the midst of enemies, it was more a risk than protection.

'Are you listening, *Sardarji*? Give me the gun. What do you need a gun for while you're staying in my house?'

'Sister, if I give you the gun I'll feel so defenceless. The gun puts confidence in my heart.'

'Give me the gun. Lower it from this side and I'll hold it. When you go away I'll return it to you.'

Harnam Singh looked at his wife's face and then quietly handed the gun down.

After parting with the gun it suddenly occurred to him that he should have removed the cartridges from it. How foolish of him to have placed a loaded gun in their hands! Then he shook his head. When life had become so uncertain what difference did it make whether the gun was loaded or unloaded? Harnam Singh heaved a deep sigh, so deep that Banto felt that even the old woman and her daugher-in-law standing below could have heard him.

As the trap door closed the attic was again plunged in darkness. How things had changed! Yesterday at this time, Banto was in her own house, taking her clothes out of her box...and now they were hiding here like rats. Yesterday her husband and Karim Khan were vehemently denouncing the riots and condemning the people

179

who were killing and looting.

And now they had lost everything. Harnam Singh was terrified. He was afraid he had made an awful mistake. Would he ever see his gun again? The gun was to him what a staff was to a blind man. Sweat broke out on Harnam Singh's face. More than himself, he was worried about his wife. How could he protect her now? People could stone them to death. All that he had lost was finally sinking in hard. He had lost everything he had amassed through devotion, wisdom and love of mankind.

'If only we knew something about Jasbir's fate,' Banto mumbled.

Harnam Singh was silent. He did not know how to console his wife. A mother's instinct—Banto was worried about her children all the time. Last night while she had been walking along the *nullah* this thought had constantly been nagging her. And now all of her fears had returned with greater intensity.

There was a commotion in the village. It appeared as if everyone had started talking together.

'O, Akran, come out. The men have returned!' one of Akran's friends called out. Akran opened the door and ran out.

Harnam Singh tensed. Banto looked up at her husband's face. It had suddenly turned pale. His soiled and crumpled clothes seemed to be disintegrating.

Through a crack in the trapdoor he could see the old woman. She stood at the door, one hand resting on her waist. Tall and straight, how stately she looked! Harnam Singh felt reassured. He would come to no harm as long as she was there.

'You believe in God. You worship Him day and night,' Banto consoled her husband. 'He will stand by you. You'll come to no harm.'

Judging by the noise, more people had assembled outside the house. They were laughing and joking; obviously, they were in a happy mood.

Then Harnam Singh heard footsteps inside the courtyard and guessed that the men of the house had returend.

After a while, Akran's father-in-law and Akran came into view in the courtyard carrying a big, black trunk.

Harnam Singh touched Banto's knee.

'Our trunk! Our big, black trunk!' he whispered. 'They must have looted our shop.'

Banto craned her neck to look into the courtyard through the crack in the door flap.

'It's still locked!' Harnam Singh muttered.

Akran's father-in-law sat down on the trunk. Then he removed his turban and wiped the perspiration from his forehead with it. His wife went up and shut the door.

'Where's Ramzan? Hasn't he come? she asked.

'Ramzan is somewhere in the lane doing some propaganda work for the League.'

Harnam Singh again touched his wife's knee. 'I know him,' he said. 'He's Ehsan Ali. He has business dealings with me.'

'*Abba*, you've brought the trunk just like that?' It was Akran speaking. 'Didn't you find out what's in it? It might be nothing but junk.'

'It's so heavy. I was bent double carrying it. It must be full of clothes. I'm sure it contains something really useful.'

'Just one trunk? Hasn't Ramzan brought something?'

'Ramzan saw it first and pulled it out of the house. It's full to the top. What more do you want?'

'Let's open it.' Akran ran into the house and came back with a small hammer. In her eagerness to lay her hands on the booty she had even forgotten to tell her father-in-law about the two infidels hiding in the attic. Her mother-in-law stood by her side, wordlessly.

'Rajo, give me some *lassi*,' the father-in-law said. 'I'm thirsty.' His wife, Rajo, went in to fetch *lassi*.

They started hammering on the lock.

Ehsan Ali was drinking *lassi* when Rajo told him that she had given shelter to a Sikh and his wife in the house.

Harnam Singh flung open the trap door of the attic. '*Beti*, don't break the lock,' he said to Akran. 'Here take the key. It's our trunk.' Then he turned to Ehsan Ali. 'I'm Harnam Singh speaking to you. Your wife has given us asylum in your house. May God bless you. This trunk is ours. But now you may regard it as your own. Good, that it has fallen into your hands. It could very well have been some one else.'

Ehsan Ali looked up, feeling very embarrassed, as if he had been caught in the act of stealing.

'*Amma* gave them shelter,' Akran cried, raising an accusing finger towards Rajo. She had stopped hammering the lock. 'I told her

181

they were *kafirs* and she should not let them in. But she wouldn't listen.'

Akran said this to please her father-in-law but he stood there looking confused. In the past Harnam Singh and he had done business together and they knew each other well.

Finally he said, 'Harnam Singh, come down!' Then, he said, 'You are lucky you took shelter in my house. If you had gone to some other house, you would have died long ago.'

Akran was eager to open the box. But Rajo had taken the key from her and refused to part with it though Akran asked for it again and again.

'Harnam Singh, you've come to me in search of shelter so I'll not do you any harm. But you must leave my house. If my son comes to know that I'm sheltering you he will not spare you. Even the villagers will get at me for harbouring you.'

'Ehsan Ali, I agree with what you say. I must abide by your wishes. But where can we go at this time of the day? They will tear us to pieces.'

Ehsan Ali fell silent and then looked at his wife accusingly.

'They were looking for you last night too,' Ehsan Ali said. 'And now if somebody comes to know that you are hiding in my house I'll be in serious trouble; they won't spare me either.You must go away from here.'

Akran brought the ladder and placed it against the wall under the attic. Harnam Singh and his wife came down without arguing any more. They appeared resigned to their fate.

Harnam Singh was about to ask for his gun when his eyes fell on Rajo, who was standing in the middle of the courtyard, her hands on her hips.

Ehsan Ali said: 'We'll put them in the fodder house. Rajo, you lock the door from outside. Here, take this lock. Now hurry up.' Then he turned to Harnam Singh, 'It's because of our past friendship,' he said. 'Otherwise my blood boils when I think of what the *kafirs* have done in the city.'

Rajo walked hurriedly away. Harnam Singh and Banto followed her. They went past a dark room and entered another courtyard at the back of the house which was equally dark. The sharp acrid smell of cowdung, decomposed fodder and animals came to them. Rajo threw open the door of a small room crammed with fodder up to the ceiling.

'Stay here,' she said. 'My husband is a kind man. I did not know that you knew each other. Make yourselves as comfortable as you can.'

Harnam Singh and his wife sat down gingerly on the floor. It was very cramped. Rajo closed the door.

The hours dragged slowly by. Their fright gradually diminished. They knew they were safe till the evening. In the afternoon Rajo brought them *lassi* and *chapatis*. The food revived them. They sat silently for a while after they had finished the food. Then Banto said: 'What do you think? Is Iqbal Singh still in the village? Or do you think he has escaped?'

'It'll be as God wills,' Harnam Singh said. 'There's a chance, he may yet live. Some good people may give him shelter.'

'Good that Jasbir is not alone. There are a lot of people of our own community living in that village. They must have assembled in one place.'

'Do you think they'll give back my gun?' Harnam Singh asked. 'I think they will.'

They talked for a long time. Then they dozed off.

They woke suddenly at the sound of heavy pounding on the door.

'Come out, you!' People outside the door shouted fiercely. 'Come out, may your mother—Get out of there!'

They heard the people outside attack the door with axes. Harnam Singh and his wife sat up thoroughly alarmed.

'Where's the key, you! How dare you give shelter to *kafirs*? May I—your *kafir's* mother!' A heavy blow fell on the door.

'Not so loud, Ramzan!' They recognized Akran's voice. Perhaps she was warning her husband to be cautious.

More axe blows fell. The door buckled under the assault.

'Stop barking, you!' It was Rajo's voice. 'Are you mad? Where's that witch, your wife? I'm going to pull out her tongue. Ah, there you are *haramzade!* I told you not to tell your rogue of a husband about these Sikhs. Why did you tell him? Can't you hold a secret in your belly? Ramzan, what are you up to? Do you want to spill blood in our house? So you want to kill them, do you? Them, to whom we have given shelter? We know this man. He has always been nice to us.'

'Ma, stop being foolish! These *kafirs* have killed two hundred Mussalmans in the city.' Ramzan attacked the door again. 'You *kafirs*, come out! You! May I—your mother!'

Two more blows. The hinges came off, the door creaked and crashed to the ground. The barn suddenly became bright as if a bushel of light had been dumped there. Holding an axe in his hand, Ramzan was panting hard, Akran standing by his side, her face gone pale. Rajo was standing a little away from them, her hands resting on her hips.

'Come out, you *kafirs*.'

Ramzan cautiously looked into the barn. Sitting there holding one another, Harnam Singh and his wife stared at him. Then Harnam Singh stood up quietly and came out without offering any resistance.

'Kill me!' he said quietly.

'—your mother!' Ramzan caught hold of Harnam Singh by the neck and pulled him down. Harnam Singh's turban fell off. Ramzan swiftly let go his neck as he recognized Harnam Singh. He had taken tea at his shop a couple of times. In an agony of indecision Ramzan raised his axe but could not bring himself to the point of striking Harnam Singh with it. It is one thing to kill a *kafir* and quite another to kill a man with whom one is familiar and who is also staying under one's roof.

Still panting with excitement, Ramzan stood there for a moment facing Harnam Singh. Then, swearing, he rushed away.

*

It was past midnight. Rajo was walked ahead with swift strides, Harnam Singh and Banto quietly following her a few steps behind.

She escorted them past as a cluster of trees. The moon hung over the trees, flooding the countryside with its light. Again the same dreamy, other-worldly atmosphere, darkness and light playing hide and seek. The stretch of land beyond the cluster of trees looked mysterious and terrifying in its vastness. Rajo looked grave to the point of sternness. She was holding Harnam Singh's double barreled gun in her hand.

They descended the slope leading to the river. Far off to the left the sky had started turning red. Harnam Singh pressed his wife's hand.

'Just look to your left,' he whispered to her. 'Do you see anything there?'

'Yes, I can see it. A whole village seems to be ablaze. *Vah guru!*' she mumbled under her breath.

Harnam Singh stopped once. On the horizon to the right there was another slash of red.

'Which village is that? It's burning.'

Without a word, Banto gazed into the distance.

They walked on. The houses in the village looked squat and stunted in the moonlight, lamps glimmering in some. In front of some doors bullock carts had been unhitched for the night.

Under a cluster of trees they noticed the white tomb of the Pir they had seen the previous night. There was no lamp burning. Perhaps they had forgotten to light the lamp.

Rajo kept walking till she reached the end of the village. Here she stopped and handed Harnam Singh the gun.

'Go, may God be with you. Go straight along this path. The rest depends on how luck deals with you.' Her voice was strained.

'If we come out of this ordeal alive we shall...' Harnam Singh's voice shook.

'I've done nothing for you. It's all dictated by one's fate. I see fire raging on all sides.'

Rajo put her hand into the pocket of her *kurta* and took out a small bundle of white cloth. 'Here, take it. It's yours,' she said.

'What's it, Rajo sister?'

'I found this in your trunk. Two pieces of ornaments. You've fallen on hard times. In such times ornaments are a great help.'

'May *Vah Guru* bless you. We must have done some good deed in our past lives that we happened to meet you.' Overwhelmed, Banto started sobbing.

'Go now. It's getting late,' Rajo said. She couldn't tell them in which direction to go, which village to go to, which door to knock on.

Harnam Singh and his wife slowly walked down the slope. Rajo stood on the embankment watching their receding figures. The path was uneven, strewn with rocks, the moonlight making of the scene a mosaic of black and white.

After walking some distance they turned round to look. Rajo was still standing on the embankment and watching their straying feet as they slowly trudged towards the unknown. Then she turned and walked away towards the village. As she disappeared

185

from sight, the wilderness around them appeared even more threatening.

Chapter 17

Ramzan was surprised at himself for having let Harnam Singh and Banto go. Especially given his brutal treatment of all the Sikhs he had met after the riots had started. Earlier, when he and his companions were returning after looting Harnam Singh's shop they had seen a Sikh running away from them. They were in a boisterous mood and thought it would be fun to go after the Sikh. *'Ya Ali'* they yelled—it was a group of twenty or thirty people—and dashed off in the direction of the Sikh. The Sikh was running in the direction of a village but he was not following the rutted path generally taken by the bullock carts.

Instead, he was running through the fields, hoping that in that manner he might escape the Muslims' atttention.

Ramzan and his companions followed the Sikh for a while, then lost sight of him.

'The *Sikhra* has hidden somewhere!' Ramzan said and quickened his pace. He must have gone about fifty yards when he saw the Sikh again. He was making his way through the dunes and the hollows. But when they reached there, he was nowhere to be seen.

'He must be hiding in some hollow,' Noordin said. 'Let us pull out the mother—!'

They started throwing stones into each hollow in the hope that they would be able to ferret him out. If the Sikh had kept running they would have certainly brought him down like a country rat, but the fellow had hidden in some dark hollow between the dunes. There were innumerable hollows and to locate him was not going to be an easy job. 'Come out, you Sikh!' Noordin shouted. They all started laughing. Noordin came from the same village as Ramzan. He carried earth and bricks on donkeys. When he laughed his red gums showed over his teeth.

Some people climbed down the dune. 'He must be in that hole!'

'Come out, you! May I... your mother!' said one of them and threw a stone into the hole. But that bore no result. It was very dark inside the crater and it happened to be very deep.

Simultaneously they started pelting stones into the hole, but to no effect.

'Let's climb right down into the hole,' Ramzan said. 'Otherwise we'll never be able to find him.'

'We must be careful, Ramzan. He must be carrying a kirpan.'

'May his—!' Ramzan laughed. But to be on the safe side he pulled out his knife. As he entered the hollow two of his companions followed him.

'Come out, you low-born!'Ramzan cried. Some more people entered the hollow.

They carefully combed the hole but there was no trace of the Sikh.

Then one of the group, who was keeping watch on top of the sand dune, cried, 'There he goes!' He pointed to a dune some distance away on which he had a fleeting glimpse of white clothes.

All of them ran in the direction of the dune, throwing stones as they ran. One of the stones hit the Sikh on the knee, but he suppressed a cry and crouched inside a crater. Then there was a shower of stones. The stone-throwing was random and most of the stones fell harmlessly against the walls of the hollow; but some stray ones hit him on the shoulder, forehead and knee, making him groan. The stones kept flying into the hole continously. After some time the mob outside heard stifled groans from one of the holes. They knew that the Sikh was hiding there. The hail of stones increased.

'Eh, stop it!' One of the group cried. 'Don't hit him!' The man who had called out considered himself the brain of the group. He planted himself at the mouth of the hollow. 'Oh, Sikh, If you agree to accept Islam, we shall let you off.'

No reply came. Only groans.

'Oh Sikh, why don't you speak? Are you willing to accept Islam? Speak up, eh. If Islam is acceptable to you, come out of hiding. We'll do you no harm. Otherwise, we shall stone you to death!'

Still there was no response from inside the hole. Some

members of the mob chucked a few more stones into it. 'Come out you! Khanjir's seed! Or do you want us to bring out your carcass?'

Still no sound came from inside the hole. They again started hurling stones into it. Ramzan came up with a huge piece of stone and stood near the mouth of the hollow.

'There's yet time!' he shouted into the mouth of the hollow. 'Or do you want to be reduced to a pulp?'

Some people laughed. They resumed throwing stones into the crater.

Then they saw the Sikh crawling on all fours out of the mouth of the crater, his turban dangling from his neck, his clothes torn and smeared with dust. Blood was oozing from his forehead and knees.

Bent over the Sikh gazed stupidly around him.

'Tell me will you read the *Kalma* or not?' Ramzan asked him.

He was still holding the big stone in his hands.

The Sikh kept staring vacantly for some time and then nodded.

A man standing behind Noordin had recognised the Sikh. He was the only one who knew him, though Ramzan if he had been able to foresee events would have been surprised that he would soon meet the young Sikh's father in his own house without guessing the relationship between the two. The young Sikh was Iqbal Singh, who had a cloth shop in Mirpur. His father, Harnam Singh, ran the tea-shop at Dhok Ilahi Buksh. Perhaps he was going to Dhok Ilahi Buksh, to his parents, when he was caught on the way. The man who had recognized him, concealed himself behind Noordin so that Iqbal Singh would not see him. He knew there was no way to help the Sikh.

'Speak from you mouth, you mother—! Speak up, or I'll crash the stone on your head!'

'I'll read the *Kalma*!' Iqbal Singh said in a faltering voice. '*Allah-o-Akbar!*' they all cried together.

'*Nara-e-Takbir! Allah-o-Akbar!*'

Ramzan threw away the stone and so did the others.

'Get up!' Ramzan said, clasping Iqbal Singh's arms.

'Now you're one of us. Our brother!'

Iqbal Singh was still in great pain. He couldn't even stand properly.

'Come, let us embrace each other,' Ramzan said and hugged

Iqbal Singh. The others also embraced him, one by one. First they would place their heads on his right shoulder and then on his left, and then again on his right shoulder. This was the Muslim way of fraternizing. Iqbal Singh's legs were shaking and his throat was parched, but after fumbling initially he learnt the ritual.

Slowly he began to hope. Perhaps they would let him go. He hadn't expected to escape so easily. They came out of the sand dunes, Ramzan supporting Iqbal Singh. They picked their way through the wheat fields, Iqbal Singh still being driven like a helpless animal. They had not been able to decide whether to present him before the main group as a symbol of their triumph, or as a prisoner, cowering at their feet. Maybe he should be presented as an initiate who had joined their fold? Iqbal Singh could not walk properly. At least five stones had hit him on the knees and he was still bleeding from the forehead. At one place, as he was struggling to cross an embankment, Noordin had given him a playful nudge, and he had fallen headlong into the field.

'Ramzan *bhai*, they are still pushing me,' he complained, as he falteringly rose to his feet like a child who is thrashed in spite of his having promised to behave himself.

'Eh, stop pushing him!' Ramzan warned his companions in a threatening tone, then winked at them.

'Eh, don't push him!' Someone walking behind said, then pushed Iqbal Singh himself.

Hate and animosity cannot so easily change into love and sympathy. They can only change into ridicule and scorn Now they couldn't beat up Iqbal Singh, but that did not stop them from making him the target of their cruel jokes.

'Look, Ramzan *bhai*, someone has again flicked his finger into my behind,' Iqbal Singh complained.

He had reached that rock-bottom stage of self-respect.

Noordin thought of a new antic. 'Eh, stop! No further!' He held Iqbal Singh's hand.

Iqbal Singh stopped, looked at Noordin.

'Take off his *salwar!*' Noordin said to his companions. 'We shall march him naked into the village. The fellow was trying to hide from us!' Noordin stepped forward and thrust his hand into the fold of Iqbal Singh's *salwar*. His companions started laughing.

'Look, Ramzan *bhai!*' Iqbal Singh said in a plaintive tone.

'I warn you. Nobody is to take off his *salwar!*' Ramzan shouted at his companions.

'But he hasn't read the *Kalma* yet. Until he reads the *Kalma* he's a *kafir* and not a Muslim. Pull down his *salwar*!'

Ramzan's defence of him put courage into Iqbal's heart.

I'll not allow you to remove my *salwar*!' he said in a challenging tone. 'Let me see how you do it.'

At this show of bravado the people around him burst out laughing.

They had arranged for the conversion to be held at Imamdin the oilman's house. The village barber was called and the *mullah* of the village mosque was also hurriedly summoned. A big crowd collected in the courtyard of Imamdin's house.

The barber's fingers started aching after a while. He was having a difficult time shearing off Iqbal Singh's crop of hair. The barber first clipped Iqbal Singh's hair short, then tied the remaining hair into small knots and rubbed horse-dung and urine into them before the final clipping. For this final stage he used a shearing machine normally used for cropping horses' hair. The machine worked its way through Iqbal Singh's hair, making grotesque patterns on his head. Then the barber shaved his head clean with a razor. They let his beard remain.

When the time came to trim his beard there were many catcalls.

'Cut it in Muslim style!' someone shouted.

'Take care of his side-burns too!' another called. 'Reduce his moustache to a thin line!' called a third.

Despite his fear-stricken eyes Iqbal Singh had begun to look Muslim.

Then Noordin came forward through the crowd. While Iqbal Singh's hair was being cut he had slipped away unnoticed. Now he returned making a lot of noise. 'Please make way for me,' he said, pushing people aside.

He sat down by Iqbal Singh. With his left hand he forced Iqbal Singh's mouth open and with his right hand he pushed a big piece of beef, dripping with blood, into his mouth.

'Open your mouth! May I...your mother! Open your mouth! Suck it up! You mother's...!'

Noordin triumphantly looked at the people standing around and laughed, baring his red-gummed teeth.

The *mullah* and an elder of the village scolded Noordin for his levity. 'You've no right to demean your brother for having embraced Islam,' the elder said, his face livid with rage.

With the arrival of the village elder on the scene everyone became more solemn. Iqbal Singh was treated with some deference. He was made to sit on a cot fetched hurriedly from inside. The remaining rites were performed with solemnity.

Holding a rosary in his hand, the *mullah* recited the *Kalma* asking Iqbal Singh to repeat it after him. The *Kalma* was read three times. The people standing around, touched their eyes with their fingers and kissed them. Finally, all those present embraced Iqbal Singh.

Following a procession to the village well, he bathed and was given new clothes; his name had been changed from Iqbal Singh to Iqbal Ahmed. The people raised loud slogans: *'Nara-e-Takbir! Allah-o-Akbar!'*

Before nightfall Iqbal Singh was circumcised. The soothing words of the elders did nothing to reduce the pain.

'We'll have your *nikah* performed and get you a beautiful wife. Kalu oilman's widow is just your age. Young and strong. One glance at her will send ripples through your body. Now you are one of us. Now you're a Sheikh—Sheikh Iqbal Ahmed.'

Before nightfall all the signs of Iqbal Singh's Sikhism had been carefully obliterated; in their place were all the external Muslim signs. From an enemy he had been transformed into a friend, not an infidel, but a believer—a Mussalman. The doors of all Muslim houses were now open to him.

Lying on a cot Iqbal Ahmed passed the night in torment.

Chapter 18

The Turks had come, but they were from the neighbouring villages. The Sikhs believed they were settling scores with their traditional enemies, the same Turks with whom the Khalsas used to battle two hundred years ago. It was just one more link in the historic chain of battles.

They fought for two days and two nights. Then the ammunition ran out, making it impossible to carry on. Behind the *chowki*, on which the Holy Book rested, lay seven dead bodies covered with white sheets. Five women lamented their heads in the laps of the dead.

Nobody came forward to claim the remaining two bodies, one of them a Nihang Sikh who had bravely held his post to the last, the other that of Sohan Singh, the peacemaker who had come from the city to meet Sheikh Ghulam Rasool. Sohan Singh's body had been deposited near the gurdwara by Muslims as a sign of their disdain for peace proposals. Apart from these, many other Sikhs had been killed but no one had time to pick up the bodies.

The dead body of the peon of the Khalsa School was still lying in the school courtyard. The peon had been given strict instructions to stay back in the school and not budge under any circumstances. The peon's wife was still alive, the village's *numbardar* (headman) having taken her under his wing. Mai Bhagan's dead body was still lying in the courtyard of her house. She had, however, succeeded in saving her jewellery by burying it outside. Raiders had set fire to her house out of spite, but Rahim, the oilman, who lived next door, promptly extinguished the fire for fear of his own house being engulfed by it. Old Sudagar Singh also lay dead outside. He had been overlooked when bodies were carried to the gurdwara.

Some dead bodies were lying outside the town, one of them face down, near a well: the man had been killed by mistake. He was the water-carrier, Allah Rakha. He had been going to the well at midnight to deliver water to the Sheikh's house when he was killed. He had just come out of his house to fetch the water when a bullet fired from the roof of the Sheikh's house hit him in the back. Another body, that of a Sikh, lay on the city road. Fatehdin, the baker, whose shop was near the approach to the gurdwara, had luckily escaped death, but two small boys working in his bakery had been killed when they rushed out of the bakery to see what was going on in the lane where flames were still rising from the Khalsa School. In the lane to the left of the school all the shops had been gutted. On the other side, three butcher shops and four houses located in the oilmen's mohalla were smouldering.

The gurdwara had nearly run out of ammunition. Sitting on the roof, Kishan Singh sporadically fired his gun just to give the enemy the impression that they were still holding out, although, in fact, they knew they were finished.

'Our ammunition is gone!' someone blurted out softly. But even those who caught the words made no comment. The ammunition had also depleted in the Sheikh's fort. Yet both sides kept on shouting slogans to keep up their morale. The cries of '*Allah-o-Akbar*' were now coming, not from one, but from three directions. The people in the gurdwara tried to match their adversaries slogan for slogan, but it was evident to the Muslims that the Sikhs were weakening.

A spy brought the news that the Muslims were expecting reinforcements, whereas the Sikhs could expect no help at all. The outside world was no longer their's to rely upon. Two people had surreptitiously been sent in the direction of Kahuta to ask for help, but they had not returned. The hastily convened council of war wanted to move for a truce, perhaps by offering the Muslims money to withdraw. In fact, they had already sent a messenger to the Sikhs.

Now the five members of the council of war were discussing the Muslims' terms with *Sardar* Teja Singh near the inner gate of the gurdwara.

'They are asking for two lakhs,' Teja Singh said in an angry voice. 'We don't have so much money.'

'What message did you send them through the Junior Granthi?' one of the members asked. The younger brother of the Granthi (Sikh priest),who was called the Junior Granthi, had been selected as an emissary when Mir Dad, the communist, who was the first choice of the Sikhs, had declined the job when he heard an exchange of money would be a pre-condition for a ceasefire. 'I had told him to indicate a figure of 20 to 30 thousand rupees at which the matter could be settled but they demand two lakh rupees.'

'They must have known that we are in a bad shape.'

'They can never know it. Not even their forefathers can,' the grocer, Hira Singh fumed. 'We are not worse off in any way, considering the way we have mowed them down. The difference would be very slight, almost negligible. It is our bad luck that we have run out of ammunition.'

'*Allah-o-Akbar!*' The slogan echoed.

'How much jewellery have we been able to collect?' another member of the war council asked.

Teja Singh walked up to the *chowki* of the Granth Saheb and picked up a box lying in front of it. Taking out the jewellery the woman had donated, he weighed them in his hands to assess their approximate value.

'Not more than twenty-five thousand rupees!' he said. 'And they want two lakhs. Where are we going to get so much money?'

'You can make up the whole amount from your own pocket,' a member of the council of war said. 'Teja Singh, you've amassed a lot of wealth!'

Sardar Teja Singh ignored this remark.

'Shall we make it fifty thousand rupees?'

'There's no harm in trying. It's only if we start low that we shall be able to settle at ,say, one lakh rupees.'

Sardar Teja Singh sent for the Junior Granthi.

'Granthi, go and settle with them for one lakh rupees. But on one condition—that they agree to send the outsiders across the river. After that they may send us three of their representatives. Our men will wait for them at the appointed spot, with bags of money.'

The Junior Granthi joined his hands together and said: 'I'll do as you bid. But if they ask for the money first and agree to send the men across the river only afterwards, what should I say?' At this the grocer flared up. 'Don't they trust us?' he asked. 'Are we from Lahore or Amritsar that we say one thing today and something else tomorrow? We are the natives of Sayyedpur. Our word is as true as a line drawn across a stone!'

It was true that the Sikhs had as much pride in being of the village of Sayyedpur as the Muslims. They were proud of its red soil, of its excellent wheat, its loquat orchards, its extreme winters and icy winds. The Sikhs, like the Muslims of this place, were known for their hospitality, generosity and joviality. And, as the riots were proving, for their volatility as well. The moon, which had disappeared behind clouds, reappeared, giving the Sikhs, more anxious moments. If the firing started again it could lead to a disastrous end for them all. Perhaps it had been a mistake to have gathered in one spot, the gurdwara, and perhaps it had been equally wrong to have broken off negotiations with Sheikh Ghulam Rasool and his men. The irony of it was that, if they were on top, the same mistakes would probably be regarded as the finer points of their strategy.

Some people sat on the platform outside Sheikh Ghulam Rasool's house, talking among themselves. They too had not been able to retrieve their dead bodies, yet they had one great advantage over the Sikhs; the gurdwara was now hammed in on all sides by the Muslim and could be attacked at will but Sheikh Ghulam Rasool's house was built on open land and he could therefore maintain contact with all the neighbouring villages.

The people exchanging notes were outsiders.

'The moment we entered the lane, the *karars* (derogatory term for Hindus) took to their heels!' one of them said. 'They had lost all sense of direction. One of the Hindu girls climbed to the roof of her house when we happened to spot her. About twelve of us climbed up to the roof. She was about to jump over the railing to the next roof when we caught her. Nabi, Lalu, Meer, Murtaza—they all had her turn by turn.'

'Really!' one of them said.

'Yes, I swear by Allah. When my turn came, she said neither "no" nor "yes" as she lay under me. She didn't even stir. And then I found that she was dead.' He gave a hollow laugh. 'I had been doing it with a corpse!'

'Really! Don't tell me that!'

'Yes, I swear by the Holy Koran. I'm telling you the truth. Ask

Jalal, if you don't believe me. He was also with us. He was there when we discovered that the girl was dead.' He twisted his mouth and spat on the ground.

Now it was another's turn to speak.

'It's all a matter of luck,' he said. 'We caught a bagri (low caste woman) in the lane. You know, we were hounding out the *karars* from their houses. Our knives were doing a real good job. Whack! A head would fall from its neck! When we confronted this girl she started screaming. *Haramzadi*! She was begging us not to kill her.'

'"All the seven of you can have me" she pleaded. "Do with me what you like but don't kill me."'

'So?'

'So what? Aziz plunged his knife into her breast. She fell down dead.'

Under the moon, the Junior Granthi slowly made his way towards the river where the representatives of the Muslims were waiting for him to negotiate the terms of the truce. There were people framed in the gurdwara windows watching the shadowy figure of the Junior Granthi descending the slope to the river. Just then those in the gurdwara heard running feet on the roof and a Nihang Sikh shouted down to them: 'The rioters are coming from the west. The enemy has received reinforcements!'

Before long they heard the familiar voices of the rioters, the beat of drums, and the cries of '*Allah-o-Akbar*!'

Teja Singh's face fell. The Senior Granthi who was standing near the window, watching his younger brother, cried, 'Mehar Singh, stop! Don't go any further. Come back!'

But his voice did not reach the Junior Granthi. Hopping over the jagged stones along the river he steadily descended the slope.

'Come back, Mehar Singh! Come back!'

Many other voices joined the Senior Granthi's voice. The Junior Granthi stopped once to look back, then resumed his walk.

Beating their drums, the rioters approached the river. In response, the people standing on the river bank raised the cries of '*Allah-o-Akbar*!' The Junior Granthi was lost in the black and white mosaic of the moonlit night.

Although he was not clearly visible through the gurdwara window those inside vaguely saw that some people had advanced to meet the Junior Granthi; they surrounded him and raised *lathis*.

Something flashed in the moonlight; it was either an axe or the Granthi's *kirpan*. Then the cries of '*Allah-o-Akbar*!'

Teja Singh's blood froze. As if dazed, the Senior Granthi cried, 'They have killed him! They have killed my brother!'

He dashed out of the gurdwara, barefooted, unarmed and ran along the lane toward the slope.

'Stop him! Stop him!' The Nihang Sikh who was posted at the gate ran after the Granthi. He was only half way down the slope when the Nihang Sikh overtook him lifted him in his arms and carried him back to the gurdwara.

As soon as the sound of the drums reached the village it resounded with the cries of '*Allah-o-Akbar*!'

Firing started again and people panicked.

'*Jo Bole So Nihal*!'

'*Sat Sri Akal*!'

The Sikh slogan pierced the air. A small contingent of Sikhs, the Senior Granthi among them, spilled out of the gurdwara gate, brandishing swords and shouting slogans. All the women and children had assembled at one place in the gurdwara near the right wall. Jasbir Kaur seemed to be in a trance, her hand firmly gripping the handle of her *kirpan*.

They started reciting the Guru Bani ... their droning voices rising.

Then they saw flames rising from behind the houses at the end of the lane, turning the sky a lurid red.

'They have set the house near the school on fire,' they cried. 'Kishan Singh's house!'

Jasbir appeared not to have heard anything. She stood in the midst of the women, in a nimbus of light, her face transformed.

The stockade on the left entrance of the lane shook and noisily crashed to the ground. People could be seen in the distance, slowly crawling up the slope. The Nihang Sikh on the roof was the first to see them and immediately pointed them out to Kishan Singh. But Kishan Singh just shook his head, as if in despair. The number of the dark figures crawling up the slope was steadily increasing. Soon they were clearly visible in the glow of the leaping flames. The Sikh defenders had no ammunition to stop the advancing enemy. Kishan Singh fired at them twice, before giving up.

Another batch of Sikhs, holding naked swords, their hair hanging loose, marched into the lane towards the left. As the barricade had given way, so they knew that the Muslims would attack from that side. Then they heard wild cries, punctuated by gun fire and the intermittent roar of '*Allah-o-Akbar*!'. With swords raised, the Sikhs disappeared into the darkness of the lane.

Then a line of women, clad in white, emerged from the gurdwara. Jasbir Kaur was at the head of the line, her eyes half-closed with excitement, emotion and religious ecstacy. All the women had removed their *dopattas* from their heads and put them round their necks. Their feet were bare. They came out of the gurdwara, one after the other, as if in a trance.

'The Turks have come! The Turks have come!' some of the women cried as they walked through the lane. Others recited lines from the Holy Book. There were still others singing. 'I go where my warrior goes!' Some had children in their arms, others dragged them along their hands. As the flames rose higher, their reflection fell across the river turning its water garish red. The roar of the rioters and the sounds of crashing doors resounded in the air. A goatpath led from the end of the gurdwara lane to a well. The silent line of women look the path, lined on both sides lay flaming houses.

A Nihang Sikh, who was standing in the middle of the lane in front of the gurdwara, yelled shrilly, 'Come, Turks, come! Cross my path, if you dare!'

The women were now within sight of the well, where they normally came to bathe, wash their clothes and to gossip. They looked unearthly in the light of the fires and the moonlight.

They made no sound as they advanced, oblivious to everything around them. Jasbir Kaur was the first to jump. She did not raise a slogan, or address any one. She simply said Vah Guru! quietly and leaped. As she fell, many more women climbed up on to the parapet of the well. Hari Singh's wife pulled up her four-year old son after her and they jumped into the well together. Deva Singh's wife followed next, her infant clinging to her breast. Prem Singh's wife also jumped in, but her small son kept standing where he was looking down in utter bewilderment. Then Gyan Singh's wife pushed him in, ensuring that he joined his mother. Scores of women, with their children, followed.

When the Muslims entered the gurdwara there was not a single woman to be seen, but they heard the screams of women and the wail of children coming from within the well; their screams merged with the cries of '*Allah-o-Akbar*!' And '*Sat Sri Akal*!'

Dawn broke, dissipating the night's ghastly spectacle. As on other mornings, a cool breeze streamed through the village. The ripening wheat swayed in the breeze. The smell of loquats mixed with the smell of wild flowers. A flock of parrots, flew over the loquat orchards. The reddened water in the river had again turned blue.

The looting had stopped. Most of the houses had escaped the ravage of fire, because, other than the houses in the gurdwara lane which exclusively belonged to the Sikhs, they were in 'mixed' localities. As the morning advanced, the fires died down. The ruins of some houses still smouldered. A light still burned in the gurdwara where all four members of the council of war remained as if waiting to meet their end. Sardar Teja Singh sat on a bag of wheat in a corner, looking forlorn. A Nihang Sikh still stood next to the door, holding a spear. Kishan Singh was still on the roof, sitting in his chair.

As the light spread, vultures, kites and crows started wheeling in the sky in large numbers. About fifteen vultures perched on a denuded tree, their small heads and big yellow beaks conspicuous against the backdrop of desolation. Many more descended on to the parapet of the well where the dead bloated and decomposing bodies floated near the top of the well. The path which led from the gurdwara to the well was strewn with women's dopattas, bangles and plaited hair strings. The doors of houses on either side of the lane stood open or hung crazily on their hinges, bearning mute witness to the rioting that had taken place the previous day. The fight had not ended. The fat butcher's son had surreptitiously worked his way to the back of the gurdwara and was sprinkling kerosene on the windows in order to set the building ablaze. He struck a match, then his hand was arrested in mid-air by a strange sound—a deep, slow, long-drawnout sound. The sound reached Teja Singh's ears as he sat dejectedly in the gurdwara. Kishan Singh, who was still keeping vigil on the roof, also heard the sound, as did the people in the Sheikh's mansion. Everyone stopped to listen to the low booming sound which grew louder with every passing minute.

Then they saw it. A large aeroplane with big, black wings was flying towards the village. Sometimes the wings turned dark and sometimes when they caught the sun they glittered like silver. Sometimes the left wing of the aircraft dipped and sometimes the other wing. It seemed to be performing aerobatics.

As the plane drew nearer, people came out to watch. They rushed out into the lane, stood up on their platforms, or climbed on to the roofs to have a closer look. The plane nosed down, then started flying at a lower altitude. The pilot, a white man, waved to the people standing on the ground. Some thought that they could see him smiling.

'Yes, he did smile!' one small boy said to another boy. 'I saw it myself, He was wearing gloves and he waved like this. 'Didn't you notice?' he asked the other boy.

All activity ceased. Nothing more would happen now. The *angrez* had got wind of the trouble. No more arson, no more firing. Hadn't the fat butcher's son, who was about to strike a match to burn down the gurdwara, suddenly withdrawn his hand? Like him, all the people now stood there, gaping at the plane.

As the pilot flew over the gurdwara he waved from the cockpit. Kishan Singh, who was standing on the roof of the gurdwara, felt that the pilot had especially singled out a fellow soldier for his greetings. In reply he clicked his heels together, stood to attention, and *salaamed* the pilot. A soldier is a soldier. To salute is second nature.

'God save the king, Saheb! God save the King!' he cried in an impassioned voice as the plane flew over. Kishan Singh particularly wanted to see whether or not the British pilot would wave to the Muslims on the roof of the Sheikh's house. Though he couldn't see what actually happened, he decided that the pilot had withdrawn his hand as he flew over the Sheikh's house. It made Kishan Singh happy.

'Saheb!' he cried, 'If only you had come two days earlier it would have saved us from so much loss and ruination. But never mind...'

Then Kishan Singh in his excitement clenched his fist and waved it in the direction of the Sheikh's house, shouting '*Muslas*, why have you stopped firing? I'm standing here. Go on, fire at me! Shoot if you dare!'

He stood gesticulating for a while, then started dancing like a mad man.

Teja Singh wanted to personally make it to the city to give a detailed account of the happenings to the Deputy Commissioner. He must make a list of the loss sustained by the Sikhs of the village. Then he wondered if it would serve any useful purpose to report at all to the high-ups. It all seemed so futile. But never mind, the Sikhs had given it to these *Muslas* blow for blow. They would never dare fight them again.

Standing at the back of the gurdwara the fat butcher's son emptied the bottle of kerosene in the drain, then hid the empty container under the platform. He threw the wood shavings into the gurdwara through a window, then struck a match to light his cigarette. Pulling hard at the cigarette, he walked towards the Sheikh's house.

The plane flew over the village thrice before it went away.

The atmosphere of the village changed. People ventured out. The fighting seemed to have stopped and dead bodies were being disposed of. People went back to their houses to assess their losses in terms of clothes and ornaments. The Nihang Sikh and volunteers began to clean and repair the gurdwara. At the Sheikh's behest the mosque was also being cleaned and swept.

The villages over which the plane had flown stopped beating their drums. The slogan-mongering also stopped and, with it, the arson and pillage.

Chapter 19

The moment you stepped out of your house and came on to the road you sensed a change in the atmosphere of the city. Across the road, in front of the mosque of *Mohalla* Qutubdin, there were four armed soldiers sitting in chairs. As you walked along the road you came across one or two armed soldiers at regular intervals standing by the roadside or sitting on the front plinth of some house. The army had been deployed in the city. On the fourth day of rioting, an eighteen hour curfew had been imposed on the city which on the following day had been reduced to twelve hours—from six in the evening to six the following morning. It was said that the Deputy Commissioner and the City Magistrate had gone round the city in an armoured car, along with armed soldiers.

Here and there, shopkeepers ventured to resume business though, as a matter of precaution, they kept only one door of their shops open. On the main thoroughfares, members of the mounted police went in pairs, riding sleek-looking horses, loaded pistols dangling from their holsters. The government offices, schools and colleges were still closed. You could still come across a handful of people holding spears in some lanes. Because of the curfew and deployment of the military, the edge of the rioting had been completely blunted. People started cautiously coming out of their houses, and went from from one *mohalla* to another; all the while looking around for lurking danger. It was said that two refugee camps were shortly going to be set up in the city and the cantonment, which would take care of the uprooted people of the twenty villages in the area. The two government hospitals in the city and the cantonment had already been thrown open for admission of riot victims. Additionally, collecting centres for dead bodies had been established. The Deputy Commissioner's name figured in every rumour. A pipe pressed between his lips, he seemed to be everywhere at the same time. It was said that while going on a round of the city just after the curfew hours he had seen a youth standing outside the hospital. He had twice challenged the youth to reveal his identity and had then shot him dead on the spot. This rumour had a salutary effect on the rioteers.

A relief centre had been opened in a school, on behalf of the Congress; people from the villages flocked there day and night. The Deputy Commissioner visited the centre thrice. The government was keen to restore normalcy in collaboration with public-spirited social bodies. Encouraged by the government's attitude, the leaders of these organizations started taking a keen interest in the centre. Even the government officials tried to promote social work with the result that the impression about the Deputy-Commissioner changed radically in political circles. They said, he may be a cog in the wheel of the Imperialistic machine but at the same time he is a truly good man. It was said that the evening he had shot the man dead in front of the hospital he had felt so remorseful that he had not been able to sleep the whole night. Professor Raghunath maintained that this man was in reality not cut out for administrative work. He was a man of wide sympathies and scholarly leanings, highly sensitive and polished. The government had been unjust to him by posting him here. Of course, some people had not stopped denigrating him; they openly said that he was the cause of all the trouble.

While making a round of the city, Richard's jeep stopped in front of the Health Officer's house. He had sent word that he would be calling at his house. The Health Officer had discarded his dress suit and instead wore a silk *kurta*, a crisply starched, flowing *salwar* and Peshawar sandals. His wife had made arrangements to serve the Deputy Commissioner coffee or tea— whatever he preferred.

As the Saheb stepped into the courtyard the aroma of his tobacco filled the air. He refused to have any tea or coffee. He talked to the Health Officer for about five minutes.

'You look fine!' he said, effusively shaking hands with the Health Officer. 'I'm glad even in such difficult times you take good care of your person. You look fine in Indian dress.'

Then he shook hands with the Health Officer's wife. 'It seems the day has not started for you! How lucky!' The Health Officer's

204

wife was still wearing a dressing gown. 'Please once again check up the water arrangements at the refugee camp,' he said to the Health Officer. 'I find they have not laid the drainage pipes yet.' He shook his head and smiled a smile which seemed to express disapproval. He had told the Health Officer about it two days ago yet nothing had been done about it till now.

'I've arranged for everything. The work will start from today.'

'Good!' The Deputy Commissioner smiled again. 'There's fear of an epidemic in the village in which the women jumped into a well. You must visit that village.'

The Health Officer looked surprised. The village people were already migrating to the city in search of refuge. What good would his visit do? But he marvelled at the Deputy Commissioner. Nothing escaped his notice.

'It's the third day,' The Deputy Commissioner said. 'The dead bodies must have started putrifying. You must disinfect the well. And you must go there tomorrow morning. I've arranged for a bus for you. There's no risk involved. Two armed policemen will accompany you.'

The Deputy Commissioner had his finger not only on the pulse of the city but also on that of the entire district.

The Health Officer's wife who had excused herself, returned. She had freshly done her hair and had changed. She pressed the Deputy Commissioner to have some tea.

The Deputy Commissioner smiled. 'There will be time for tea, Mrs Kapur. But not now. Thank you.' Then he added: 'Well, you'll have to help us a little. Two thousand cots will be delivered at the refugees' camp this afternoon. We have also to arrange for clothes. It's rather urgent. It will help if we can form a small relief committee.' Richard smiled.

This was one great thing about Richard. Though he gave people the impression that he was seeking advice, in effect he was laying down orders. But it was all so subtly done. The Health Officer's wife, for instance, felt honoured by what Richard had said; she would get an opportunity to work with the Deputy Commissioner's wife. What more could she ask for? But before she could say anything the Deputy Commissioner had already crossed the vestibule along with the Health Officer.

'How about disposing of the dead bodies? I think the Municipal Committee should be entrusted with the job. We must not allow

205

the public to meddle with it. It will only create more trouble.'

The Health Officer was in complete agreement with his views.

'It has been done before. Throw the dead bodies *en masse* into a big hollow and burn them. If they are allowed to take out funeral processions for each one of them it will only increase the tension.'

The Health Officer again whole-heartedly approved of the Deputy Commissioner's suggestion and said: 'First they fly at each another's throats and then they want the government to take care of their dead.'

The Deputy Commissioner glanced at the Health Officer 'Well, let's get going. We've no time to waste.' He nodded thoughtfully and got into his jeep.

Ten minutes later he was in the office of the Relief Committee where some prominent figures of the city had been called and was giving them an account of the relief measures proposed by the government.

'The bazars have opened,' he began. 'Four wagons of coal have arrived at the railway station. Ten more will arrive by Tuesday. We must continue the dusk to dawn curfew for a few days more. The army will also stay on for a couple of days more. The police will continue its daily rounds. The dead bodies have been removed from the city. The government will itself undertake their disposal. The post offices will re-open this afternoon but the delivery of the mail that has piled up cannot be taken in hand immediately. All the mail has been collected at the Head Post Office. You need not fear. All the registered letters and packets have been taken good care of and will be duly delivered.'

Richard continued: 'I would appreciate it if our social bodies could assist the government at the refugee camps. Adequate arrangements have been made for the supply of rations. Tents have been pitched. We shall now require some doctors and many more volunteers to look after the refugees.'

Richard had recognized many of the men in the audience. He had even been able to guess some of what they were thinking. For instance, he had seen Manoharlal standing near the door. Dark and fat Manoharlal stood there with his hands awkwardly folded against his chest, a fixed smile on his face. His eyebrows would go up at the Deputy Commissioner's each sentence. Richard knew the man required watching. For it had not been in his interest to stop the riots nor was he sympathetic to the government.

The other man he looked for was the Communist, Devdutt. Over the past year Richard had twice sentenced him to three months in jail. The man had, however, tried his best to prevent the rioting and indeed had not in any way relaxed his efforts while the riots were on. He had tried all along to get the Congress and the Muslim League to come together and devise some means of maintaining the peace. Even now he stood for peace.

The Congress was represented by Bakshi and a few others. He knew all of them—most of them being lawyers with whom he came in contact in the course of his duties. In the same audience he spotted another man who swore both by the Congress and the Socialist Party and was at the same time in the C.I.D.This man could put up a show, shout slogans at a meeting, stage a walkout or abuse the government.

Richard tactfully avoided antagonising any section of the audience. He merely put forward his suggestions and sat down.

The moment he sat down, Lala Lakshmi Narain got up and said. 'We would like to assure the Deputy Commissioner Saheb that all the civic and social bodies and the public at large will co-operate fully with the government. It is our good fortune that we have such an able and sympathetic officer at the helm of affairs in this district...'

Richard stood up. He took leave of the Relief Committee and left Lakshmi Narain and some lawyers ran out to see him off. The meeting had not lasted for more than fifteen minutes. Then those standing and watching Richard's jeep drive off heard someone whispering in a voice filled with scorn. 'Here we have only toadies, ever ready to lick the government's shoes. But we are not afraid of any one. We have the courage to call a spade a spade. Who's responsible for these riots? Now the government has imposed the curfew. Why didn't it impose the curfew then? What was the Saheb Bahadur doing at that time? I'm not afraid of any one. I've the courage to speak the truth... 'The man was Manoharlal.

Someone said: 'Let things alone. It will serve no purpose to raise controversies at this stage.'

The members of the Relief Committee were about to disperse when Bakshiji said to Manoharlal, 'You may abuse the government to your heart's content. But its not going to work. How are you going to benefit by abusing the government?' You had better ply the spinning wheel and clean the streets. Politics is not meant for you.' Bakshiji said, 'What good is your shouting like that? Don't I know that the Britishers are at the root of this rioting? Gandhiji has said so a dozen times.'

'Then what have you done about it?' Manoharlal asked.

'What haven't we done, tell me that first? We have been to the Muslim League asking it to help us in maintaining peace in the city. We have been to the Deputy Commissioner asking him to call in the army and stop these riots. Tell me, what more can we do? Now that the harm is done should we help the people in distress or abuse the government? You call yourself a revolutionary. Is this all that the revolutionaries are capable of?'

'Bakshiji, I know how things are. Don't force me to open my mouth. The Congress members are there because they want to benefit by bagging contracts for making supplies to the refugee camps. Do you want me to name these persons?'

'If these people go in for contracts it is their affair not mine. Tell me, where do I come into the picture? I'm just not concerned.'

'You've given these very persons positions of importance in the Congress.'

A volunteer came up and putting his arm around Manoharlal's waist drew him away from the scene.

'Leave me alone, *yaar!*' 'Manoharlal protested. 'I know these people, the class they belong to. Gandhiji, sitting far away at Wardha calls the tune and these people dance to it blindly. They are not capable of thinking for themselves. Tell me, what was the point in calling the Deputy Commissioner for this meeting?'

Manoharlal's friend dragged him away. At the gate Manoharlal said. 'Have you got a cigarette on you?' he asked his friend. 'I feel like blowing some smoke.'

They sat down by the gate.

The Deputy Commissioner gone, Bakshiji was now free to air his views.

'True, it's the Englishmen who foment trouble,' he said to himself. 'First, they let the sparks fly and then they put out the fire. First they starve the people and then they feed them. They drive the people out of their houses and then rehabilitate them.'

Since the start of the riots, Bakshiji's mind had remained clouded; he could not think clearly. The Englishman, he thought, had again scored over him. He could see that it was the Englishman who had again master-minded the whole game.

*

As Richard did his rounds of the city, Liza sat in the bungalow, feeling utterly bored.

She came out of her bedroom into the hall. The *almirahs* were crammed with books to the point of bursting. They were such an eyesore to her. Time seemed to have come to a standstill; nothing moved, as if everything was struck dead. If anything possessed life, it was the Buddhas' and the Bodhisattvas' eyes which looked at her from dark corners, weaving webs of treachery and deceit. She was afraid of coming into this big room in the evenings. The stone figurines, resting in various corners of the room, looked like poisonous serpents ready to strike with their deadly fangs.

She moved into the dining room. She always felt more at ease in this room. It was softly lit and had flower vases. She liked flower vases, but not statues of stone or books. In the mellow light of the dining room one could easily forget so many unpleasant things. In fact, soft light like this was so conducive to making love, to lazing about, to relaxing. Tears stung her eyes. Suddenly the mellowness of the room seemed to have changed into a disagreeable stillness. Suppressing a sob, she got up and going into the verandah shouted for the bearer.

'Yes, Mem Saab!' the bearer's voice came from far off, through many layers of walls.

A duster resting on his shoulder, the bearer soon came trotting along on flat padded feet and stood before her. It was getting on to four. He knew what she wanted. She generally gave up the struggle at about this time. 'Beer!' she would howl at the bearer. 'Get me a cold beer!'

Bitterly Liza returned to the dining room. She had appeared before the bearer wearing only a house-coat, its waist sagging open, untied...In this wilderness she had nothing to fall back upon except beer—the only thing which could help her forget herself.

Richard returned at about eight in the evening. Liza had passed out and was asleep on the sofa. There was still a small quantity of beer left in the bottle beside her. Liza's head hung down from the sofa and her dishevelled hair covered half her face. Her housecoat had pulled up, exposing her legs to the knees.

'To hell with this country! To hell with such a life!' Richard muttered as he stood before the sofa.

When he returned to the bungalow he always felt as if he had been transported into another world. Inside the bungalow he had created a small England for himself. The outside world existed for him only as a means to earn a living wage, whereas his real life began and ended within the confines of the bungalow—his books, his statues—his very own life. He sat down on the edge of the sofa and kissed Liza on her cheek. The body which he held in his arms at night as a matter of duty and courtesy now looked to him inert, lifeless and unattractive—no more than a lump of flesh. Liza had again started putting on weight and crow's feet had formed under her eyes. When he saw her in this state he only felt a dull anger.

'Liza!' he bent down and shouted in her ear, pushing away her hair from her forehead.

Liza was in a semi-conscious state. Richard shook her shoulders. Then finding her in no condition to join him at dinner, he carried her into the bedroom, and put her to bed. Her housecoat felt damp against him and he looked at the sofa. There was a patch of wetness on it. Liza had pissed again on the sofa.

Richard's mind filled with revulsion. The sharp, acrid smell of the urine leapt to his nose and he shook his head. So the same story was repeating itself. Liza had only recently returned from London and already she was in the state she had been in before she left. Did she mean to go away again? So soon? Either he must let her go or get himself transferred to some other station where life would be more congenial for her.

As he looked at the sofa Richard was reminded of something and he smiled. When he was transferred here he had bought the sofa from Mr. Lawrence, the Commissioner, who was himself going on transfer to Lucknow. When he had removed the sofa cover, Richard had seen a similiar stain to the one he could see now. He had heard that the Commissioner's wife was also bored most of the time, drank heavily and frequently wet the sofa. As a result, the Commissioner sought transfers from place to place in the hope that he would at last find a place that would please his wife. Eventually Lawrence's wife had deserted him and married a young captain in the army. Richard looked at his wife and then at the sofa. Would he also meet a similar fate? Liza stirred into life.

'What's the matter, Richard? Where are you taking me?'

'Your gown is wet Liza. I am taking you to your room.'

Liza shook her head petulantly.

After dumping Liza on the bed Richard sat down on a chair by her side.

'Care to have dinner, Liza?' he asked.

'Dinner? What dinner?'

Richard felt like clutching her shoulders and shaking them violently to wake her up. But he checked the impulse and just stared at her as she lay sprawled on her bed.

Lifting her head she asked suddenly:

'Richard, are you a Muslim or a Hindu?' She gave him a faint smile.

'When did you come? I never saw you coming. Have you come for lunch or for dinner?'

For an instant, Richard thought that she was saying all this in jest, that she was feigning drunkenness. He sat down on the edge of her bed and put his hand her shoulder.

'I've no respite from work these days. You know that, of course,' he said. 'They have burnt down the grain market and one hundred and three villages in the countryside have been affected by fire.'

'You mean as many as one hundred and three villages!' Liza exclaimed. 'I knew nothing about it. I just kept sleeping while the villages burnt,' Liza continued in a plaintive voice. 'You should have told me, Richard. You should have woken me up and told me about it. Such a terrible thing has happened and you didn't whisper a word to me about it.'

'Go to sleep, Liza. Change your clothes and go to sleep. You're feeling sleepy.'

'Lie down by my side. I can't sleep alone.'

'Sleep Liza! I've still a lot of work to do.'

'So many villages have been burnt down. Now what more work remains for you to do?'

Richard looked sharply at her. Was she joking? Had she started hating him that she talked to him like that? Or, perhaps like all

211

drunk people she was just babbling.

She got up, staggered forward sat down in Richard's lap.Placing her arms round his neck she cuddled up against him.

'I know you don't love me,' she said , fondling his head. 'I know everything. Richard, how many of them were Hindus and how many Muslims? You must know everything. What's a grain market?'

Richard looked at her, wordlessly. He felt a great revulsion for her, more so because she was drunk. The more she drank the more he disliked her. At such times she was nothing but a lump of flesh for him. Such a relationship did not last long. Richard's eyes remained fixed on Liza's face. Should he leave her? He had to think of her in the context of his career! A decisive moment had arrived in his career. He must ensure that he handled the situation with finesse and tact, that the people's discontent did not go to the extent of throwing his government off its balance. Till now he had handled things with great shrewdness. People had been impressed by his honesty and integrity. What he had done so far had had the desired effect. Perhaps it would be best to suffer Liza for a while, specially at this stage.

He bent down and kissed Liza on her cheek. 'Listen, Liza,' he said with forced heartiness. 'Tomorrow I've to go to Sayyedpur. I must have that well thoroughly disinfected in my presence. Several women committed suicide there. It would be nice if you could come with me. From there we can make a detour to Taxila. The museum at Taxila is worth a visit. How about coming? It's a beautiful area.'

Liza looked at Richard with sleepy eyes.

'Why do you want to take me there?' she asked. 'To see burning villages? I don't want to see anything, or go anywhere with you.'

'No, no, you must come. There's no sense in sitting at home all the time. Now conditions have changed. Now you can freely move about. The countryside around here is really very beautiful.' Richard kept up his attitude of cheeriness with an effort. 'The other day while passing through an orchard near Sayyedpur,' he continued, 'I heard a lark singing. I was really surprised. A lark in a warm climate! But larks migrate here in the thousands during this season. There are many other species of birds which you've never seen before.'

'Is this the same place where those women were drowned?'

'Yes, the very same place. The river flows by the well and we have orchards across the river.'

Liza smiled. Then the smile vanished. She said:

'What kind of man are you, Richard? Even in such places you've an eye only for birds. You can only hear the larks singing.'

'There's nothing very surprising about it. The Civil Service hardens our feelings. If we turned sentimental we wouldn't be able to carry on the administration even for a day.'

'Even when one hundred and three villages burn down?'

'Not even then.' Richard said after a brief pause. 'It's not my country. Nor are they my countrymen.'

Liza gaped at Richard.

'Richard, you said you were going to write books about these men. Books about their origin.'

'Writing is something different. It has nothing to do with administration.'

Seeing that Liza was silent, Richard continued: 'Today I asked the Health Officer's wife to collect clothes for the refugees. We are establishing two camps for the refugees from the villages. I've assured her that you will help her. We want clothes for the refugees and food and toys for their children. This will also give you an opportunity to go round the city.'

Liza was still silent. Richard bent down and kissed her cheek and stroked her hair.

'I'm sorry, Liza. I can't spend more time with you. I've a lot of work to do. Infact I should have been at my desk long ago.' He got up. 'See you later. Don't wait for me, dear. And as for a visit to the country side you must be ready in the morning. We shall start at eight.' He left the room.

Liza sat there a long time, staring blindly at the open door. She felt sick and frightened. The empty room seemed suddenly very threatening. She shivered.

Chapter 20

'We want statistics, nothing but statistics. Just try to understand! I don't want stories. I want the bare figures—how many died, how many were injured and the extent of their financial loss!'

The Records Clerk of the Relief Committee, a register lying open before him, flared up regularly but nothing seemed to register on the minds of the refugees. And though one did the same thing day after day one discovered so many loopholes. And the worst of it, one had not covered even two villages.

It was so difficult to make these people understand. One could not be gruff with them and turn them out of the office. They all barged into the office and started speaking at the same time. Sometimes the Records Clerk wondered in great distress whether he was working in an office or whether in a railway station. Imagine hundreds of them shouting together to catch his ear, bursting with tales of their woes. But how could one be hard on them? They were homeless, down and out, utterly ruined. They would lean over his table and plead with him to hear them out. And once they started they would go on and on. At this rate it would take two months to compile the data of one village alone.

'I don't want your stories!' the *Babu* admonished the man in front of him. 'I want figures...'But Kartar Singh, who was sitting in front of his table with folded hands, continued as before: '"Imdad Khan!" I reminded him again, "we have played together, grown up together. You seem to have forgotten me. The morning has just begun. Do you think I'll start the day with a lie? Oh, no, not me! May *Vah Guru* save me from telling a lie." The truth is Imdad did not take the initiative. He did not attack us first...'

The *Babu* looked at Kartar Singh annoyed. He wanted figures and these people were wasting his time by showing him their wounds.

'The chopper hit me on my forehead, just over my eye. *Babu*ji, would my eye be saved? Grandfather said, "Banta Singh, you must be careful. Don't remove the bandage from your eye." And as you can see, I've not removed the bandage...'

These were no figures, just mad words. And one person had monopolized the table.

The *Babu* questioned the next man without taking his eyes off his register.

'Name?'

'Harnam Singh.'

'Father's name?'

'*Sardar* Gurdial Singh.'

'Village?'

'Dhok Ilahi Buksh.'

'Tehsil?'

'Noorpur.'

'How many Hindu and Sikh homes?'

'Only one Sikh house. My house.'

The scribe raised his head from the register and looked at the man. He was old and looked tired.

'Rather surprising. But how did you escape?'

'I was on good terms with Karim Khan. In the evening when...'

The scribe raised his finger, gesturing him to stop. 'Any loss of life?'

'No. My wife and I escaped, complete in our limbs. My son, Iqbal Singh, was in Noorpur. But I've no news of him. My daughter, Jasbir Kaur was in Sayyedpur. She jumped into a well and died.'

The scribe again raised an admonitory finger. 'I'm asking you, was there any loss of life?'

'I've told you my daughter jumped into...'

'But she didn't die in your village?'

'No, not in my village.'

'Then keep to the facts. I'm not concerned with what relates to another village. Any financial loss?'

'My shop was burnt down. They looted everything. I had a trunk. That was also stolen. But two gold bangles that were in the trunk...I myself gave away the trunk to Ehsan Ali. Rajo, his wife was a very kind hearted woman. She...'

The scribe again lifted his finger in warning. Harnam Singh fell silent.

'How much was your shop worth?'

'Banto, how much was our shop worth?'

'I'm asking you. Tell me the total cost including the value of contents. Hurry up! I've other things to do.'

'Say, seven to eight thousand rupees. There was some land attached to it, at the back of the shop. And some...'

'Should I write down ten thousand rupees?'

'Yes sir, you may...'

'Do you want anything to be recovered?'

'Yes sir, a gun. A double barrelled gun. It's lying in Jalal Din *Subedar's* house in Adheron.'

'But you don't belong to Adheron, do you? You're from Dhok Ilahi Buksh, aren't you?'

'We had to flee from Dhok Ilahi Buksh. We kept walking the first night along the river bank. We spent the day in Ehsan Ali's house. At night we again resumed our journey. On the second day Jalal Din gave us refuge in Adheron. He's a good man. He gave us separate utensils for our use so that we could cook our own food untouched by any hand.'

'Stop. Tell me the name and address of that *Subedar*.'

Harnam Singh was bursting to tell the whole story. There were so many enquiries to be made. Was his son alive? But the scribe would not let him proceed. Every time he would raise his finger and ask him to keep to the question he was asking. And then he packed him off. 'You may go!' he said.

The Records Clerk always only jotted down what he thought was relevant. But although he tried his best to keep to facts, the Records Clerk could not help listening to the victim's stories which moved him deeply.

'Babuji, my Sukhwant may not have jumped into the well. Who knows, she may still be hiding somewhere in the village with her small son. I went running through the lane into my house to get my cot. At that time I saw many women emerging from the gurdwara, Sukhwant among them. How could I know where she was going? She was walking with lifted hands. She had lifted her hands while walking and had thrown her *dopatta* round her neck. When I returned with the cot, Sukhwant was still standing in the lane. I had seen her following the other women and then she stopped and stood there. My son, Gurmeet, was standing on the steps of the gurdwara. At that time the school building, which was immediately behind the gurdwara, had been set ablaze. When the flames leapt skywards it became intensely bright. Then they would dip down, creating weird patterns in light and shade. Sukhwant looked worried. Usually, she never lost her composure but that day she looked really worried. She didn't want to leave her son. She just stood there in the middle of the lane, watching the flames, her body shaking with fear. 'Sukho, what are you doing, standing there?' I shouted out to her. But there was no time to talk or think. If she had seen me she wouldn't have taken Gurmeet along. She would have left him to my care. She falteringly walked up to her son and then stopped. How could I know what was in her mind? Then a big roar went up outside the village, *'Ya Ali! Ya Ali!'* I saw Sukhwant rushing up to Gurmeet and lifting him in her arms. I stood there watching her. She had joined the other women. When I saw her last, she was still running, carrying Gurmeet in her arms, her green *dopatta* flying in the breeze. She was lost to sight round the corner and that was the end of it. I am only saying that after all Sukhwant might not have jumped into the well. Or she might have left Gurmeet behind before jumping. It could as well be that Gurmeet did not drown in the well. He may still be roaming about in the vicinity of the well. Why, sir, can't we find out what eventually became of him?'

But it was not the *Babu's* job to track down lost persons. To find out lost persons was Devraj's responsibility. To locate buried gold, to identify lost clothes, was Devraj's job.

'*Sardarji*, you must go to Devraj if you want your son to be traced. It's no use wasting your time with me. It's the third time that you've come to me. You keep repeating the same story. It's not my job to listen to your stories.'

But the *Sardar* made no sign of getting up from the table. He just sat there looking sadly at the Records Clerk. What brought the man to him, the clerk wondered. How to tell him he could do nothing for him?

In the end the clerk said : 'Next Tuesday a bus is going to your village. I'll tell Devraj to take you along. But don't tell anybody. Otherwise, the entire village will come flocking to me.'

The sentence, however, seemed to have created no impression on the *Sardar*. 'I must see everything with my own eyes', he said, as if explaining the matter to himself. 'It's just possible the boy is hiding somewhere. One can never be sure. The moment his eyes land upon me he will come bounding to me. "Can you find me? Tell me, where am I?" Every day he used to play blindman's bluff with me. He would hide now behind one door and now behind another.'

The Records Clerk slowly got up from his chair and went out into the balcony. A huge crowd was still waiting outside the office. They were sitting in small groups in the courtyard. The long platform behind the courtyard was crowded with them. This was where Vanprasthiji used to deliver his sermon every Sunday, bringing out the greatness of Vedic religion and philosophy.

'Ganda Singh, stop crying,' a voice fell on the clerk's ears. An old man was consoling his equally aged companion. 'Don't cry, Ganda Singh. Those who are gone have become dear to *Vah Guru*. They have sacrificed their lives for the sake of religion. They have become immortal.'

Vah Guru! Satnam. Sache Padshah!' Three Sikhs sitting on the steps muttered together.

The Records Clerk had just come onto the balcony when another Sikh approached him. The clerk smiled. Big protruding eyes, dough-like flabby body—the man pestered him every day. 'Any news for me?' he asked now. 'Have they made any arrangement for taking me to the village? I know the bus will be going there. But when?'

'I'll let you know as soon as it is arranged. It's not my job, though. Lala Devraj...'

'But you're going to help me, aren't you?' the man whispered. 'Remember, I'll sweeten your tongue...'

The clerk looked at the man, peeved. 'O, *Sardarji,* you must learn to talk sense. You know that twenty-seven women jumped into that well. How will you recognize your wife among them?'

'Leave that to me, brother. I can recognize her from her gold bangles. They weigh five *tolas* each. And she has a gold chain round her neck. I know she's dead. She must have met the same fate as the other twenty-six women. But how can I forget the bangles and the chain? Am I right, brother?'

He spoke with his mouth near the clerk's ear. 'You'll get your cut, of course. I mean it. That good woman should have thought of it in time. She knew that she was going to die. She should have removed the bangles and the chain and handed them to me before taking the plunge. What do you say to that, brother? Of course, I'll sweeten your tongue. But you must help me out first. Don't tell anybody about it. It's between you and me only.' Then he stood back and stared at the clerk. 'It's not necessary to carry anyone else in the bus. Only you and I.'

'Oh, *Sardarji*, her dead body must have swollen up by now and filled the whole well. How will you remove the bangles from her swollen wrists? You must learn to talk sense. Besides, you have to reckon with the government. Will the government allow you to take away the bangles?'

'Why not? She's my wife and they are my things. I had the bangles made with my hard-earned money. I've not stolen those bangles. We shall take a small chisel along. If it comes to that, we can also take a goldsmith's assistant with us. He can finish the job within minutes. As you know, where there's a will there's a way.'

'Oh, *Sardarji*, I'm asking you, when will you learn to talk sense? In the first place, the government will demand proof that she's your wife. It'll ask you to produce witnesses. It's not an easy job to identify a decomposed body.'

'Brother, that's where you come into the picture. It's your job. Haven't I promised to sweeten your tongue? Won't you do this small thing in exchange for what I've promised you?'

'*Sardarji*, that's exactly what I'm trying to hammer into your head. It's not my job. I only compile facts and figures. I've jotted down your wife's bangles and neck chain under 'Financial Loss'. It's not my job to retrieve these for you.'

The *Sardar* caught the clerk's hand. 'Don't be angry. Don't be angry, Babuji. The world's work goes on.' He sidled up to the clerk and, holding up his hand, ticked off three of its fingers. 'Right? So you agree, don't you?'

Three fingers stood for three score rupees.

'*Sardarji*, why are you wasting your time? There's nothing I can do about it.'

At this the *Sardarji* let go of the clerk's fingers and stood there scowling. Then he threw his *chaddar* about his shoulders and walked towards the stairs. He stopped at the top of the stairs.

'Oh, *Babu*, look!' He raised four fingers. 'Agreed?'

The clerk turned away.

'Have pity on us. We have lost all we had.' The *Sardar*, seeing the clerk wouldn't budge, sighed and climbed down the stairs.

219

The Records Clerk came down into the courtyard. He found it difficult to sit at his table for long stretches of time especially as he had to remain in the office till late in the evening. All the data collected in the course of the day was tabulated and classified in the late hours of the evening when the representatives of various newspapers turned up to collect the latest figures. One copy of the figures was sent to the Congress office. One copy was retained on file.

The mortality figures were more or less accurate. There could be two Hindus more or two Muslims less dead but that didn't matter. The financial losses mostly pertained to the Hindus and the Sikhs. Devdutt would often drop in to check the figures.

'What are today's figures?' he had asked one evening.

'Today we have compiled data relating to Noorpur Tehsil. The death figures relating to Hindus, Sikhs and the Muslims are more or less even. There are as many Hindus and Sikhs dead as there are Muslims.'

Devdutt had taken the register and stood there turning its pages and carefully scrutinizing the figures.

'Add one more column to the register,' he had said, returning the register. 'Of the dead, how many were rich and how many poor.? We must have a record of that also.'

'What's the big point? You always drag in the rich and the poor in every discussion.'

'There's a point, of course. This is also an important aspect of statistics. We must know how many haves and have-nots died on each side. This will have an important bearing on our social and economic set-up.'

The Records Clerk now recognized many of the refugees in the courtyard. He would find the same girl sitting by the side of the stairs. As on other days, she would sit there with her head bowed. Nobody had been able to find out whether her husband was still living or dead. Further on, he saw Harnam Singh, the man who owned the double barrelled gun. He looked distracted. His wife sat by him. The clerk turned his face away for he knew if Harnam Singh caught sight of him he would begin pestering him. A few Congressmen were having a heated discussion in one corner of the courtyard. Kashmirilal said: 'First answer my question. If someone attacks me how am I supposed to act. Should I join my hands and say, "Kill me! I believe in non-violence."'

'Who would want to kill you?' Shanker said with a laugh. 'You are the size of a sparrow. What good will it do anybody to attack you?'

'Why, does one ever attack a hefty wrestler?' Jeet Singh countered. 'One always attacks a weakling.'

'I'm not joking,' Kashmirilal said. 'I'm serious about it. I want to know how should one act on an occasion like this. What does the creed of non-violence enjoin upon us?' He looked at Bakshiji. But Bakshiji ignored his question.

'Bakshiji, I'm asking you,' Kashmirilal said with an edge to his voice. 'Don't try to evade my question.'

'I wasn't listening. What's it you want to know?'

'Bapuji says we should eschew violence. If someone attacks me during a riot how am I supposed to conduct myself? Should I face my assailant with folded hands and say, "Beat me up! Hack off my neck!" Tell me, what am I expected to do?'

'Gandhiji asks us not to give ourselves up to violent impulses. He does not say that we should not resist if someone attacks us.'

'Then what am I supposed to do?'

'If someone attacks you, ask him to wait, and run up to the Congress office and seek instructions,' Jeet Singh said.

'Bapu asks us to eschew violence. Tell the man that what he is doing is immoral. It's a sin. He's doing something wrong.'

'I say you must face him boldly,' Master Ram Das said.

'Face him boldly with what? I've only a spinning wheel in my house.'

'You're yourself the biggest spinning wheel to have come up with this discussion when the riots are over.'

'Don't try to laugh it off,' Jeet Singh said flippantly. 'It's a very serious matter.'

'Listen, sons,' Bakshiji, who had been listening quietly to the discussion, said, 'Our General had never to face a dilemma so far as this problem was concerned. He had never worried himself about how he was going to protect himself. He was semi-literate, slightly eccentric but he knew what to do if someone attacked him.'

They all became silent. They felt his loss deeply.

'These are nothing but pious sentiments,' Kashmirilal said, after a long pause.

'Listen,' Bakshiji said again. 'Eschew violence! That's point

221

number one. Try to bring the oppressor to your point of view, if there's time for it. That is point number two. And if he doesn't relent, face him boldly. A blow for a blow. That's point number three.'

'Bakshiji, you are absolutely right!' Jeet Singh said. 'That's what they call clear thinking. Kashmirilal, that should answer your question. Now shut up.'

But there was no stopping Kashmirilal. 'But you haven't told me how I am going to face him. With a spinning wheel as my weapon?'

'No, not with a spinning wheel!' Jeet Singh said. 'With a sword, of course? I'm permitted to carry a sword.'

'So I've a right to use a sword?' Kashmirilal said. 'Am I right Bakshiji?'

Bakshiji was silent.

'You can own a pistol too!' Jeet Singh said.

'No, not a pistol!' Shanker said. 'A pistol is the embodiment of violence. It's loaded with violence. Five times over!'

'And a sword—doesn't it stand for violence?'

'Yes. it does. But one has to use one's own strength to handle a sword. As for a pistol, you've only to press the trigger and the man falls dead.'

'So, may I keep a sword, Bakshiji?' Kashmirilal asked.

The Records Clerk sighed and resumed his walk. This kind of discussion sounded very silly to him.

Near the door opening into the verandah, sat a group of ten or twelve people laughing and joking among themselves. Between them lay sprawled an old Sikh, his laughing eyes showing through a thick pepper and salt beard. The people around him, apparently his friends, laughed as he banged his heels on the ground.

'Would you like to go back to your village, Nathu Singhji?' one of them asked.

Folding his legs, Natha Singh turned on his side, and, placing his hands on his thighs said, 'No, I won't go.'

'Why won't you go?'

'No, I won't go,' The man replied in a firm voice and pressing his knees together, swung his head from side to side.

'But why not? Surely, there must be a reason.'

'They circumcise you there!' He laughed again.

The school peon had his room across the verandah, on the

other side of the courtyard. He was sitting outside his room with his wife. His young daughter who lived in the village was missing and he had learnt that a coachman was keeping her in his house. The peon had approached the Records Clerk repeatedly to beg him to get his daughter back.

The clerk stopped in front of the peon and told him that a bus, escorted by armed police, would be leaving for Noorpur the following morning and he could go in that bus to locate his missing daughter.

The school peon, a Brahmin by caste, raised his head and looked at the clerk with lustreless eyes and then shook his head. 'It's no use,' he said. 'There's not a chance. I won't get my Prakasho back.'

'But you told me that a man in your village is keeping her in his house,' the clerk said. 'Surely, the police can retrieve her.'

The peon made no reply but his wife said: 'It's too late now. They must have already forced the 'bad thing' into her mouth.'

'Babuji,' the peon added, 'We don't even have two paisas in our pockets. How can we feed her when we ourselves have nothing to eat?'

The peon's reply did not cause the clerk any suprise. By now the words had become familiar.

Prakasho and her mother had apparently been collecting fuel-wood in the fields when trouble started in their village. Allah Rakha, who had had his eye on Prakasho for some time suddenly appeared along with his friends. He had rushed up and carried her away, wailing and struggling. He had then forced her to marry him.

For two days Prakasho refused to eat. She lay there crying all the time. Then she would sit up and keep staring at the walls with abstracted eyes. But on the third day she washed her face and accepted a bowl of buttermilk. She kept thinking of her father and mother but she knew that her poor, weak father was no match for Allah Rakha. Sometimes she would look out of the room she was imprisoned in. Outside the house, under a tree, she would see Allah Rakha's *tonga*. Prakasho was familiar with this *tonga*. Allah Rakha had invited her to have a ride in his *tonga* several times. He had harassed her when she had refused his invitations but she had never complained to her father about it. What could he do? And then during the riots, Allah Rakha had waylaid her in the fields and carried her away.

Prakasho was sitting on a cot in Allah Rakha's room when he came in and sat down in front of her.

'Eat!' he commanded her, untying a handkerchief in front of her.

'Eat! You daughter of a pig, eat!' he repeated. 'I've brought sweets for you.'

Prakasho raised her head and looked at the sweets. Three days had gone by since she had been abducted but she still did not have the courage to look at Allah Rakha.

'Eat!' Allah Rakha shouted. 'Why don't you eat, you daughter of a pig? Is it poison I'm asking you to eat?'

Forcing Prakasho's mouth open, he forced a piece of *burfi* into it.

She sensed Allah Rakha was trying to be kind, but how could she eat anything touched by a Mussalman's hand?

'I've picked it up from a Hindu shop!' Allah Rakha said, as he understood why she was reluctant to eat. 'Daughter of a pig, eat!' He laughed good-humouredly.

Prakasho looked at him now. She had seen him often but never so close. He had a thin black moustache. He had put collyrium in his eyes and oil in his hair and wore new, freshly pressed clothes.

Slowly chewing the piece of *burfi* she looked once again at Allah Rakha and her eyes fell on the black thread around his neck from which a talisman dangled. How clean and tidy he looked in his striped shirt.

'You eat also!' she said shyly.

Allah Rakha looked at her, startled. 'So you've spoken at last!' he cried.

Then he leaned over and clasped her in his arms. Timidly Prakasho hugged him back. She was amazed to find herself actually enjoying herself.

'When I went to fetch water from the stream why did you throw pebbles at me?' she asked.

'Because you refused to speak to me.'

'I had no business to speak to you.'

'But you're speaking now.'

Prakasho was silent for a while. Then she asked in a low voice:

'Where's my mother?'

'How should I know? Is she not at home?'

Tears came into Prakasho's eyes. She knew she had lost her parents and would never meet them again.

*

Most of the people in the courtyard of the Relief Office had undergone awful experiences. But they lacked the capacity to weigh, assess and understand if not forget those experiences. All they could do was stare vacantly into space or listen to the horror stories of the others. The Records Clerk's heart went out to them but what could he do? None of them knew what they wanted even if he had been able to help them. They didn't even have a hazy outline of the future. Time moved on relentlessly but they had no control over it. If hungry, they scurried about for food. If they remembered something, they just wept. Otherwise from morning until evening they just sat there listening to one another's tales.

Chapter 21

People started collecting in the college hall for the peace meeting. It was an appropriate venue, for the college was not run by the Hindus or the Muslims but by Christian missionaries. Its Principal too was not an Indian but an American missionary, Reverend Herbert, who was very popular with everyone. As there was still time for the meeting some of those present were pacing the verandah in small groups of twos and threes. Others were standing in the hall, exchanging views and comparing notes. All the people there were hand-picked representatives of various associations and organizations.

A stockily built, short-statured Hindu contractor was telling Sheikh Noor Ilahi: 'Now is the time to buy property. The prices are bound to go up later. I tell you, Sheikh Saheb, I know what's what. If you mean business I can talk it over with them. I can negotiate on your behalf.'

'One never knows. The prices may fall instead of going up,' Sheikh Saheb said.

'I can assure you, the prices are not likely to fall any further. I've myself sold at fifteen hundred rupees in that area.' He took Sheikh Ilahi by the elbow. 'Sheikh Saheb, tell me, when conditions revert to normal and peace is restored will prices come down or go up?'

'All right, just give me some more time to think.'

After the rioting in the city Hindus and Sikhs were pulling out of Muslim areas and Muslims were evacuating from the Hindu and Sikh pockets. So there was lots of land for sale.

'Yes, make up your mind,' the contractor said.

'But there's no time to waste. I'll try and bring it down by another fifty rupees or so. It's a good bargain, you shouldn't miss it. You want a house in a Muslim locality and one located on the

226

main road, don't you?'

'Well, I'll let you know soon.'

If Sheikh Noor Ilahi had lingered there for another two minutes the Contractor Munshi Ram would have clinched the deal with him. But Sheikh Saheb managed to escape from the Contractor's clutches and joined a group of Municipal Commissioners who were standing close by. Munshi Ram looked around and spotting Babu Prithvi Chand walked up to him.

'Is the house adjacent to yours still on sale?'

'Call it a house? It's a pigeon hole.'

'Even if it is a pigeon hole I'll advise you to buy it. It will be going dirt cheap. If you join it up with your own house it will make a spacious house.'

'And if Pakistan comes into being?'

'Forget about it. These are nothing but politician's fibs. What harm is it going to do to you even if Pakistan is established. People are not going to run away from here. They will stay where they are.'

Munshi Ram did not want to waste time for rarely were so many affluent people assembled at one place.

'If peace is restored nobody is going to desert his own locality,' Babu Prithvi Chand said.

'What makes you say so, Babuji?' Munshi Ram said. 'You had better get rid of this idea. From now on no Hindu will live in Muslim *mohallas* and no Muslim in Hindu *mohallas*. What I'm saying will come to pass. Regard it as a line etched on stone which cannot be obliterated. Pakistan or no Pakistan it is very clear that each community is going to live in watertight *mohallas*.'

Sheikh Noor Ilahi saw Lala Lakshmi Narain in the distance. As he drew nearer, Sheikh Noor Ilahi said, 'There comes a *karar!* So you have brought it off! You had a big hand in this rioting, I learn.' The people standing around started laughing.

Lala Lakshmi Narain and Noor Ilahi were very free with each other. Both had studied together in the Mission School. Both had interests in the cloth business.

'One can never trust a *karar*! Don't you agree?' Sheikh Noor Ilahi teased, deep laughter lines appearing under his eyes.

Seeing the banter between the two men *Sardar* Mohan Singh, who was standing a little apart from them, turned to his neighbour and said: 'We have all to live here. Madness may get the better of us for a while but it's a fact that we have all to live together. Ordinary, day-to-day quarrels don't mean anything, really. Even the kitchen utensils when put together battle. Neighbours quarrel but still they live together. A neighbour is like one's right hand.'

Lala Lakshmi Narain and Sheikh Noor Ilahi hugged each other. Though they were fundamentalists they had grown up playing together. Good friends, there was a lot of affection between them. But now it was difficult to say where Sheikh Noor Ilahi's innocent raillery ended and his hatred for the Hindus began.

'I had your bales removed from your godown in good time,' the Sheikh said to Lakshmi Narain.

Lakshmi Narian smiled at him gratefully.

'First, I said to myself, let the things burn,' the Sheikh laughed. 'They are Lakshmi Narain's bales, not mine. Let them burn. Then I said, no, he's my friend, after all!'

The people standing around were deeply touched.

A harmless joke and the tone was just right. But it lacked that something which brings two friends closer. At heart both were estranged. But both were traders and they knew now to mask their real feelings. Their self interest dictated that they should feign friendship.

Leaning against a pillar, Hayat Baksh was describing a city he had recently visited.

'A beautiful city, Sardarji,' he said. 'Beautiful like a bride. In the evening when the lights were on, everything started dazzling along the sea. I wish I knew how to describe it. It was like a bride. Clean, beautiful roads. You didn't feel like taking your eyes off the scene.'

'Hayat Baksh, which city are you talking about?'

'Rangoon. A beautiful city. I had gone there during the War. I just can't describe its beauty.'

All the people there were deliberately avoiding a serious discussion of the riots. Otherwise, what had a beautiful city to do with a burning grain market and devastated villages?

At the other end of the verandah, old Prithvi Chand was talking in his thin shrill voice to the people gathered round him. 'I tried to drive some sense into their heads,' he said in his thin piping voice. "Don't be foolish," I said. "You think you can protect yourselves by putting up an iron gate at the mouth of your lane?" What a silly idea! "Have some sense," I told them. "If an outsider wasn't able to get in, neither would you be able to get out. Surely, you don't want to have a prison gate at the entrance to your lane!"'

Lala Shamlal, a member of the Congress Committee, had collared the Records Clerk. Pushing him into a corner he said : 'Come, let's have a chat. Whom have they selected as the Congress candidate from our ward for election to the Municipal Committee?'

'I don't know, Lalaji. At present they are all preoccupied with relief work.'

'Not everybody. You're, of course, engaged in this work. I can vouch for that. But not everybody. Surely, you must have heard some name or the other. Who is it?'

'Lalaji, I really don't know. But I doubt if there will be any Municipal election this time—not under these circumstances?'

'The world's work never stops, son. Work must go on. I've already met the Deputy Commissioner and I know. The election will be held two months from now. June 15 is the last date for filing nominations. Which means there's very little time left.'

'I know nothing, Lalaji.'

'Son, one should keep one's eyes and ears open. We are not going to last for long. You young men will have to step into our shoes.' He whispered to the clerk. 'I'm going to stand for election this time.'

The Records Clerk looked at Lalaji surprised.

'I hear the Congress had decided to give the ticket to Mangal Sain,' Lalaji said.

'Lalaji, what do you require a Congress ticket for?' The clerk asked and immediately realized that had asked a stupid question. No Hindu could hope to win an election without the support of the Congress, nor could a Muslim win without the League's backing. People now regarded the Congress as a purely Hindu organization.

'Won't the Congress earn a bad name by adopting a person like Mangal Sain as its candidate?' Lala Shamlal asked the clerk. 'I tell you, Mangal Sain runs a gambling joint. Not one, but two. He runs them with the connivance of the police. When Gandhiji or Nehru come to the city he dances attendance on them. But tell me, does that make him a Congressite? He does not even wear khadi.'

'Yes, he does.'

229

'He might have started wearing it now. In fact, he started wearing khadi only two years ago. He never wore it before. In fact no one else wears khadi in his house.'

Lalaji had got a willing listener and so he became garrulous. 'He even drinks beer,' he said. 'If you don't believe me go to the Company Bagh Club and check up for yourself. Even his father was a notorious person. And so is the son.' Lalaji looked disdainful. 'Do you know the father was suffering from fistula. He died of fistula, in fact. Mark my word, the son will also die of the same disease.'

The clerk didn't know what kind of a disease fistula was. He wondered why Lala Shamlal disliked Mangal Sain so much.

'If I take the lid off his misdeeds,' Lala Shamlal continued, 'he will stand exposed before the public. But I tell myself what's the use. I believe in live and let live. How am I concerned with what he does and what he does not do? All I want him to do is stop cheating people.'

'Lalaji, Mangal Sain is a member of the District Congress Committee whereas you're not even a four-anna member. How can you establish your claim to a ticket? You're not entitled to it.'

'Who's asking for a ticket? All I want is that the Congress should not nominate a candidate from my ward. Let everyone stand as independent candidates.'

Some distance from them, Lala Lakshmi Narain was discussing a herbal medicine with Hayat Baksh. It was good for stones in the kidney. Hayat Baksh prepared the medicine and distributed it free. Only, he did not tell anybody the formula for he had a superstition that if he did so the medicine would lose its efficacy.

Lakshmi Narain's son, Ranvir, had hurt himself. He had stumbled over a drain, spraining his foot and grazing his knee. Hayat Baksh listened carefully to Lakshmi Narain while he was describing the nature of the injury. 'No, no, no oil massage!' he said emphatically when Lakshmi Narain told him how he proposed to treat the wound. 'It has a 'cold' effect on the system. I've a special oil which Ashraf has brought from Lahore. It will relax the veins, bringing quick relief. I'll send some of it for your son.'

Then, he lowered his voice, and asked, 'How did the poor boy get hurt?' Getting no reply, he dropped his voice to a whisper and said: 'I've heard he has joined some fundamentalist organisation. Take my advice and send him away for some time. He may fall foul of the police. It's risky.'

Lala Lakshmi Narain looked blankly at Hayat Baksh and said, 'He's just fifteen. Of what use can he be to a secret organization?' But secretly he approved of Hayat Baksh's suggestion. He must send his son away for some time.

Two college peons were sitting on a bench outside the college gate talking. One of them said 'Only foolish people like us suffer in these riots. The rich and those coming from good families don't fight. The Hindus, the Sikhs and the Muslims—they are all here. Just watch them. How friendly they are with one another!'

All the political leaders had arrived, except Bakshiji. Devdutt, of the communist Party, had personally gone round and left word with each one of them. Bakshiji arrived. Devdutt was glad that at long last the leaders of the Congress and the Muslim League had assembled in one place. It was a measure of Devdutt's shrewd- ness that he had suggested the name of Principal Herbert as Chairman of the meeting. An American mature in years, Principal Herbert had taught three generations of the city's families. He took the chair to the accompaniment of thunderous clapping.

At the very start an argument started between a young Muslim Leaguer and a Hindu Congressman.

'We shall claim Pakistan by force!' the young Muslim cried.

'Bakshiji, stop this trickery. You must accept the fact that the Congress is a Hindu organization and can represent only the Hin- dus. Own this fact publicly and I'll hug you to my heart right now. The Congress cannot represent the Muslims.' It was the same argument that had been bruited about before the riots started.

Someone shouted. 'Pakistan Zindabad!'

'Silence! Silence!' Scores of voices protested.

Principal Herbert addressed the gathering : 'I strongly feel the time has come to improve the atmosphere of the city. Most of the prominent people of the city are present in this meeting, their words will have a salutary effect on the people. I suggest we should form a Peace Committee which will propagate peace in each *mohalla*, street and lane of the city. The Peace Committee should comprise all important political institutions of the city. If we can arrange for a bus, fitted with a microphone and a louds- peaker, to go round the city it will have a very positive effect on the people...'

The proposal was greeted with loud clapping.

'I take it upon myself to arrange for the bus,' offered Shah-nawaz. More clapping.

Devdutt stood up and said; 'I hear that the government is arranging for the bus.' Clapping again.

'In that case I'll meet the cost of the petrol,' Shahnawaz said.

'Wah! Wah!' There was a loud chorus of approval.

A man got up. 'Gentlemen, before we setttle the programme won't it be proper that we form the Peace Committee? We must select its members in a constitutional manner.'

Devdutt rose to his feet and said: 'I propose that we should have three Vice-Presidents on the Committee. In this connection I propose the name of Janab Hayat Baksh...'

'Wait!' Another man stood up. 'Let us first decide on the number. I personally think that we should have five Vice-Presidents. The more Vice-Presidents we have, the more effective would be the committee.'

A *Sardarji* had his own views on the matter. 'I'm of the opinion that we should have only three Vice-Presidents,' he said. 'A Hindu, a Muslim and a Sikh. You can enlarge the Executive Committee if you so desire and represent all interests on it.'

Devdutt said: 'Please remember one thing. It's a Peace Commit-tee. We must not think in terms of Hindus and Muslims.'

2'I suggest that all political parties should find a place on the Committee,' another man said. 'We should have Janab Hayat Baksh on behalf of the Muslim League, Bakshiji on behalf of the Congress and Bhai Jodh Singh should represent the Gurdwara Managing Committee. They should be given the positions of Vice-Presidents.'

'If you want to proceed on the basis of political parties why not have their Presidents on the Peace Committee. It is not necessary to recount their names.' It was Lala Lakshmi Narain speaking.

A man got up, excitedly. 'It pains me to note that you have mentioned three political parties but have completely ignored another political party. I mean the Hindu Sabha. Is the Hindu Sabha not a political party?'

'No, it's not a political party.'

'Then by the same token neither is the Gurdwara Managing Committee.'

Five or six persons stood up simultaneously.

'It's an insult to the Sikh community!' they said. Only the

232

Gurdwara Managing Committee represents the Sikhs.'

Devdutt got up in a huff. 'Gentlemen,' he cried, 'if we argue in this manner we won't transact any business. We must wage a war against the communal elements. It is not necessary to represent each community on the Committee. The point is that the Peace Committee should take care of every interest and we should have faith that its members will be able to speak for the Hindus, the Muslims and the Sikhs alike. Keeping that aspect in view I suggest that Janab Hayat Baksh, Bakshiji and Giani Jodh Singh should be appointed as the Vice-Presidents of the Peace Committee.'

'We agree! You're right! Please proceed!' the audience said. Someone started clapping. There was more clapping, giving those who were opposed to the suggestion no opportunity to speak. The proposal was carried unanimously.

Master Ram Das stood up, 'I propose Comrade Devdutt's name for the office of the General Secretary. He is a tireless worker and as you know it is through his efforts that we have today assembled here. The next few days are very crucial for all of us. The Peace Committee will have to conduct itself with great care and tact. For this, I feel Comrade Devdutt is the most suitable choice.'

'Are all young men of the city dead?' The question had been asked by Manoharlal who was, as usual, standing against a wall, his arms crossed over his chest. 'I ask, are only traitors, toadies, stooges of the government and Communists left for this job? Are all the well meaning young men dead? This election is a farce. I walk out from this meeting!' He turned to go out of the hall.

'Stop! Stop, *yar* Manoharlal! Must you oppose everything?'

Manoharlal, was in no mood to relent. 'Let me be, *yar*!' he said, 'I've seen the likes of them. Manoharlal believes in calling a spade a spade. He's not even afraid of his own father!' Some Congress members barred his way. One of them pushed him back into the hall.

'They are all stooges. I know them, one and all!'

'Silence! Silence!'

'I second Comrade Devdutt's name!'

'I support it!'

Clapping. The proceedings got under way. Many names were suggested for members of the Executive Committee—Lakshmi Narain, Maya Das, and Shahnawaz, among them.

Suddenly, at the back of the hall, many Muslims made for the door, Maula Baksh taking the lead. He cried as he walked: 'The Hindus, being in a majority, dominate this Committee. We can't join this Committee. We knew in advance that the Hindus were conspiring against us.'

Ten men, including Devdutt, rushed forward to stop them from going out. They kept arguing in the door for a long time. At last, after a protracted discussion, it was agreed that the Executive Committee would comprise fifteen members—seven Muslims, and eight Hindus and Sikhs in the proportion of five and three respectively.

Shahnawaz, Mangal Sain and Lakshmi Narain figured on the committee. Lala Shamlal was one of the persons who failed to find a place on the Committee. Nobody proposed his name. He kept pulling at the Records clerk's coat all the time, but the clerk hesitated. Finally Lala Sham Lal himself got up. 'I would request you to give me an opportunity to serve on the Committee,' he pleaded.

'All the seats have been filled,' Mangal Sain said, glaring at him. 'Please sit down!'

Another person promptly got up, 'I see no harm in it,' he said.

'One Hindu, one Muslim and one Sikh can easily be added to the committee.'

'No, that's not possible,' Mangal Sain said. 'There will be no end to it, once you start.'

They were still wrangling over it when they heard the loud honking of a vehicle. Devdutt rushed up to the Chairman and proclaimed: 'Gentlemen, the peace bus has arrived. Our first round will start from here. I would request our President, the Vice-Presidents and other members—as many of them as can be accommodated in the bus—to join us on this important mission. A loud-speaker has been fitted on the bus. The bus will address the public, turn by turn.' The bus was painted in large red and white stripes—the bus of peace. From the four corners of its roof flew Congress and Muslim League flags.

'Where's the Union Jack?' Manoharlal quipped.

Then the slogan shouting began.

'Hindu Muslim unity zindabad!'

'Peace Committee zindabad!'

People on the road looked at the bus curiously. A man sat next to the driver's seat holding a microphone and shouting slogans.

Many people did not know who he was but others did. Nathu had died in the riots. But if he were alive it would have taken him no time to recognize the man. It was Murad Ali—the dark-faced Murad Ali with the pointed moustache, his thin stick resting between his legs and his beady eyes darting in every direction.

Before the bus started there was another brief argument over who would occupy which seat. Who would sit in front and who at the back. Again, what kind of slogans would be raised and who would shout the first slogan.

It was decided that the Presidents of the Congress and the Muslim League would not sit one behind the other but would sit side by side near the driver.

For some time there was utter confusion. There was a general scramble for a place in the bus. People wanted to be dropped at their houses.

Manoharlal was very angry. 'It's either me or that Communist! I refuse to ride this bus with a traitor to our country!'

Devdutt who was standing on the footboard of the bus said: 'Manoharlal Saheb, it is not in my nature to talk behind others' back. We aren't the stooges of the Congress. We are revolutionaries, for we go by our convictions. It is necessary to establish peace in the city at this juncture. The leaders of all parties should join hands in achieving this. All of them have to be brought together on one platform in the interests of peace.'

'What peace are you talking of?' Manoharlal asked testily.

'Your white Saheb has already established peace—the peace of the grave.'

Standing on the verandah, Lala Shamlal kept talking about his candidature for the municipal elections. While he was busy laying everybody who came his way, Mangal Sain, his rival, jumped into the bus.

'Nobody told me that the bus was ready to leave!'

Lala Shamlal shouted as the bus started. He ran frantically after it and just managed to squeeze in. Bakshiji who was sitting by the side of the President of the Muslim League stared blankly at the road. He looked sad and pensive, 'Vultures will fly over the city!' he mumbled to himself.

'Many more vultures than you can see now.'

Just then Murad Ali, who was occupying the seat next to the driver, shouted a slogan loudly. The bus lurched forward on its peace mission to the echo of that slogan.

*

In the dim light of the dining room Richard and Liza were sitting at the dining table. Both wondered what the future would be like. Liza pulled herself together and looked quite composed. Richard didn't have much work to do. The city was fast reverting to normal and junior officials had taken charge.

'I wish I could stay here a little longer,' Richard said. 'I had some work to do at the Taxila Museum. But I'm afraid I may have to leave.'

Liza was secretly pleased at the news.

'Are you being transferred?' she asked. 'Does it mean a promotion?'

Richard made no comment. He just smiled.

'Why don't you tell me? Are you being promoted?'

'There's no question of promotion, Liza. It's the government's policy to transfer an officer from a station where rioting has taken place. A new officer takes over from him.'

'When are you going? Soon?'

'Maybe. I'm not certain though.'

'But you wanted to stay here. Didn't you? You said you wanted to spend some time at the Taxila Museum. To gather material for your book.'

Richard shrugged his shoulders. Then he lighted his pipe and stretching his legs under the table, relaxed. He smiled and said: 'Where do you want me to start?'

'Start what, Richard?' Liza looked surprised.

'You wanted to know what happened here, didn't you?'

This time it was Liza's turn to shrug her shoulders as if she wanted to say that it made no difference to her whether he told her or not.

MORE ABOUT PENGUINS

For further information about books available from Penguins in India write to Penguin Books (India) Ltd, B4/246, Safdarjung Enclave, New Delhi 110 029.

In the UK: For a complete list of books available from Penguins in the United Kingdom write to Dept. EP, Penguin Books Ltd, Harmondsworth, Middlesex UB7 0DA.

In the U.S.A.: For a complete list of books available from Penguins in the United States write to Dept. DG, Penguin Books, 299 Murray Hill Parkway, East Rutherford, New Jersey 07073.

In Canada: For a complete list of books available from Penguins in Canada write to Penguin Books Canada Ltd, 2801 John Street, Markham, Ontario L3R 1B4.

In Australia: For a complete list of books available from Penguins in Australia write to the Marketing Department, Penguin Books Australia Ltd, P.O. Box 257, Ringwood, Victoria 3134.

In New Zealand: For a complete list of books available from Penguins in New Zealand write to the Marketing Department, Penguin Books (N.Z.) Ltd, Private Bag, Takapuna, Auckland 9.

UNDERSTANDING THE MUSLIM MIND
Rajmohan Gandhi

Through the lives and philosophies of eight prominent Muslim personalities—Sayyid Ahmed Khan, Fazlul Haq, Muhammad Ali Jinnah, Muhammad Iqbal, Muhammad Ali, Abul Kalam Azad, Liaqat Ali Khan and Zakir Hussain—the author sketches a fascinating and insightful picture of the Islamic community in the subcontinent today.

'Rajmohan Gandhi's excellent book should waken us to the many why's of Hindu-Muslim relationships that remain unanswered to this day'. —M.V. Kamath in the *Telegraph*

'At long last we have a dispassionate analysis of the making of Indian Muslims psyche'. —*The Hindustan Times*

BHOPAL:
The Lessons of a Tragedy
Sanjoy Hazarika

The chilling story of the world's worst industrial accident that occurred at the Union Carbide factory in Bhopal, the capital of the central Indian state of Madhya Pradesh. Years after thousands of people died when a deadly gas leaked from a storage tank at the Carbide pesticides factory, no one knows what really happened. Who was really responsible for the disaster? Was it an accident or was it sabotage? Will the billions of dollars being fought over in the courts ever get to the victims of the tragedy? The book seeks to answer these and the larger questions Bhopal raised—the degradation of the environment by big industry, the irresponsible business methods of large multinational corporations, the problems of development in the Third World—by thoroughly examining every aspect of the tragedy, its aftermath and similar tragedies that have happened before.

UNVEILING INDIA:
A Woman's Journey
Anees Jung

The women in this book are neither extraordinary nor famous and yet their stories and testimonies provide a passionate, often deeply touching, revelation of what it means to be a woman in India today. They tell of marriage an widowhood, unfair work practices, sexual servitude, the problems of bearing and rearing children in poverty, religious discrimination and other forms of exploitation. But they also talk of fulfilling relationships, the joys of marriage and children, the exhilaration of breaking free from the bonds of tradition, ritual and religion. Taken as a whole, the book is essential reading for anyone wishing to understand the women of India—the silent majority that is now beginning to make itself heard.

'An extremely valuable investigation into the lives of ordinary women in India'
—*The Hindustan Times*